SNOOPY

─ A BEAGLE OF ─

MARS ™

PEANUTS

SNOOPY: A BEAGLE OF MARS, June 2020. Published by KaBOOM!, a division of Boom Entertainment, Inc. Peanuts is ™ & © 2020 Peanuts Worldwide, LLC. All rights reserved. KaBOOM!™ and the KaBOOM! logo are trademarks of Boom Entertainment, Inc., registered in various countries and categories. All characters, events, and institutions depicted herein are fictional. Any similarity between any of the names, characters, persons, events, and/or institutions in this publication to actual names, characters, and persons, whether living or dead, events, and/or institutions is unintended and purely coincidental. KaBOOM! does not read or accept unsolicited submissions of ideas, stories, or artwork.

BOOM! Studios, 5670 Wilshire Boulevard, Suite 400, Los Angeles, CA 90036-5679. Printed in China. Second Printing.

ISBN: 978-1-68415-326-8, eISBN: 978-1-64144-179-7

Designer
Chelsea Roberts

Associate Editor
Jonathan Manning

Editor
Chris Rosa

For Charles M. Schulz Creative Associates

Chief Creative Officer
Paige Braddock

Senior Editor
Alexis E. Fajardo

Special thanks to the Schulz family, everyone at Charles M. Schulz Creative Associates, and Charles M. Schulz for his singular achievement in shaping these beloved characters.

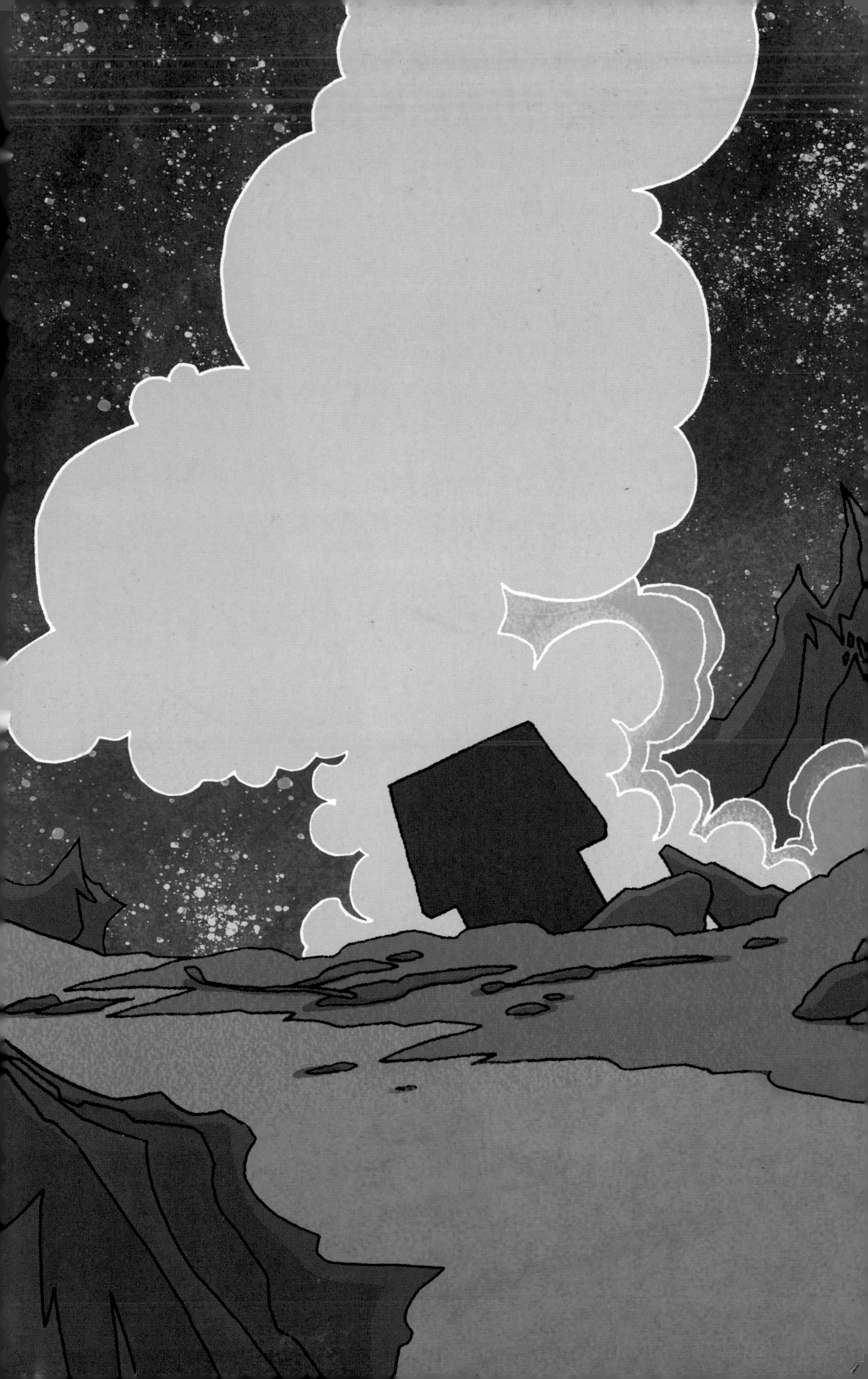

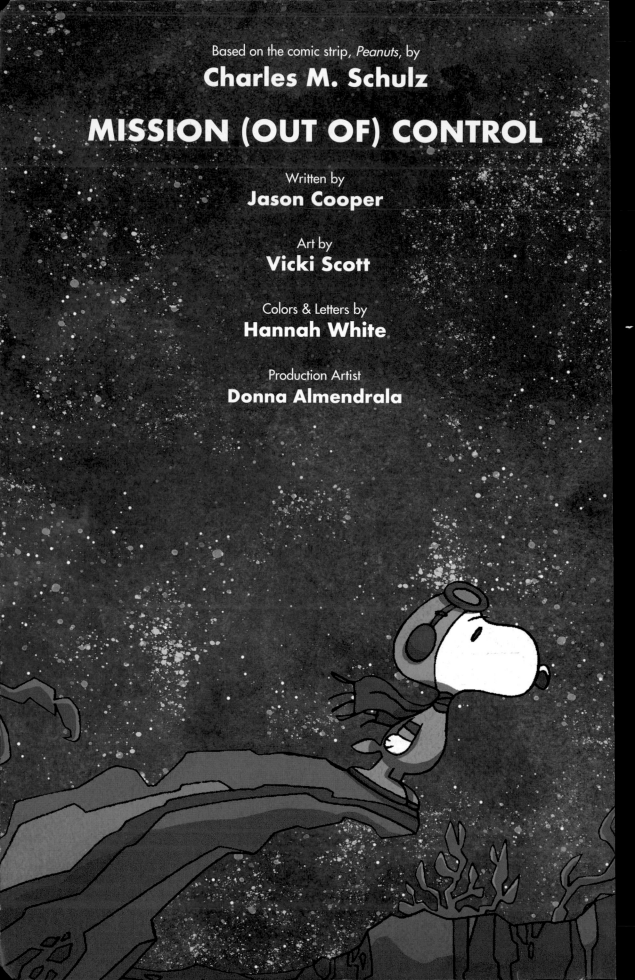

Based on the comic strip, *Peanuts*, by
Charles M. Schulz

MISSION (OUT OF) CONTROL

Written by
Jason Cooper

Art by
Vicki Scott

Colors & Letters by
Hannah White

Production Artist
Donna Almendrala

SNOOPY: A BEAGLE OF MARS

Written by
Jason Cooper

Art by
Robert Pope

Colors by
Hannah White
with color assists by **Jewel Jackson**

Letters & Post Production by
Donna Almendrala &
Bryan Stone

Cover Illustration by
Robert Pope
with colors by **Hannah White**

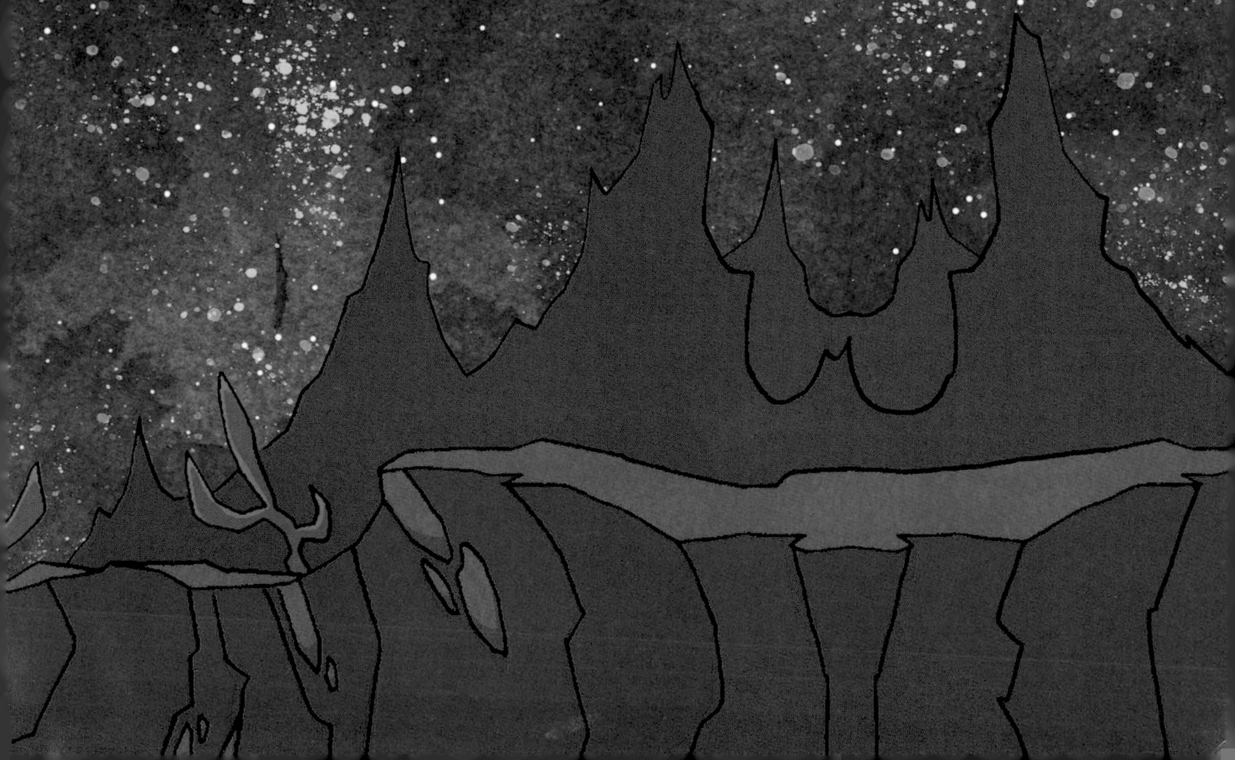

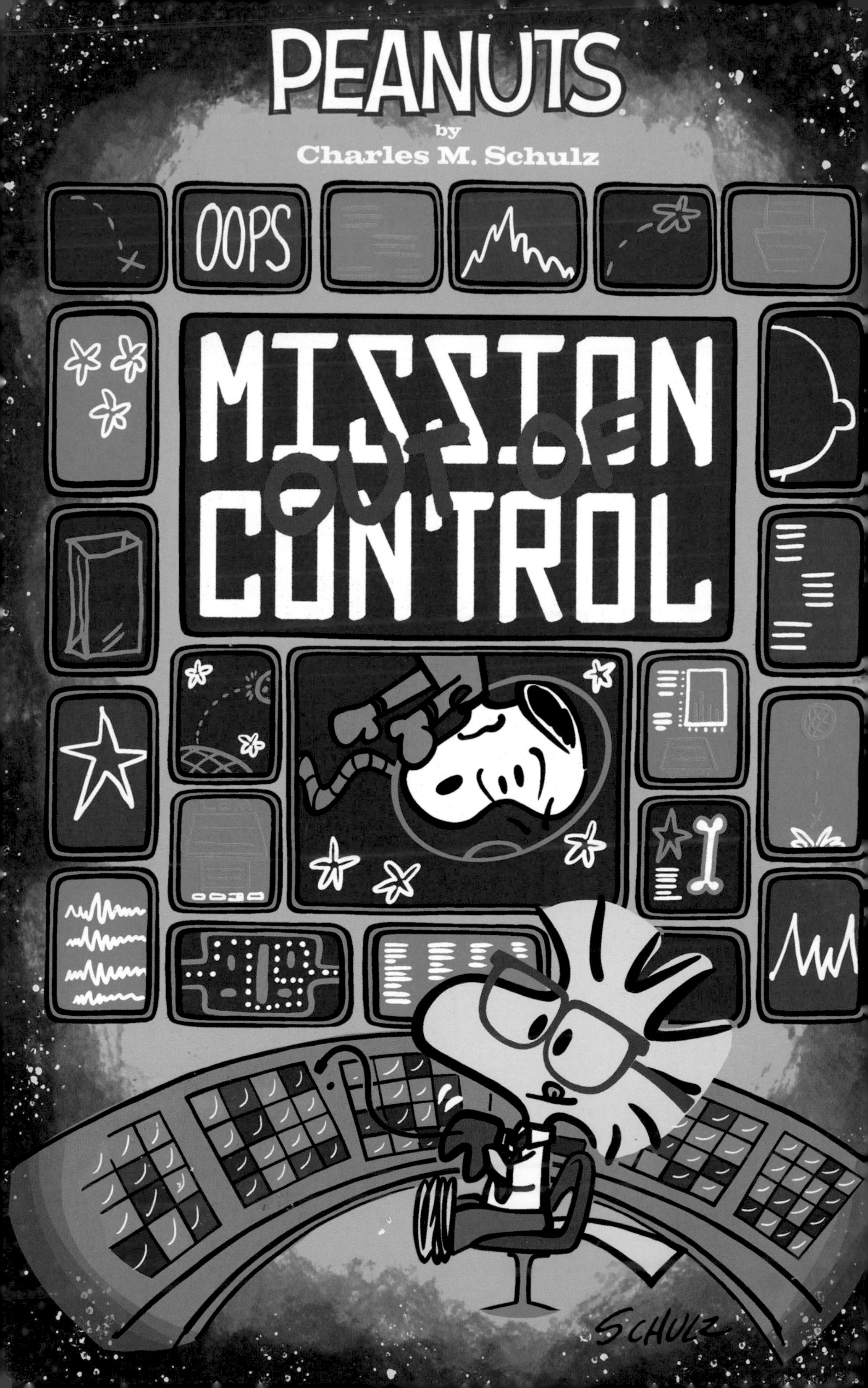
PEANUTS
by
Charles M. Schulz
OOPS
MISSION OUT OF CONTROL
SCHULZ

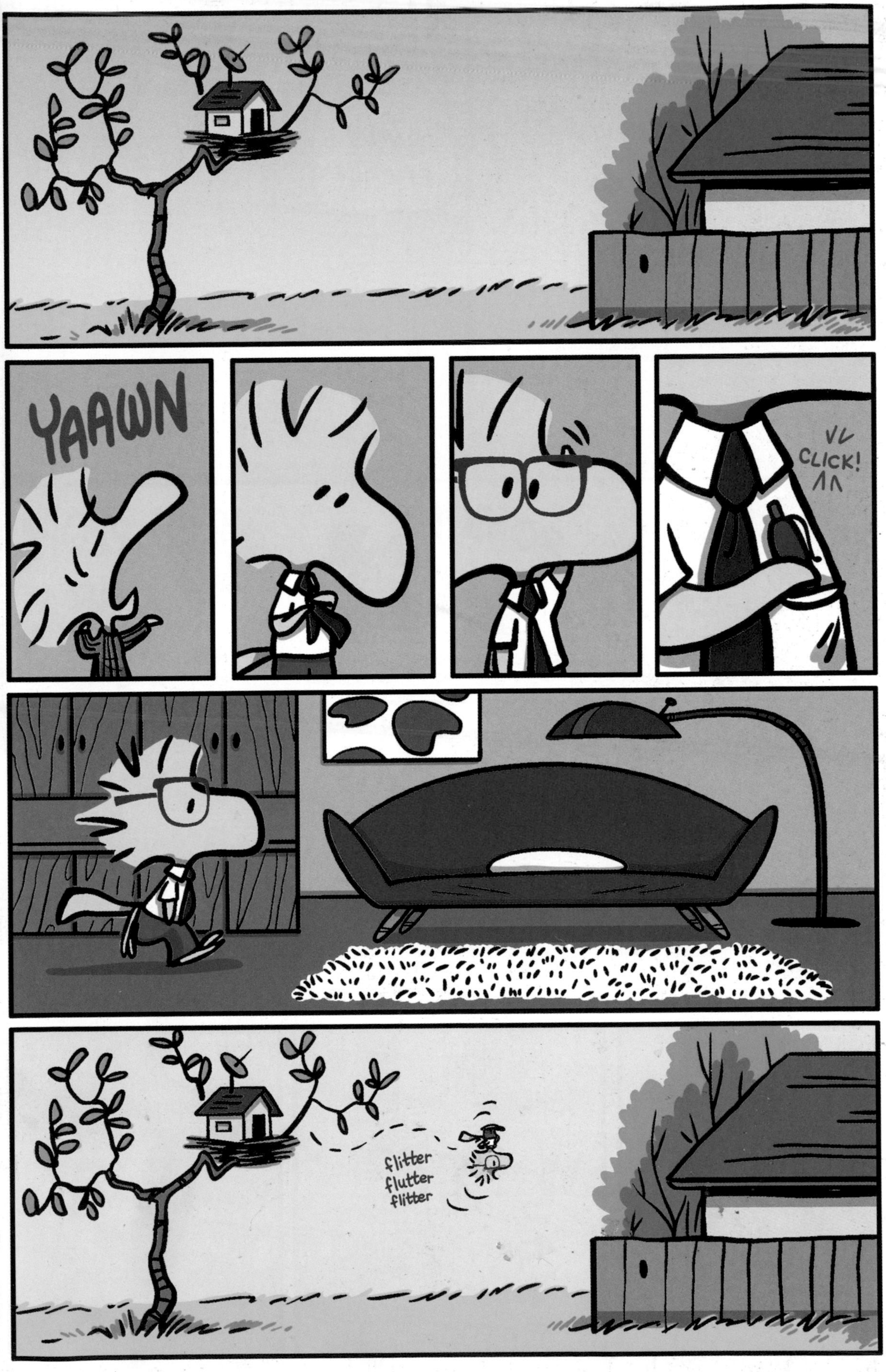
YAAWN
CLICK!
flitter
flutter
flitter

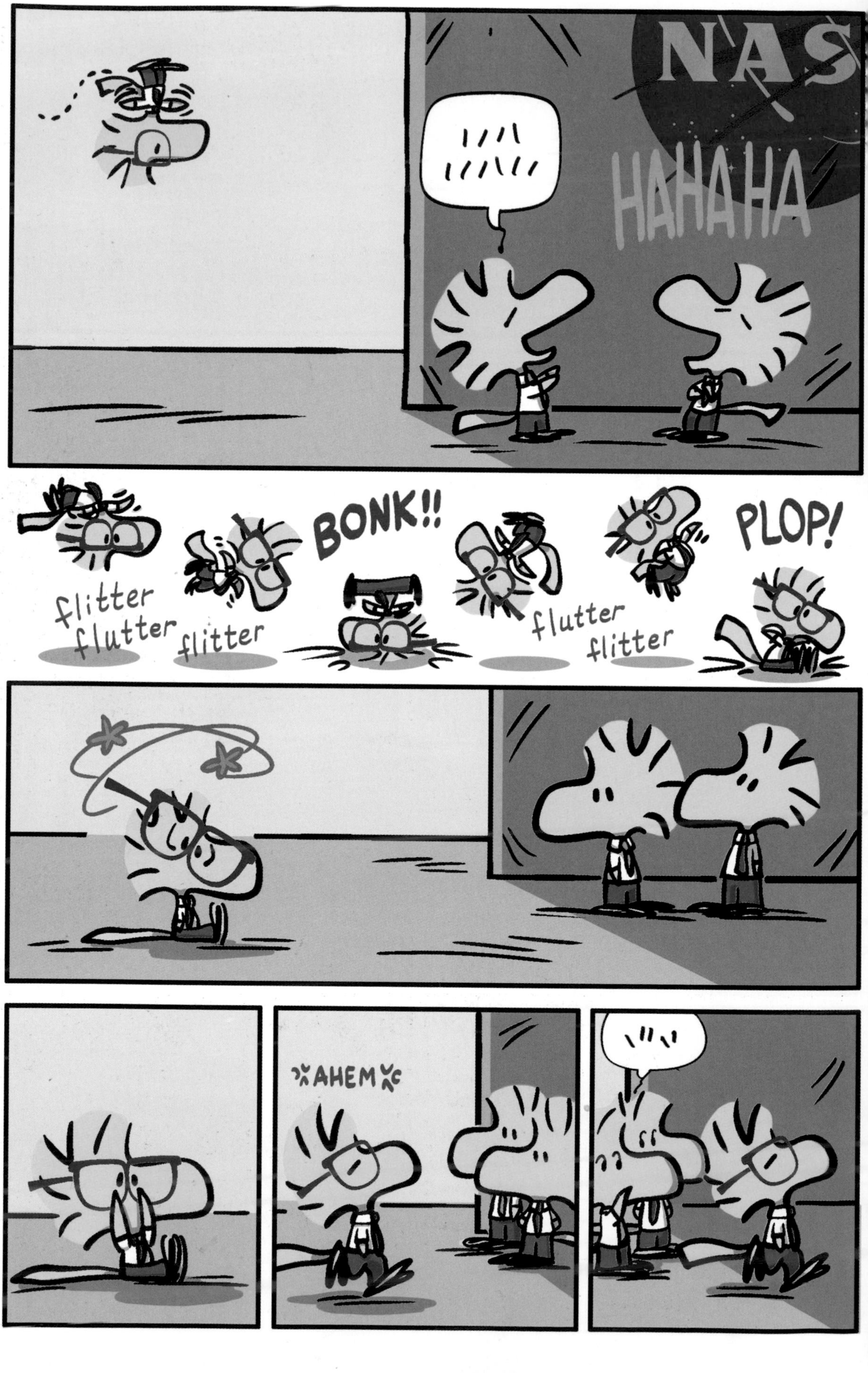
NAS
HAHAHA
flitter
flutter
flitter
BONK!!
flutter
flitter
PLOP!
AHEM

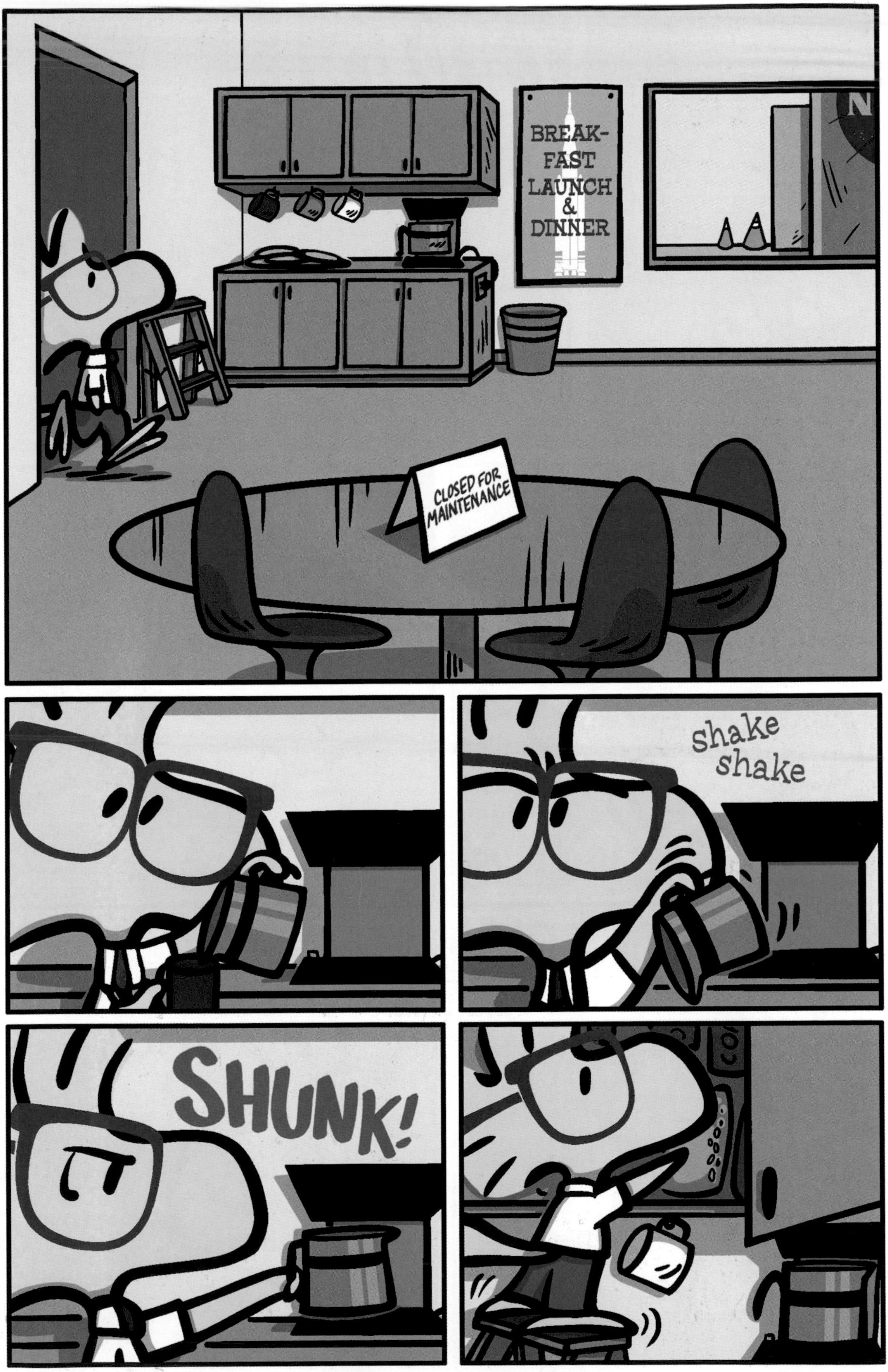
BREAK-FAST LAUNCH & DINNER
CLOSED FOR MAINTENANCE
shake shake
SHUNK!

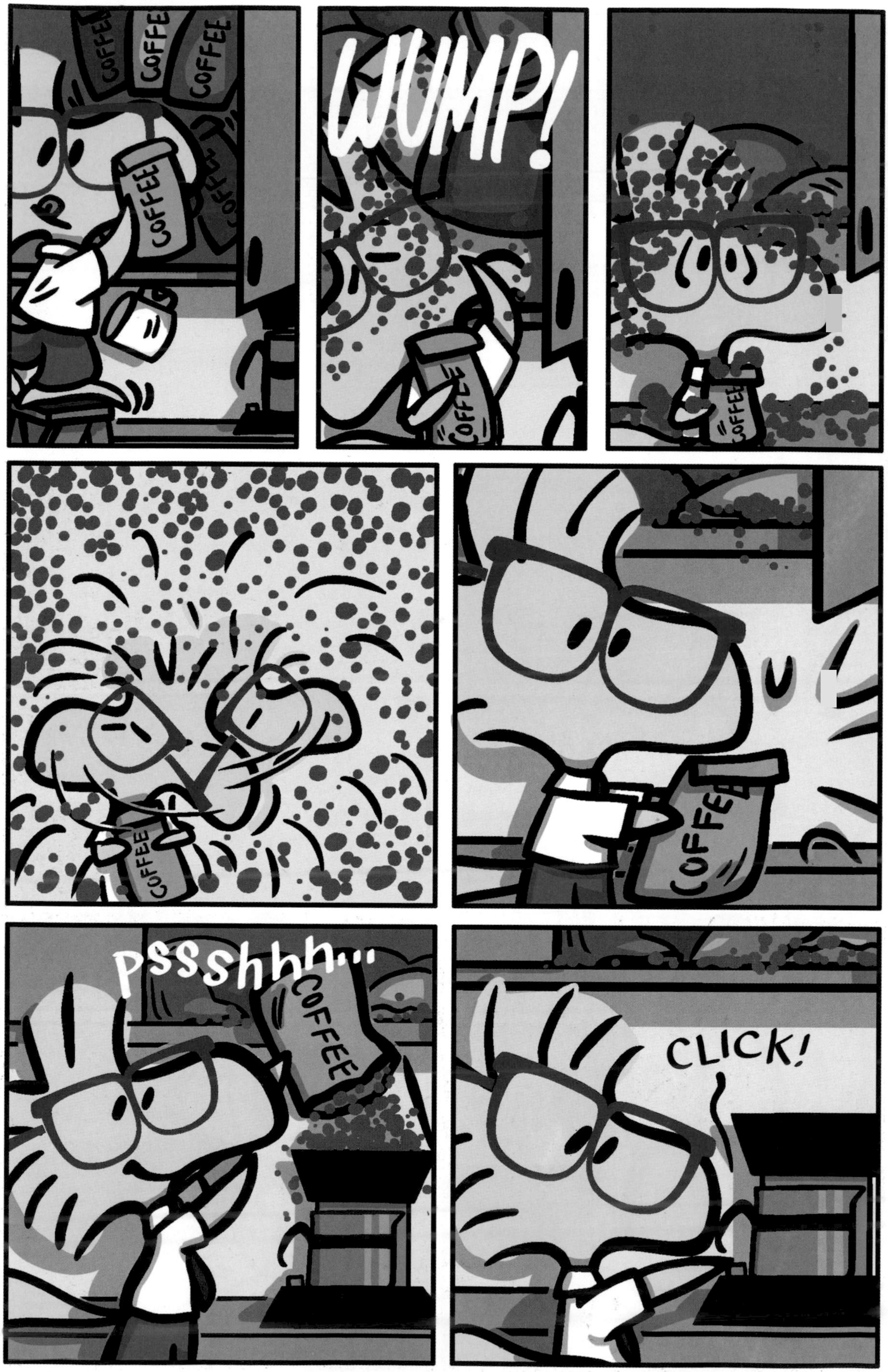
COFFEE
COFFEE
COFFEE
COFFEE
COFFEE
WUMP!
COFFEE
COFFEE
COFFEE
COFFEE
PSSShhh...
COFFEE
CLICK!

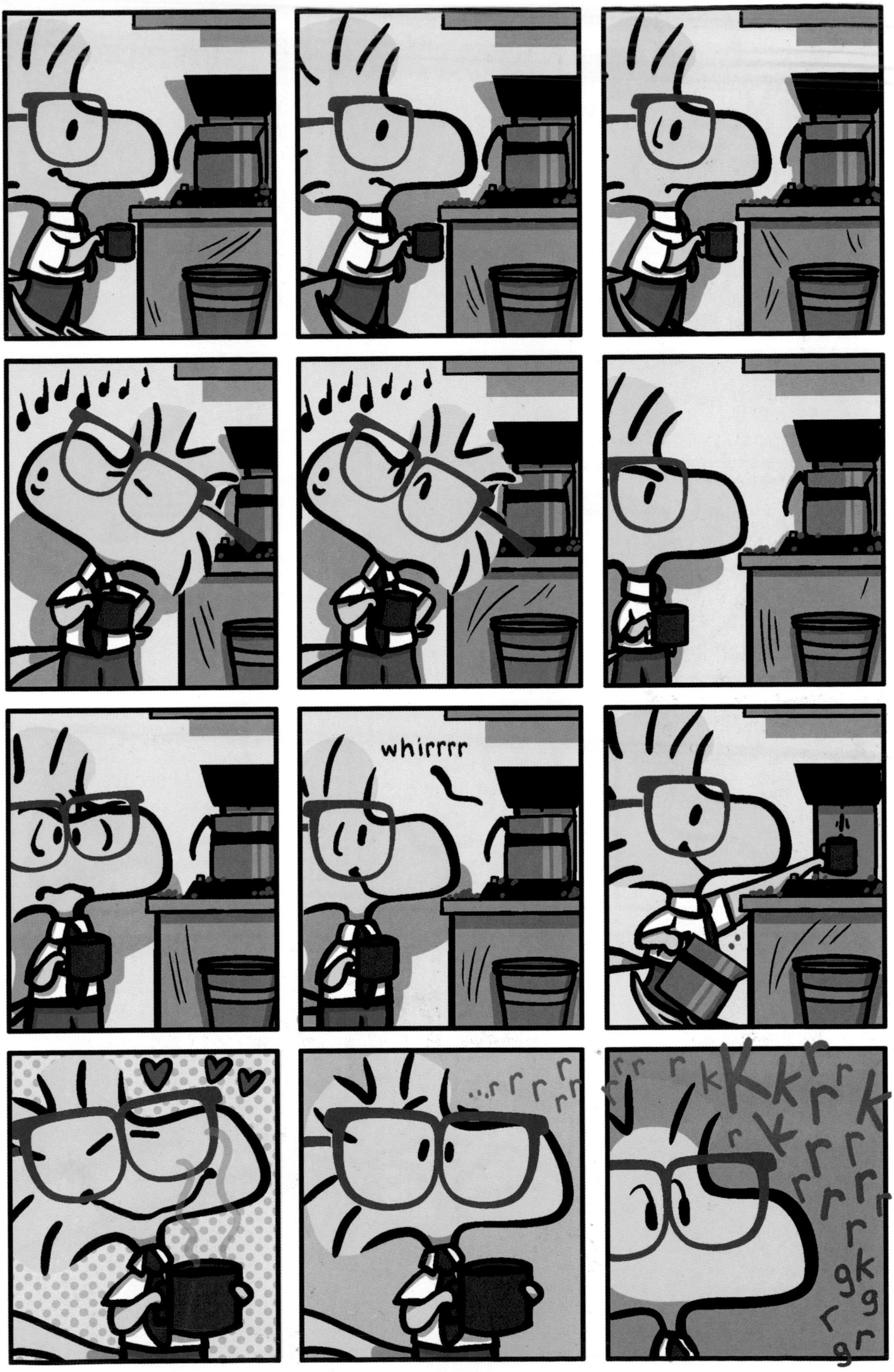
whirrrr

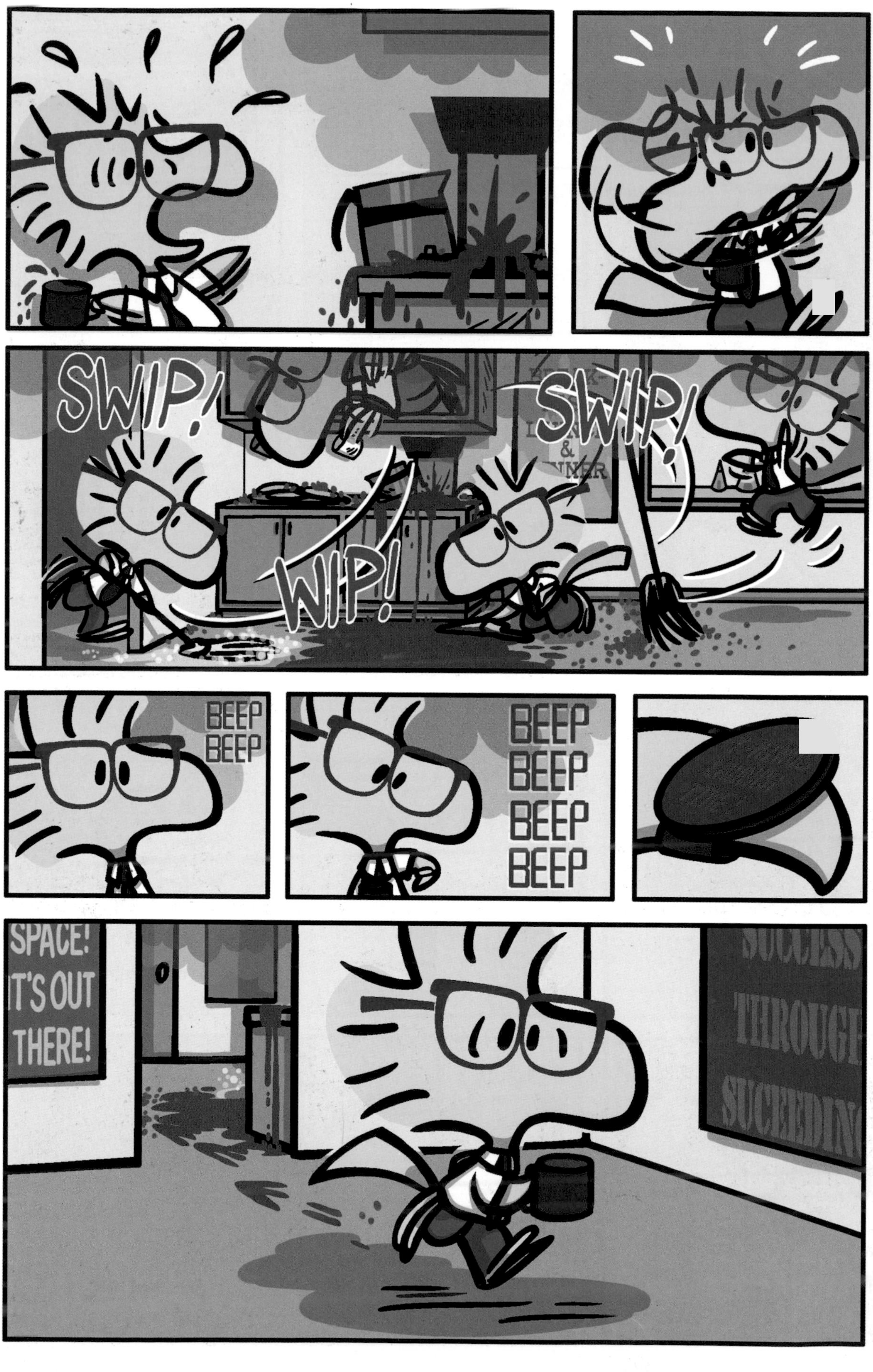
SWIP!
SWIP!
WIP!
BEEP BEEP
BEEP BEEP BEEP BEEP
SPACE! IT'S OUT THERE!
SUCCESS
THROUG
SUCEEDIN

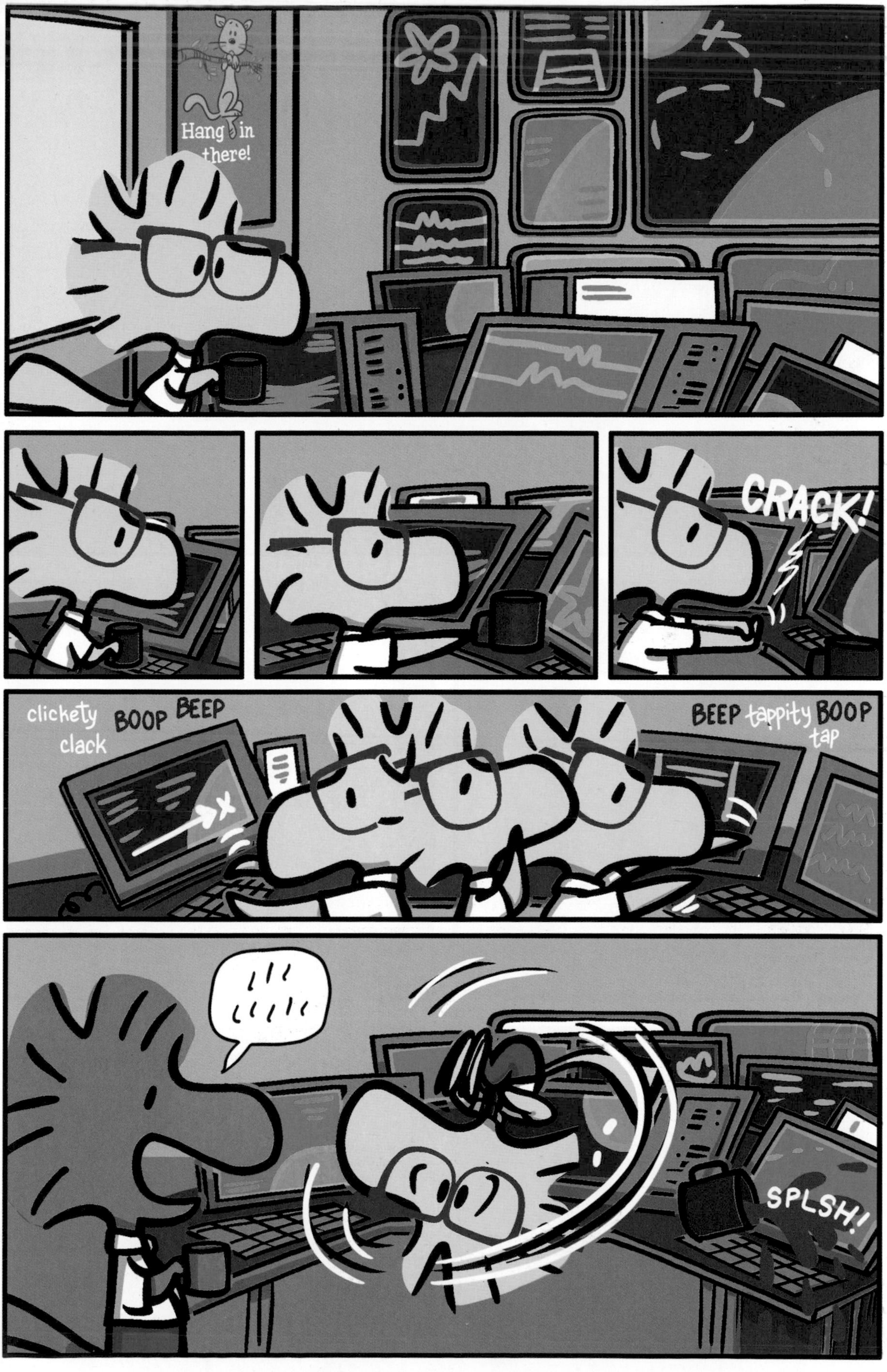
Hang in there!
CRACK!
clickety clack
BOOP
BEEP
BEEP
tappity
BOOP
tap
SPLSH!

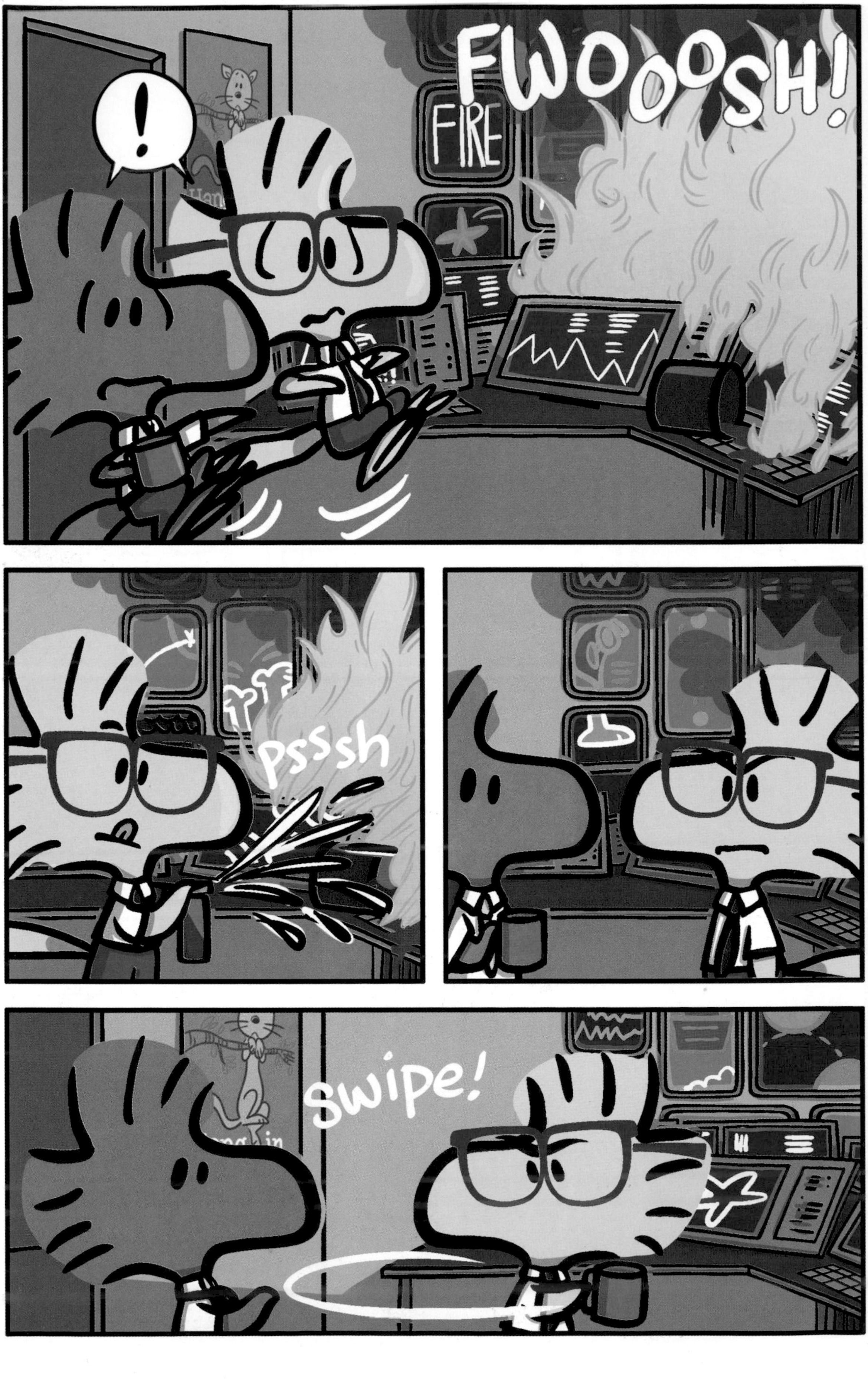
!
FIRE
FWOOOSH!
psssh
swipe!

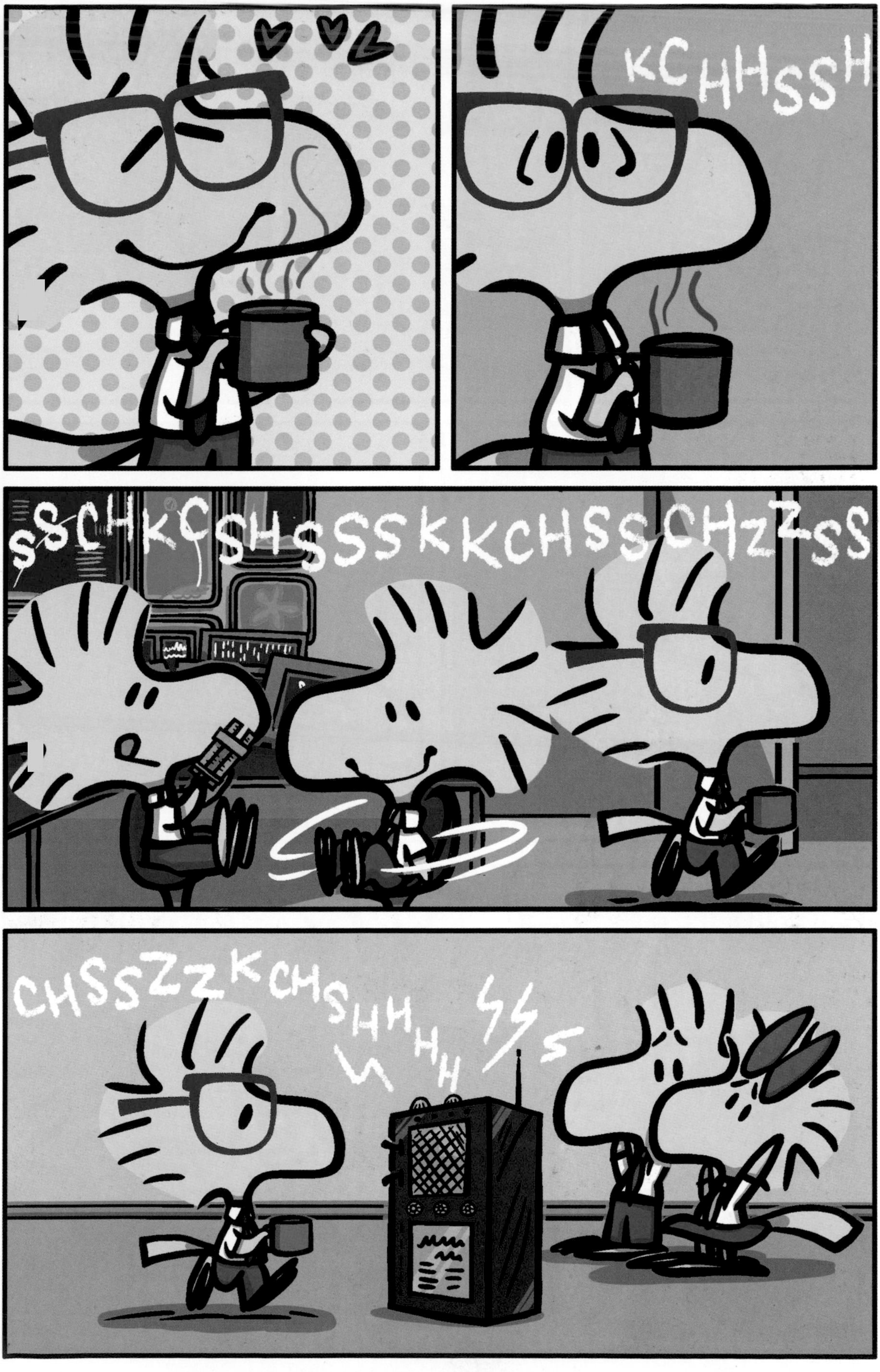
KCHHSSH
SSCHKCSHSSSKKCHSSCHZZSS
CHSSZZKCHSHHHH
S

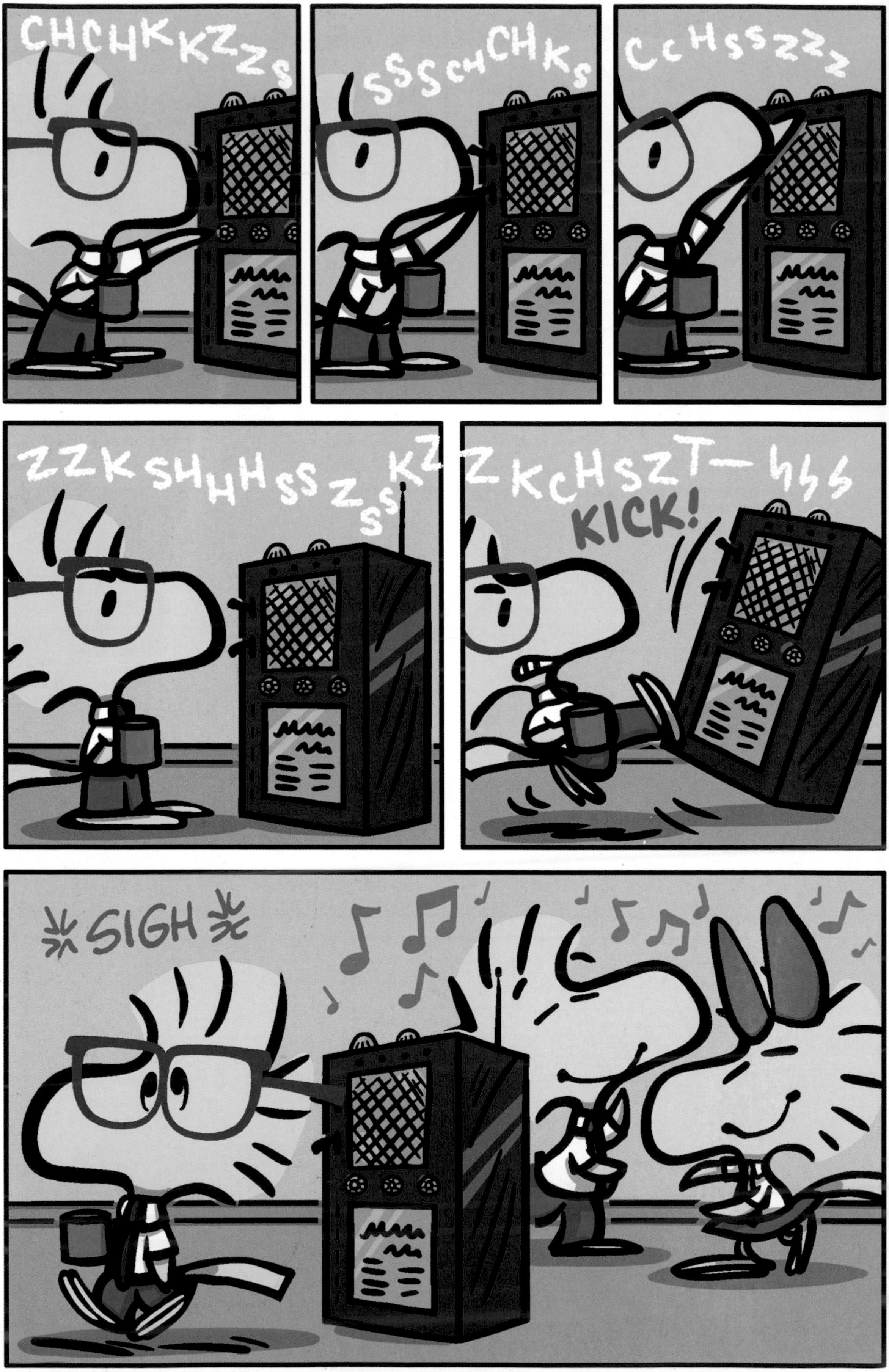
CHCHKKZZZS
SSSCHCHKS
CCHSSZZZ
ZZKSHHHSSZSSKZZ
ZKCHSZT—HSS
KICK!
SIGH

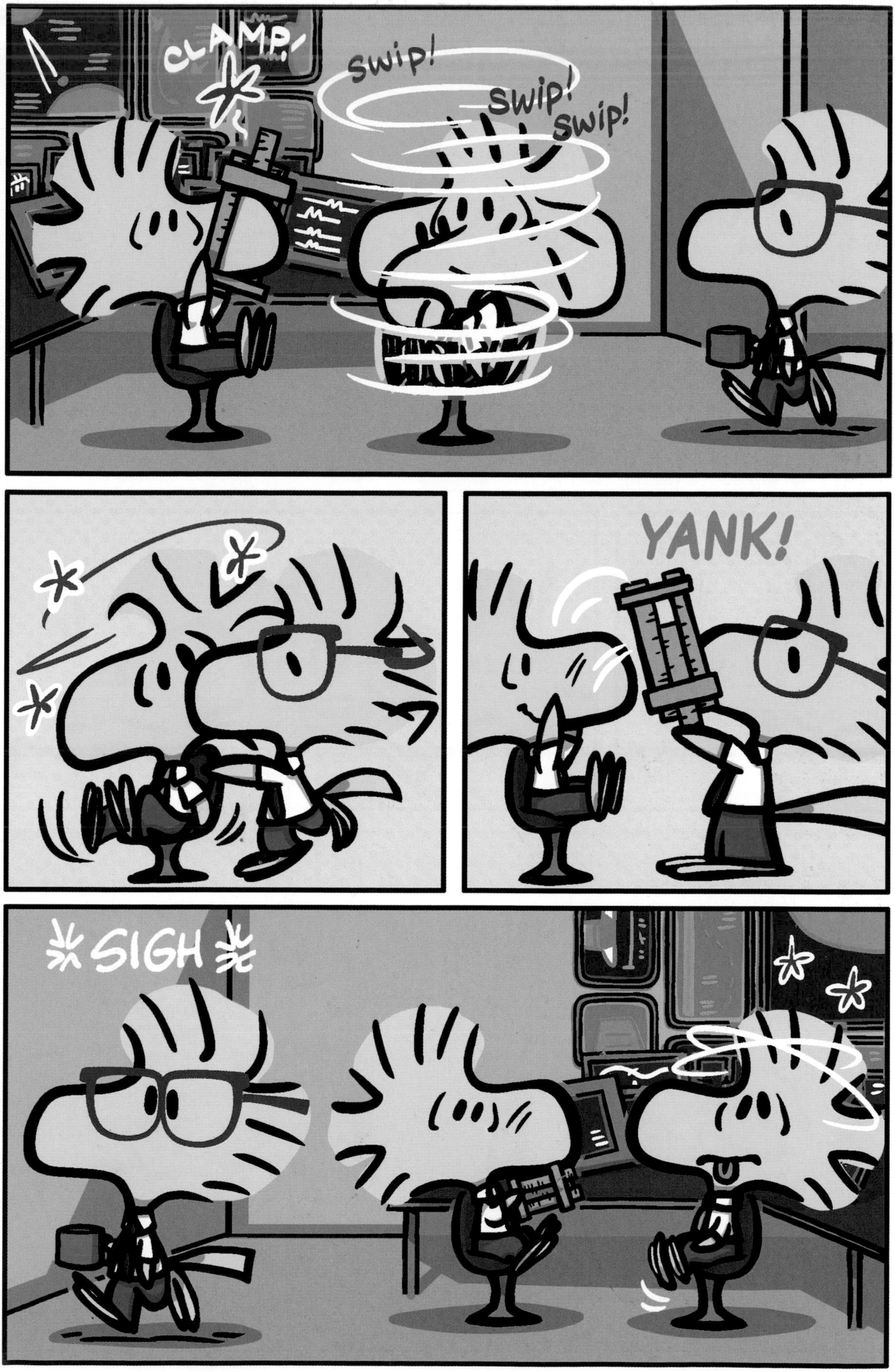
CLAMP!
SWIP!
SWIP!
SWIP!
YANK!
SIGH

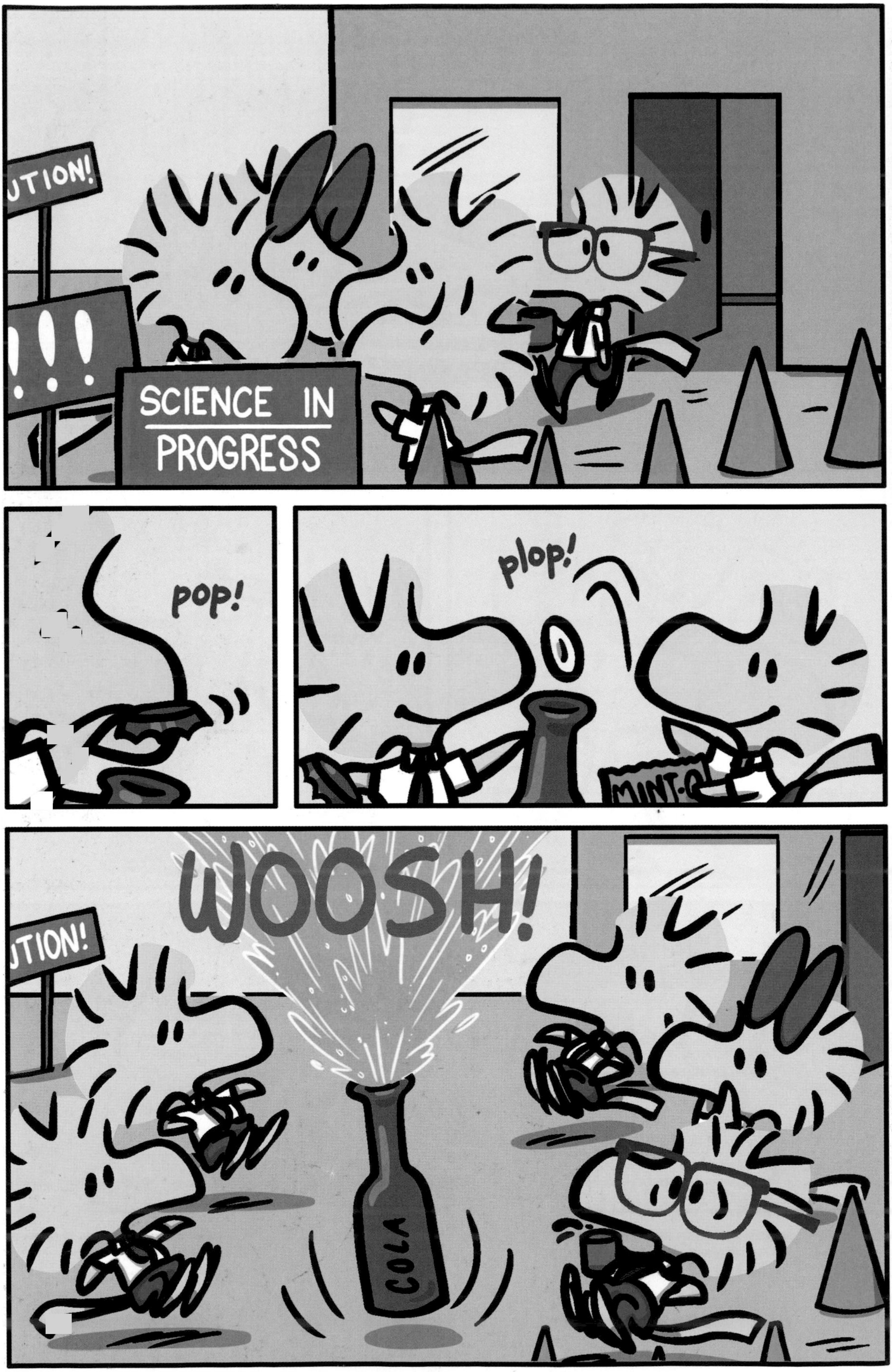
UTION!
SCIENCE IN PROGRESS
pop!
plop!
WOOSH!
UTION!
COLA

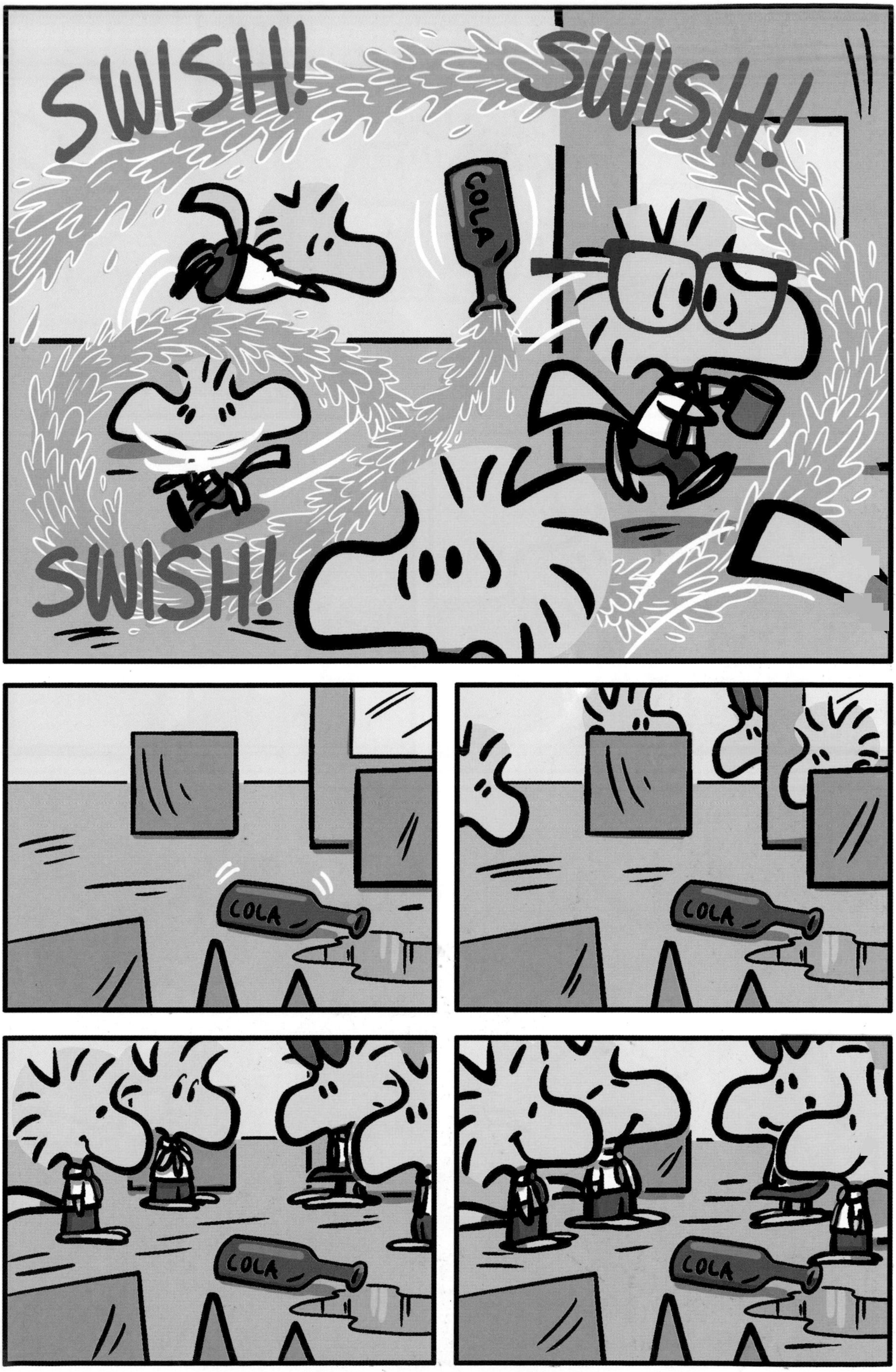
SWISH!
SWISH!
COLA
SWISH!
COLA
COLA
COLA
COLA

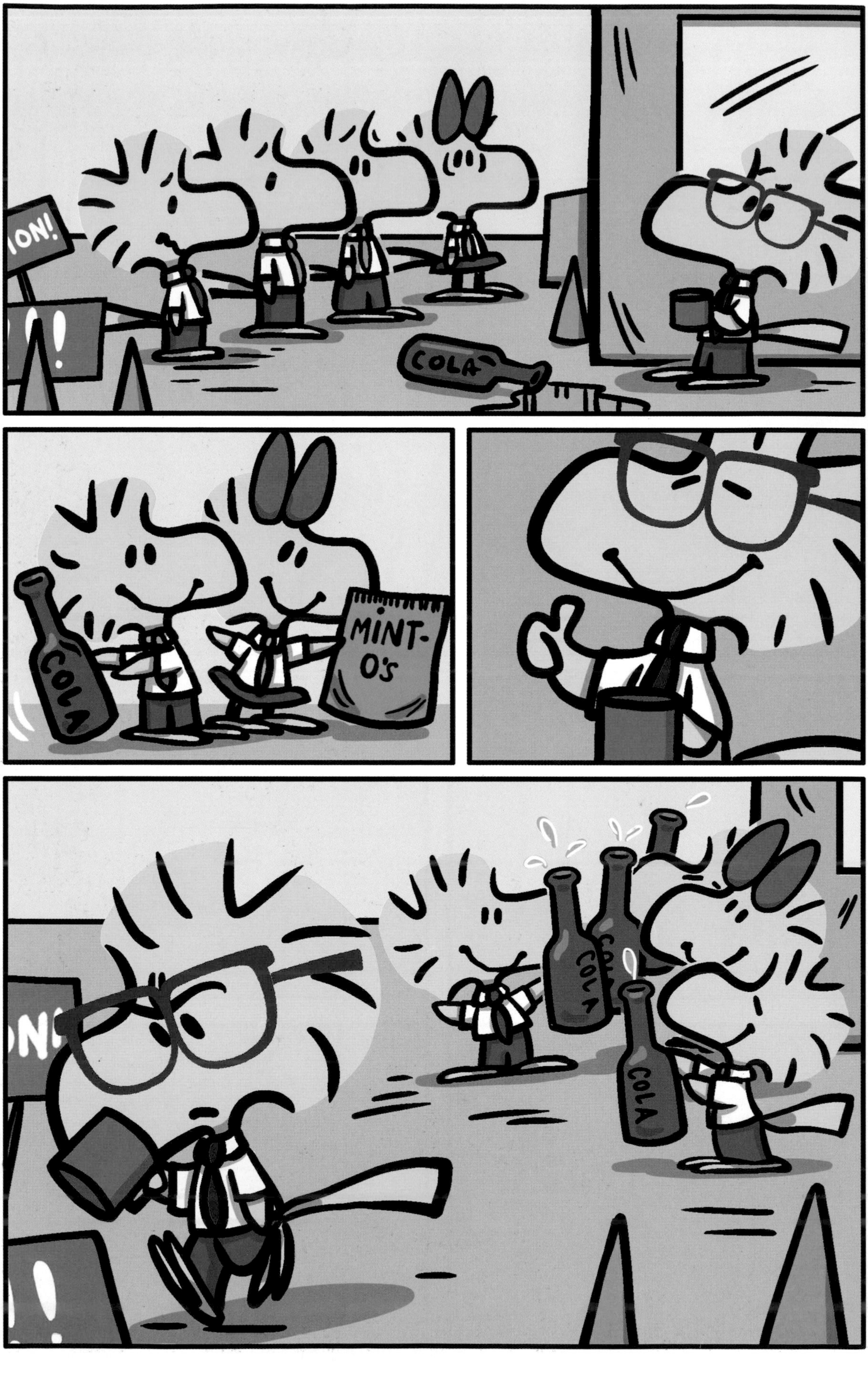
ON!
COLA
COLA
MINT-O's
COLA
COLA

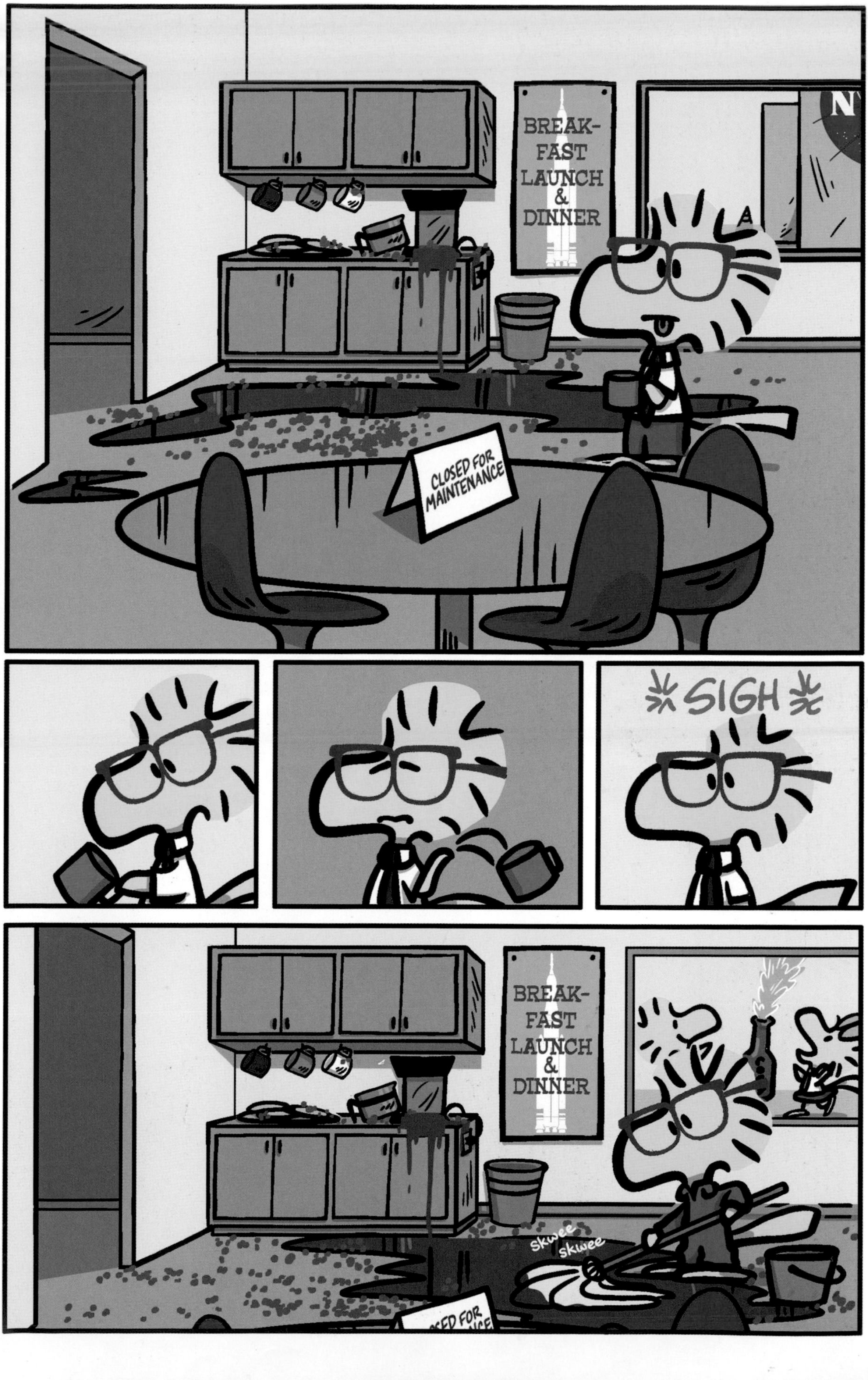
BREAK-
FAST
LAUNCH
&
DINNER
CLOSED FOR MAINTENANCE
SIGH
BREAK-
FAST
LAUNCH
&
DINNER
skwee
skwee

SNOOPY:
A BEAGLE
OF MARS

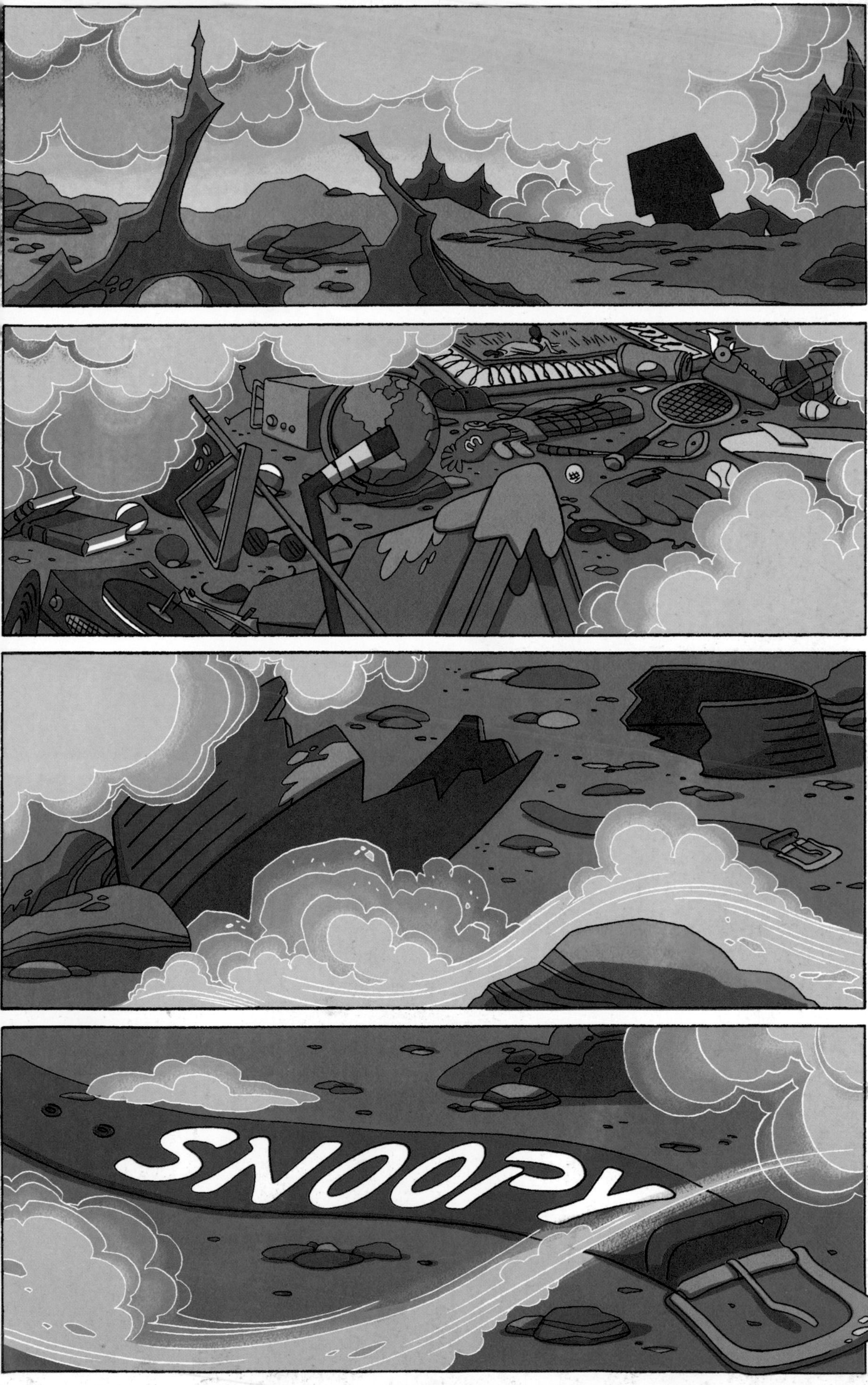
SNOOPY

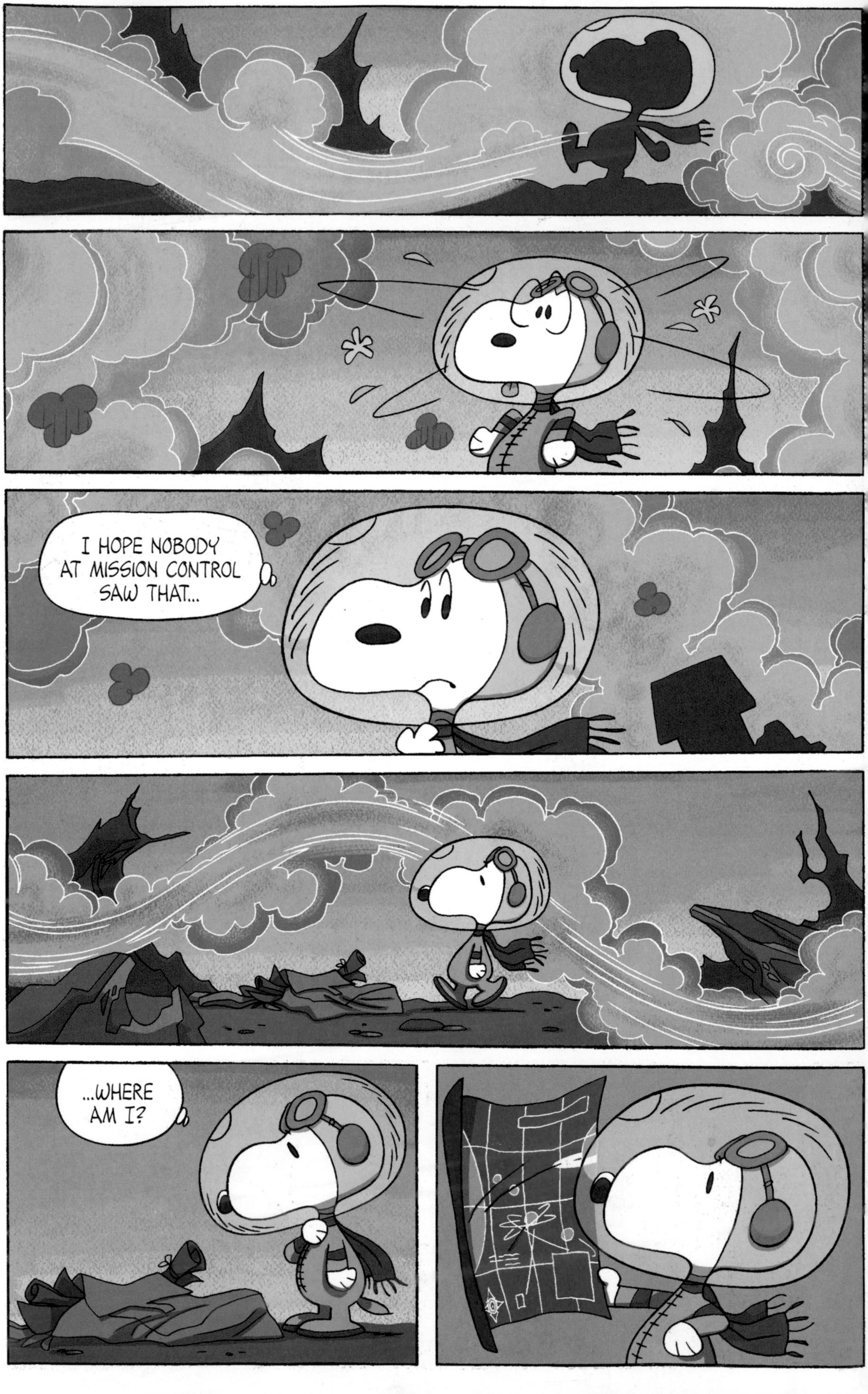
I HOPE NOBODY AT MISSION CONTROL SAW THAT...
...WHERE AM I?

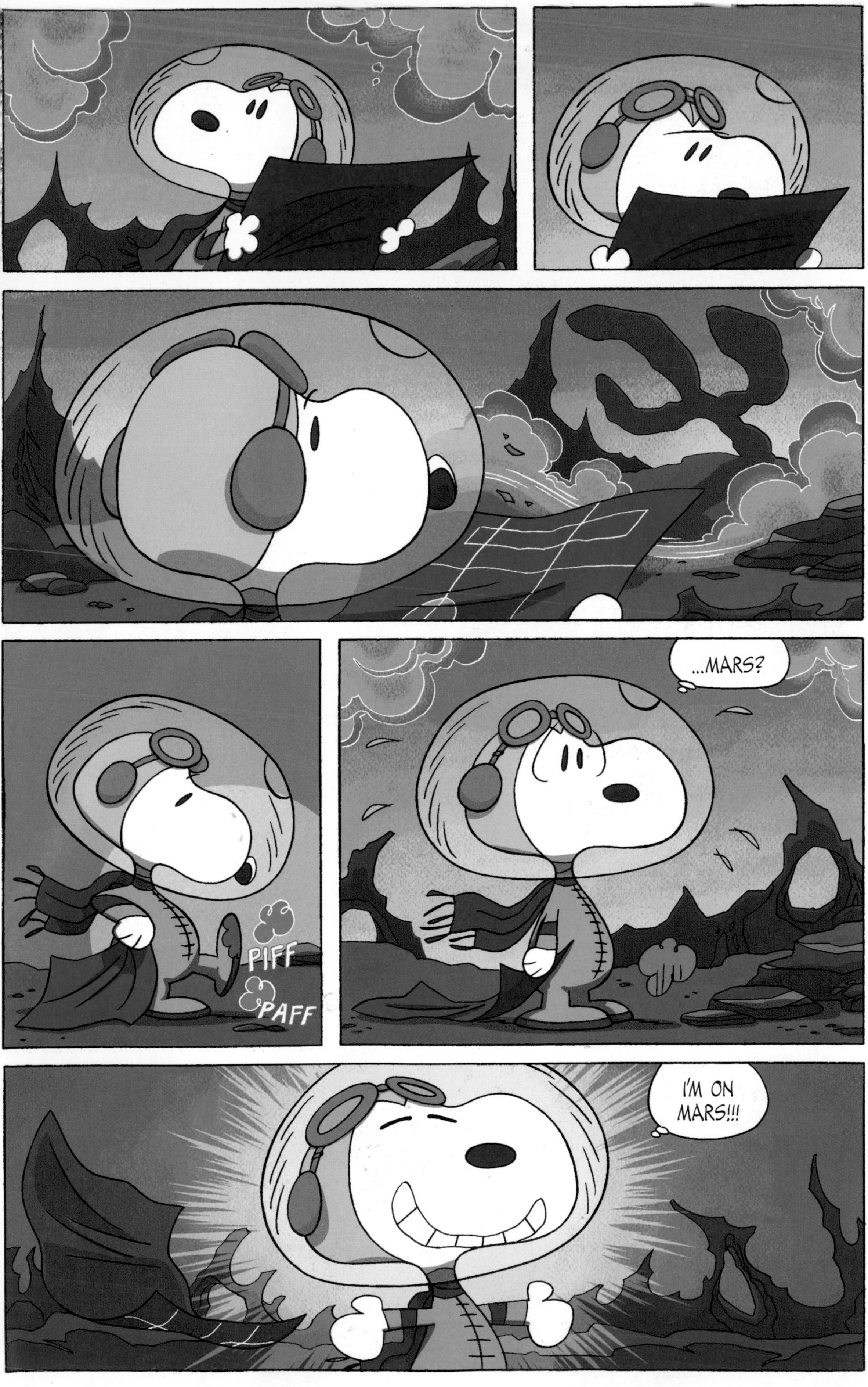
PIFF
PAFF
...MARS?
I'M ON MARS!!!

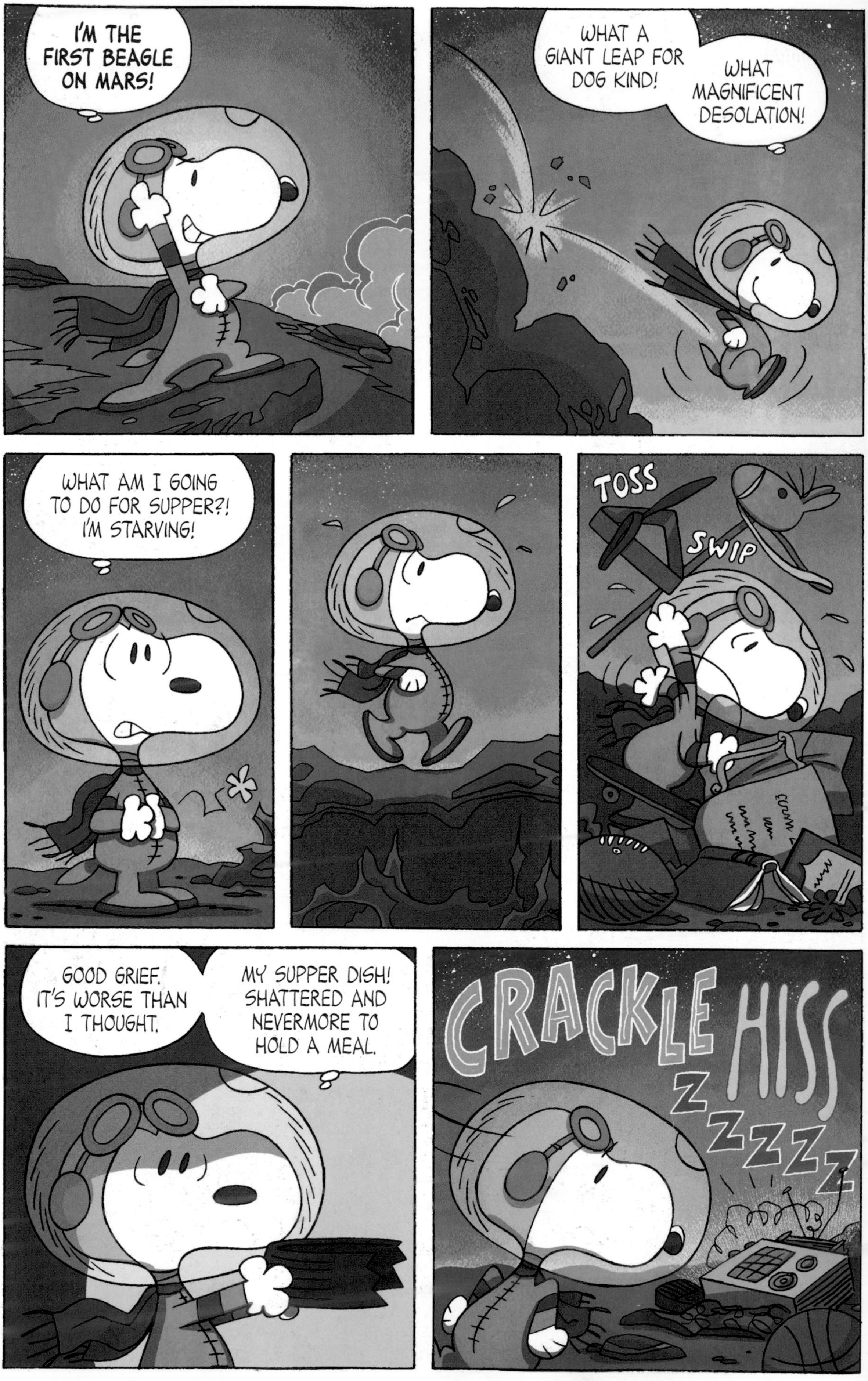
I'M THE FIRST BEAGLE ON MARS!
WHAT A GIANT LEAP FOR DOG KIND!
WHAT MAGNIFICENT DESOLATION!
WHAT AM I GOING TO DO FOR SUPPER?! I'M STARVING!
TOSS
SWIP
GOOD GRIEF. IT'S WORSE THAN I THOUGHT.
MY SUPPER DISH! SHATTERED AND NEVERMORE TO HOLD A MEAL.
CRACKLE
HISS
ZZZZZ

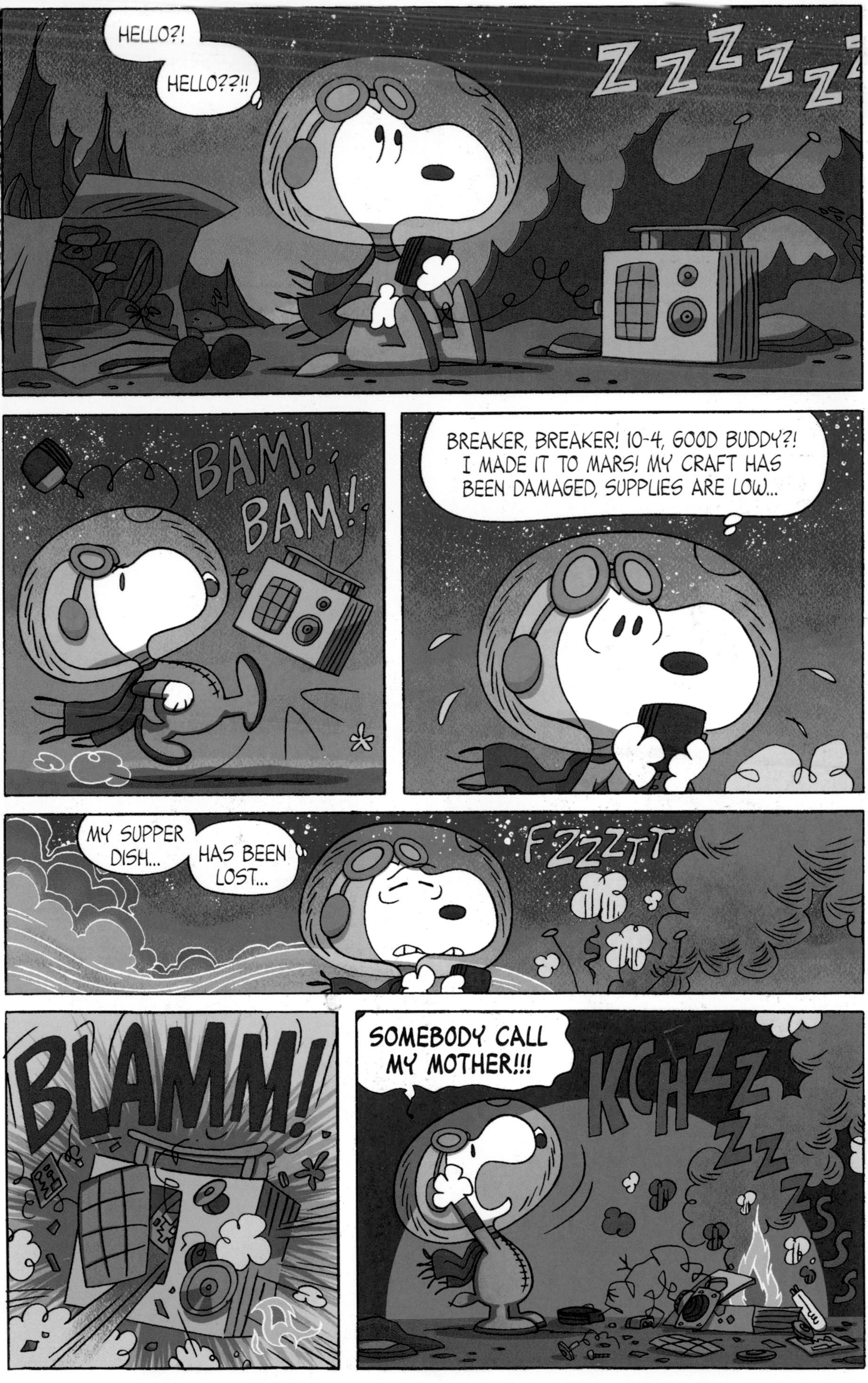
HELLO?!
HELLO??!!
ZZZZZZZ
BAM!
BAM!
BREAKER, BREAKER! 10-4, GOOD BUDDY?! I MADE IT TO MARS! MY CRAFT HAS BEEN DAMAGED, SUPPLIES ARE LOW...
MY SUPPER DISH...
HAS BEEN LOST...
FZZZTT
BLAMM!
SOMEBODY CALL MY MOTHER!!!
KCHZZZZZSSS

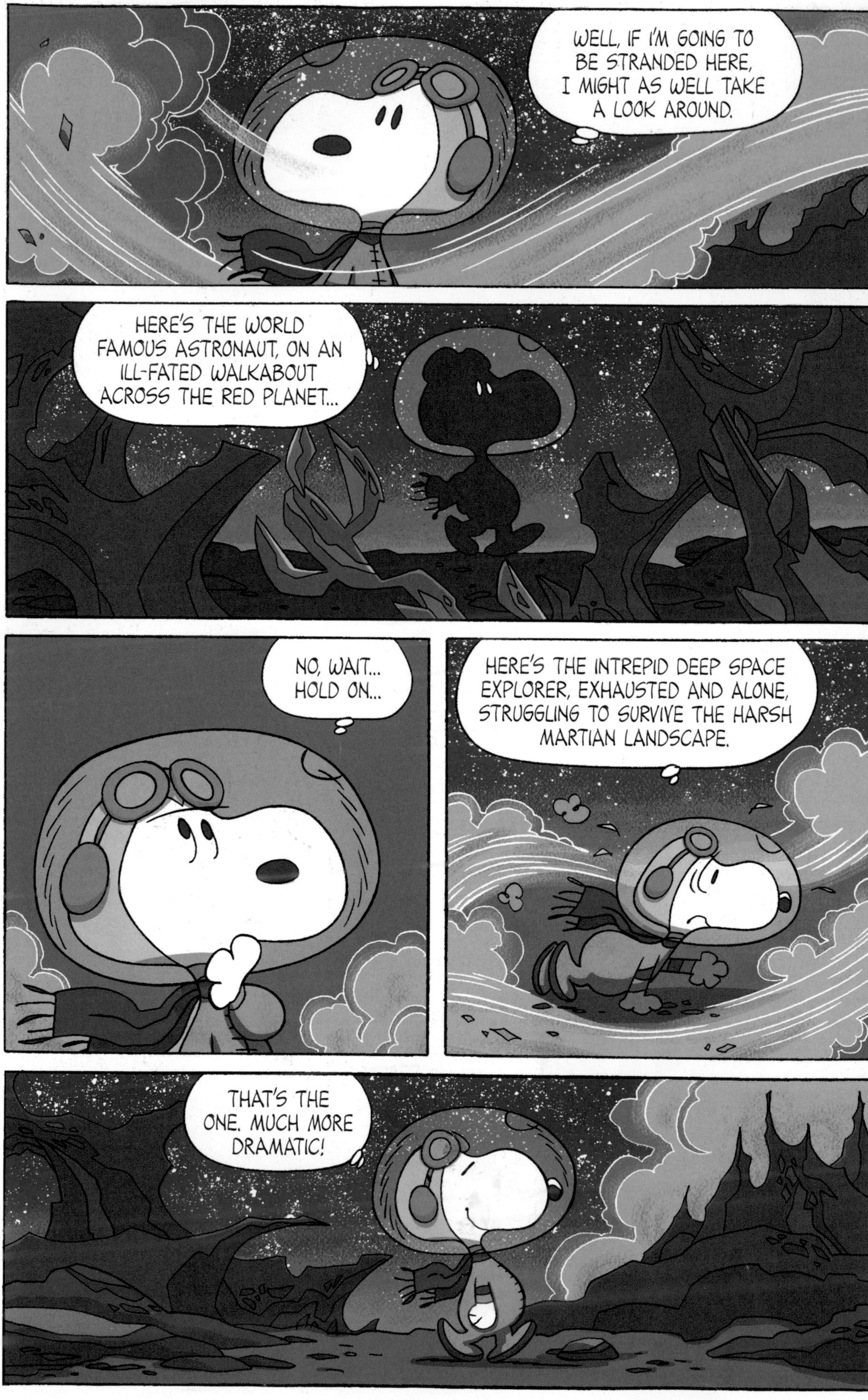
WELL, IF I'M GOING TO BE STRANDED HERE, I MIGHT AS WELL TAKE A LOOK AROUND.
HERE'S THE WORLD FAMOUS ASTRONAUT, ON AN ILL-FATED WALKABOUT ACROSS THE RED PLANET...
NO, WAIT... HOLD ON...
HERE'S THE INTREPID DEEP SPACE EXPLORER, EXHAUSTED AND ALONE, STRUGGLING TO SURVIVE THE HARSH MARTIAN LANDSCAPE.
THAT'S THE ONE. MUCH MORE DRAMATIC!

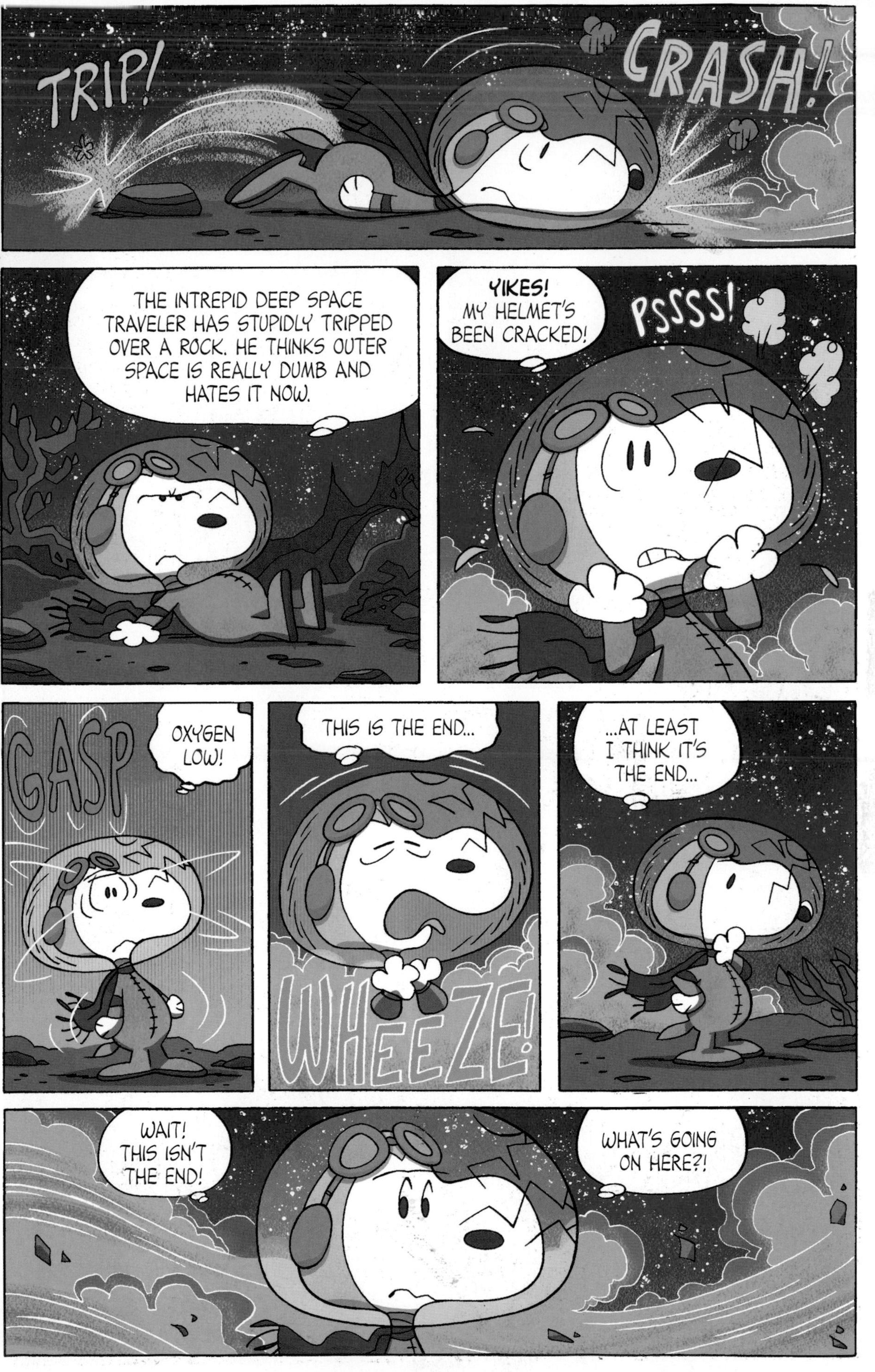
TRIP!
CRASH!
THE INTREPID DEEP SPACE TRAVELER HAS STUPIDLY TRIPPED OVER A ROCK. HE THINKS OUTER SPACE IS REALLY DUMB AND HATES IT NOW.
YIKES! MY HELMET'S BEEN CRACKED!
PSSSS!
GASP
OXYGEN LOW!
THIS IS THE END...
WHEEZE!
...AT LEAST I THINK IT'S THE END...
WAIT! THIS ISN'T THE END!
WHAT'S GOING ON HERE?!

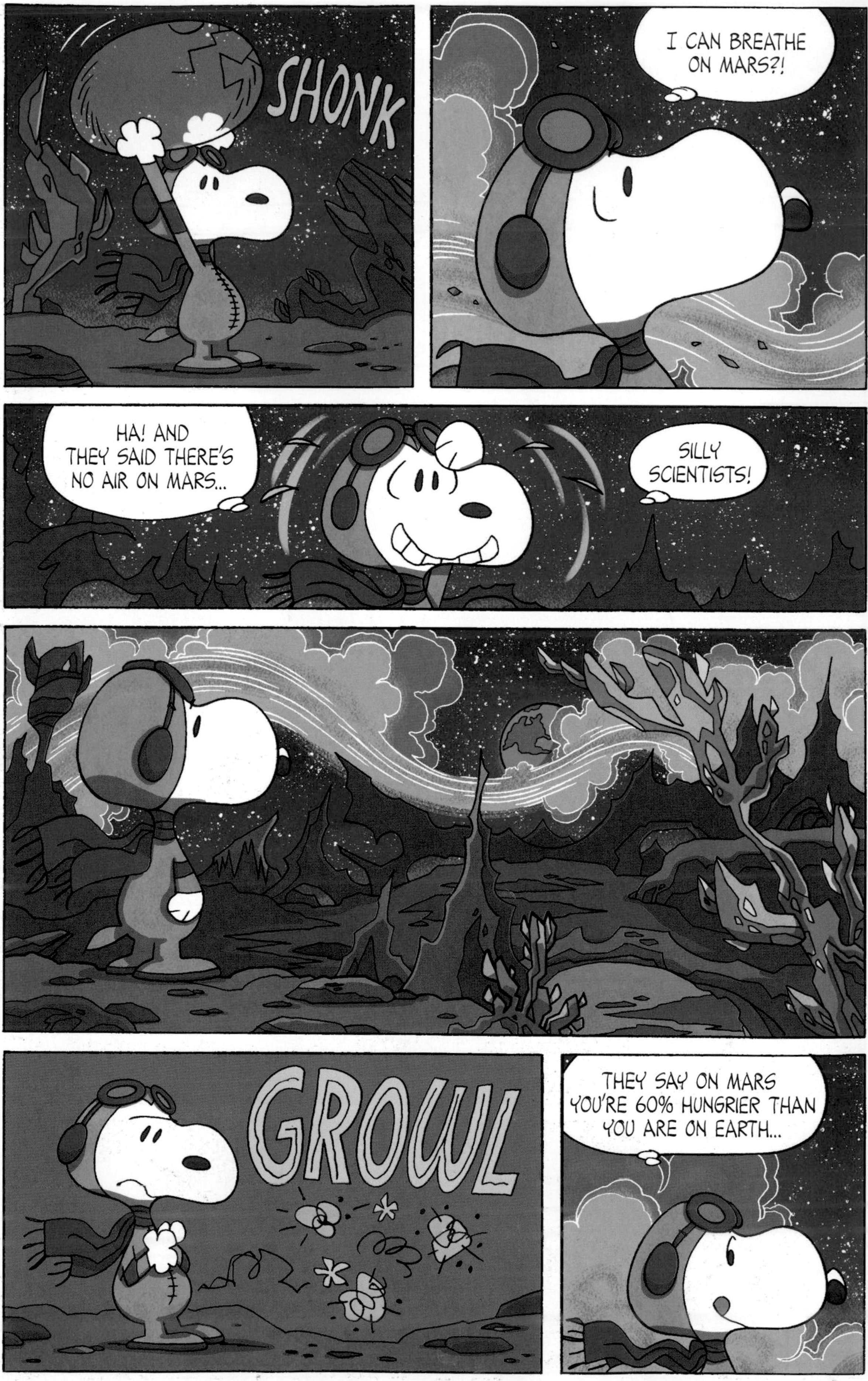
SHONK
I CAN BREATHE ON MARS?!
HA! AND THEY SAID THERE'S NO AIR ON MARS...
SILLY SCIENTISTS!
GROWL
THEY SAY ON MARS YOU'RE 60% HUNGRIER THAN YOU ARE ON EARTH...

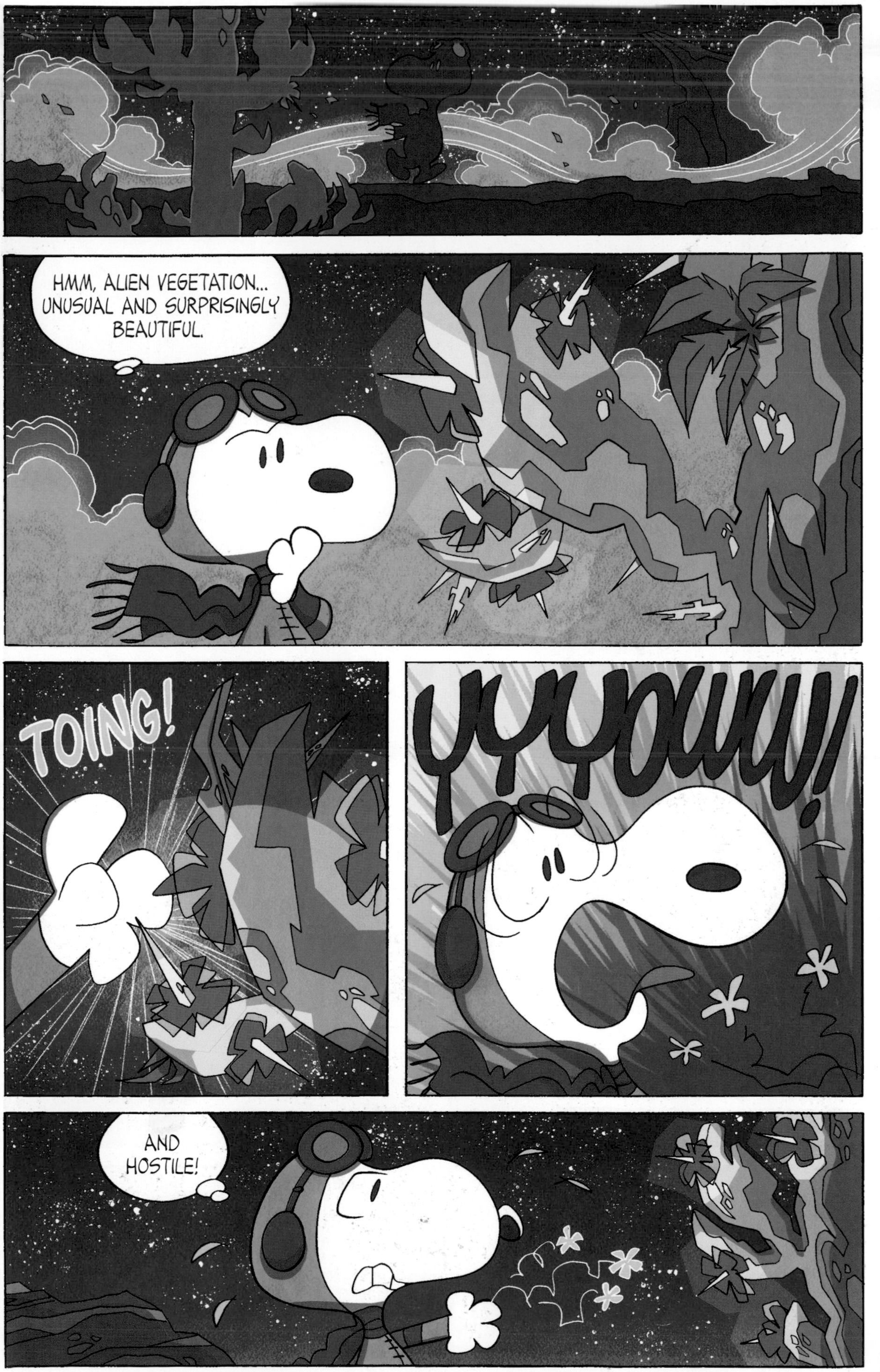
HMM, ALIEN VEGETATION... UNUSUAL AND SURPRISINGLY BEAUTIFUL.
TOING!
YYYOWW!
AND HOSTILE!

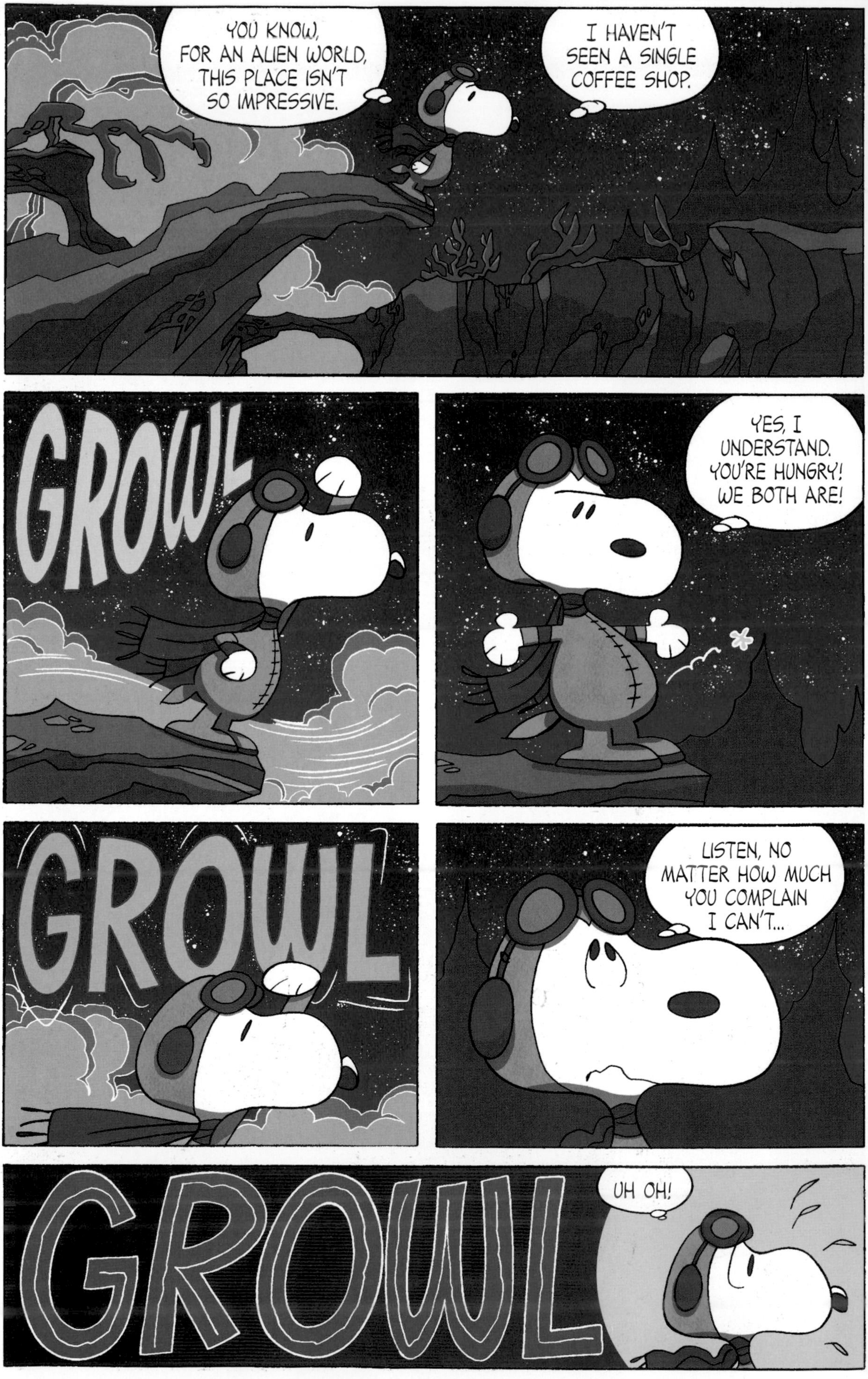
YOU KNOW, FOR AN ALIEN WORLD, THIS PLACE ISN'T SO IMPRESSIVE.
I HAVEN'T SEEN A SINGLE COFFEE SHOP.
GROWL
YES, I UNDERSTAND. YOU'RE HUNGRY! WE BOTH ARE!
GROWL
LISTEN, NO MATTER HOW MUCH YOU COMPLAIN I CAN'T...
GROWL
UH OH!

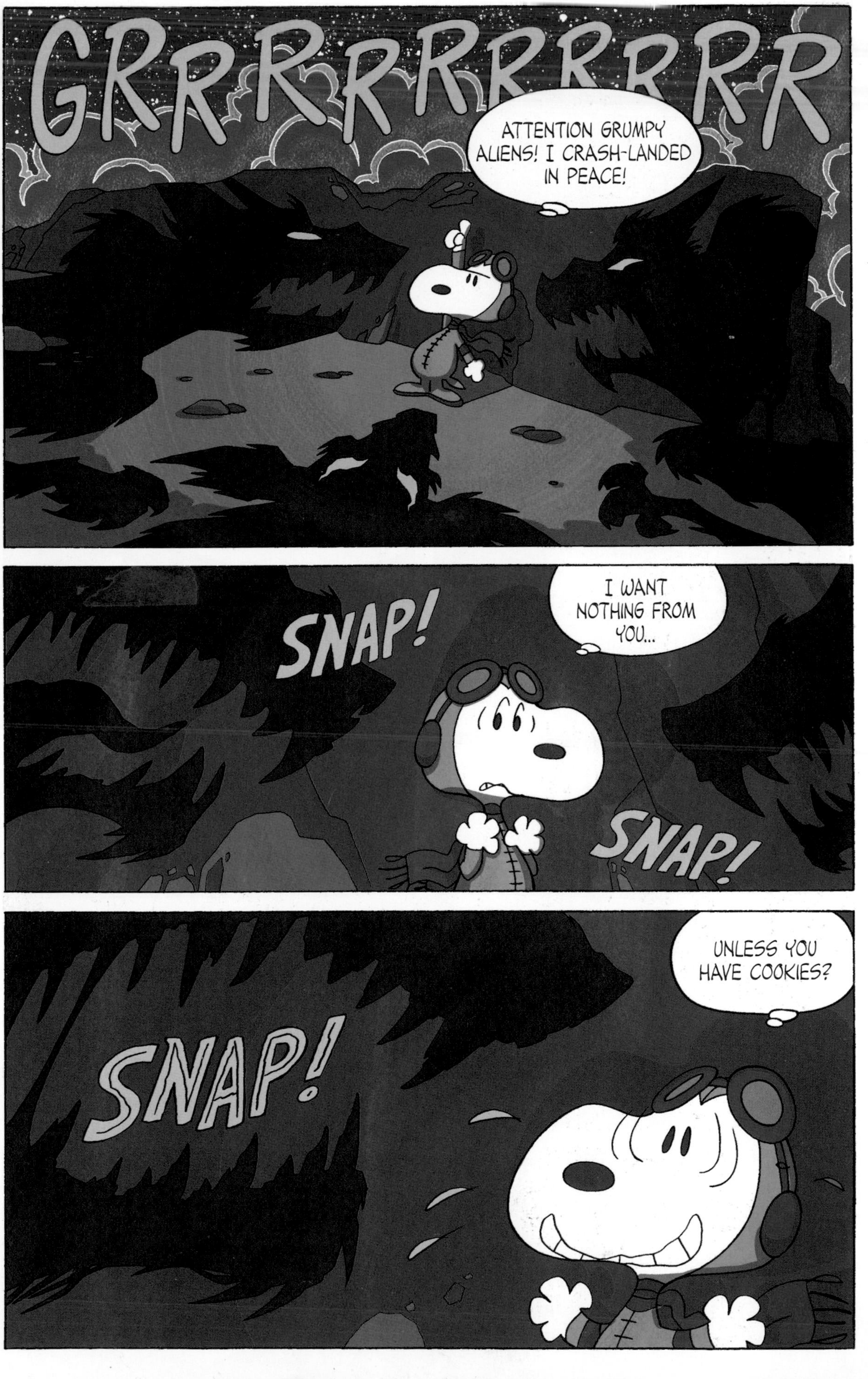
GRRRRRRRRRR
ATTENTION GRUMPY ALIENS! I CRASH-LANDED IN PEACE!
SNAP!
I WANT NOTHING FROM YOU...
SNAP!
UNLESS YOU HAVE COOKIES?
SNAP!

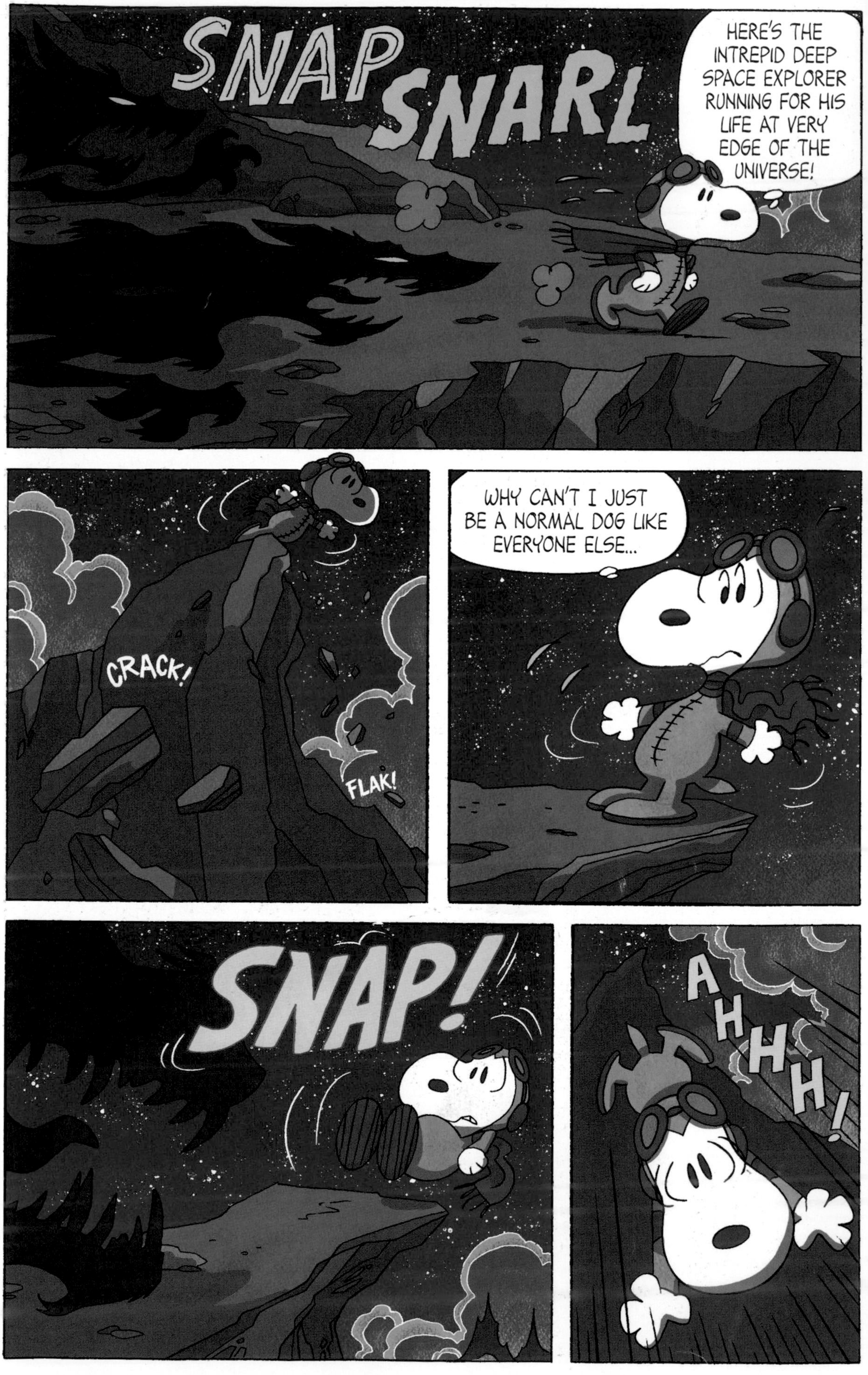
SNAP SNARL
HERE'S THE INTREPID DEEP SPACE EXPLORER RUNNING FOR HIS LIFE AT VERY EDGE OF THE UNIVERSE!
CRACK!
FLAK!
WHY CAN'T I JUST BE A NORMAL DOG LIKE EVERYONE ELSE...
SNAP!
AHHHH!

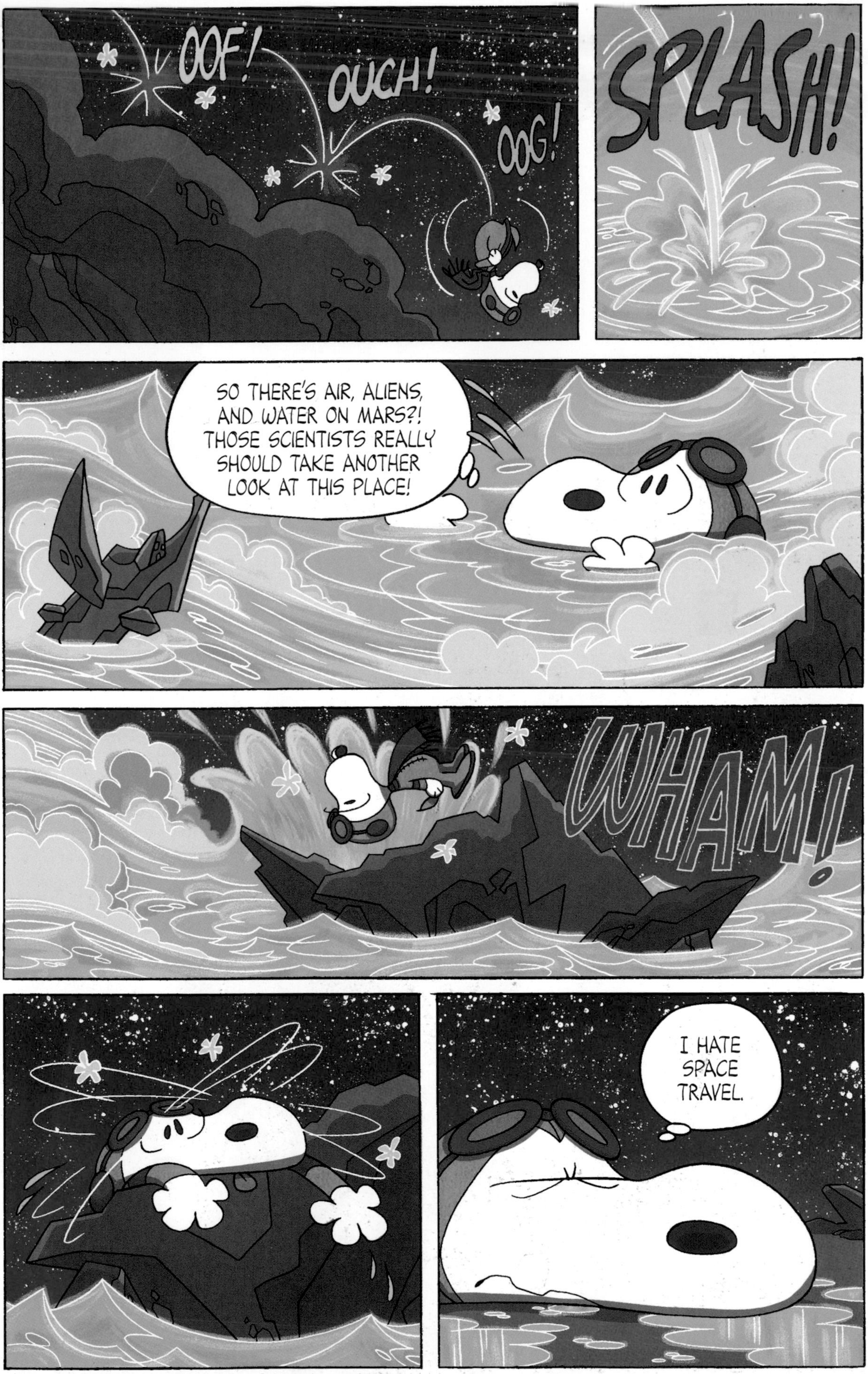
OOF!
OUCH!
OOG!
SPLASH!
SO THERE'S AIR, ALIENS, AND WATER ON MARS?! THOSE SCIENTISTS REALLY SHOULD TAKE ANOTHER LOOK AT THIS PLACE!
WHAM!
I HATE SPACE TRAVEL.

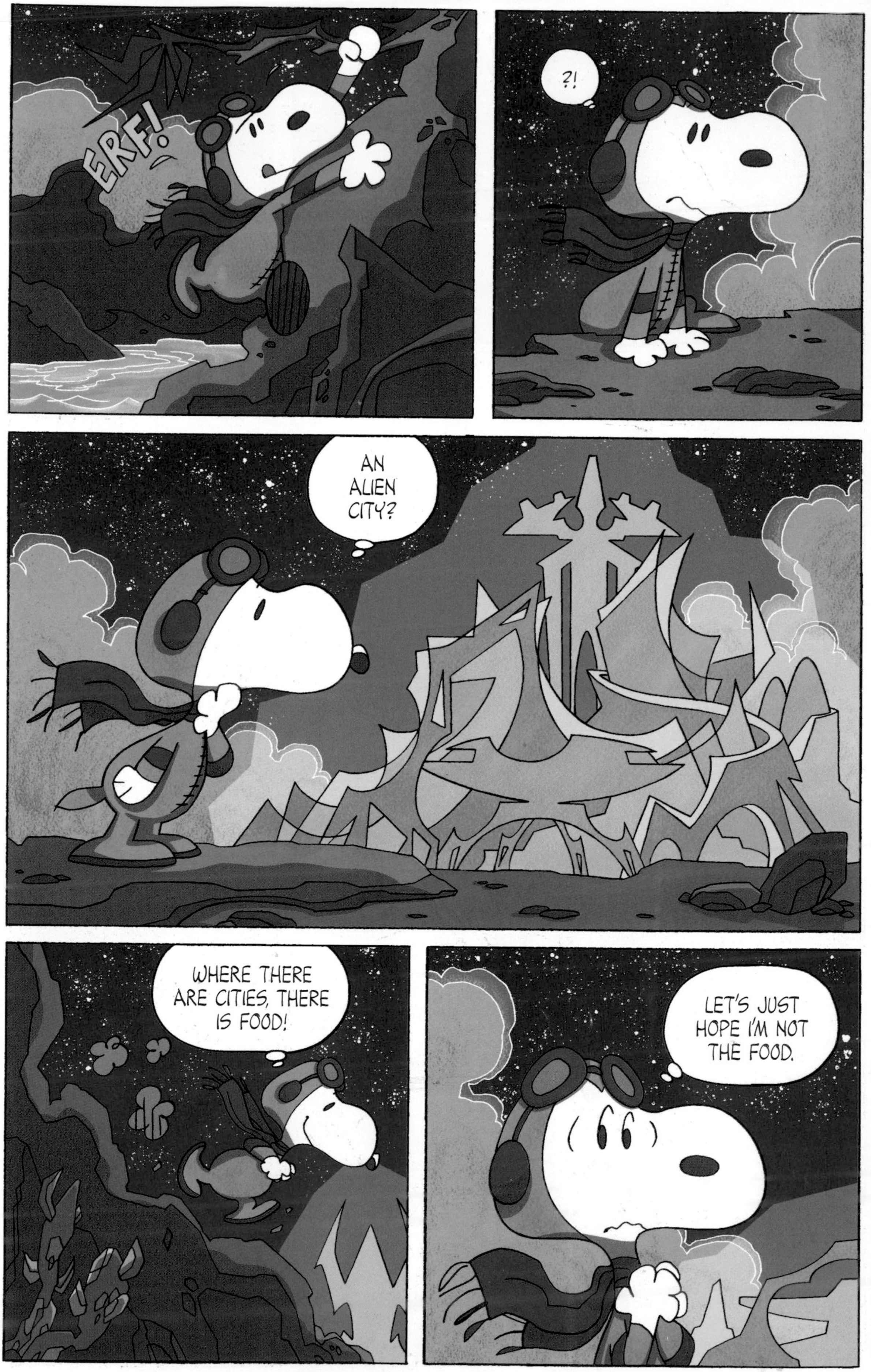
ERF!
?!
AN ALIEN CITY?
WHERE THERE ARE CITIES, THERE IS FOOD!
LET'S JUST HOPE I'M NOT THE FOOD.

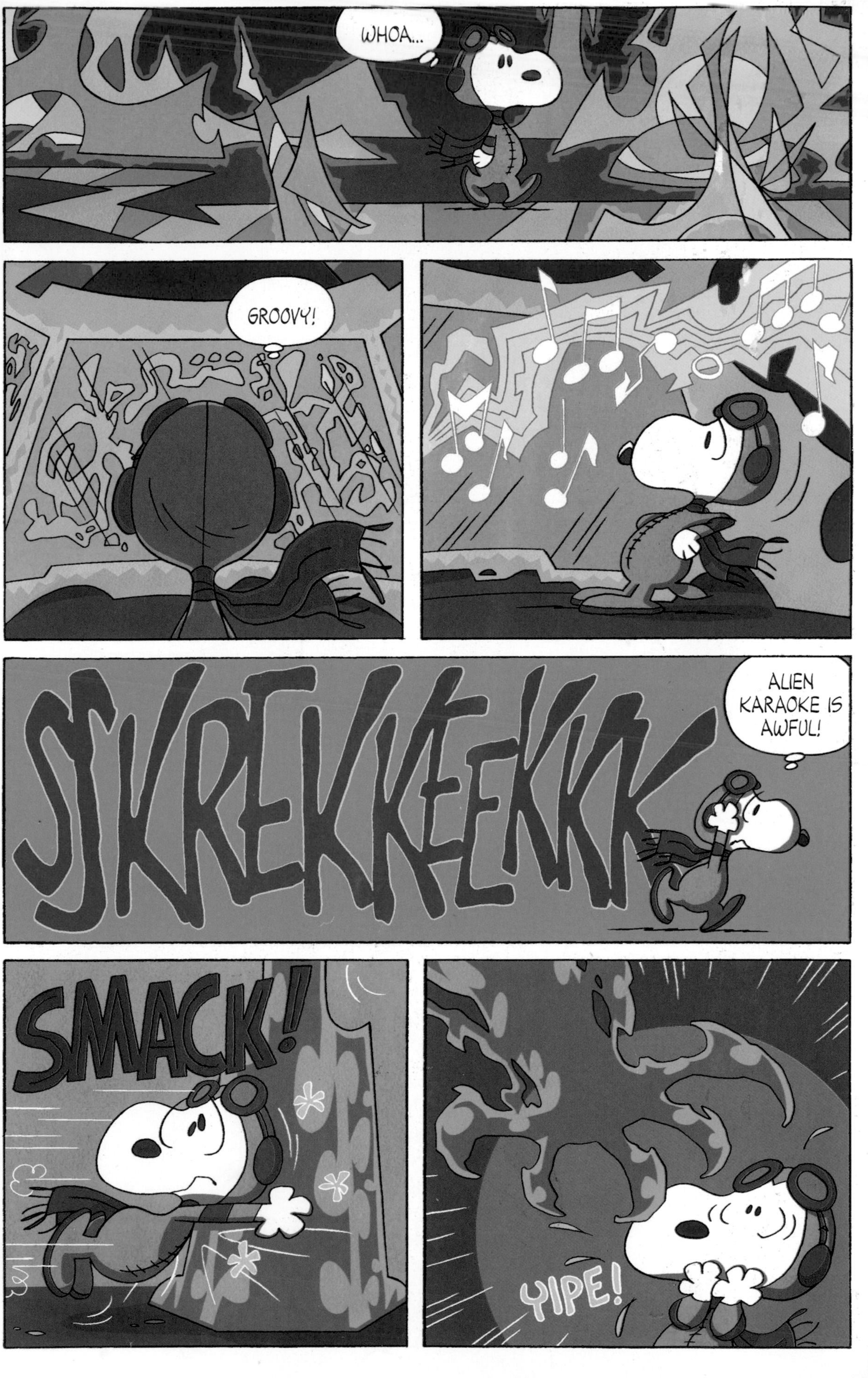
WHOA...
GROOVY!
SKREKKEEKKK
ALIEN KARAOKE IS AWFUL!
SMACK!
YIPE!

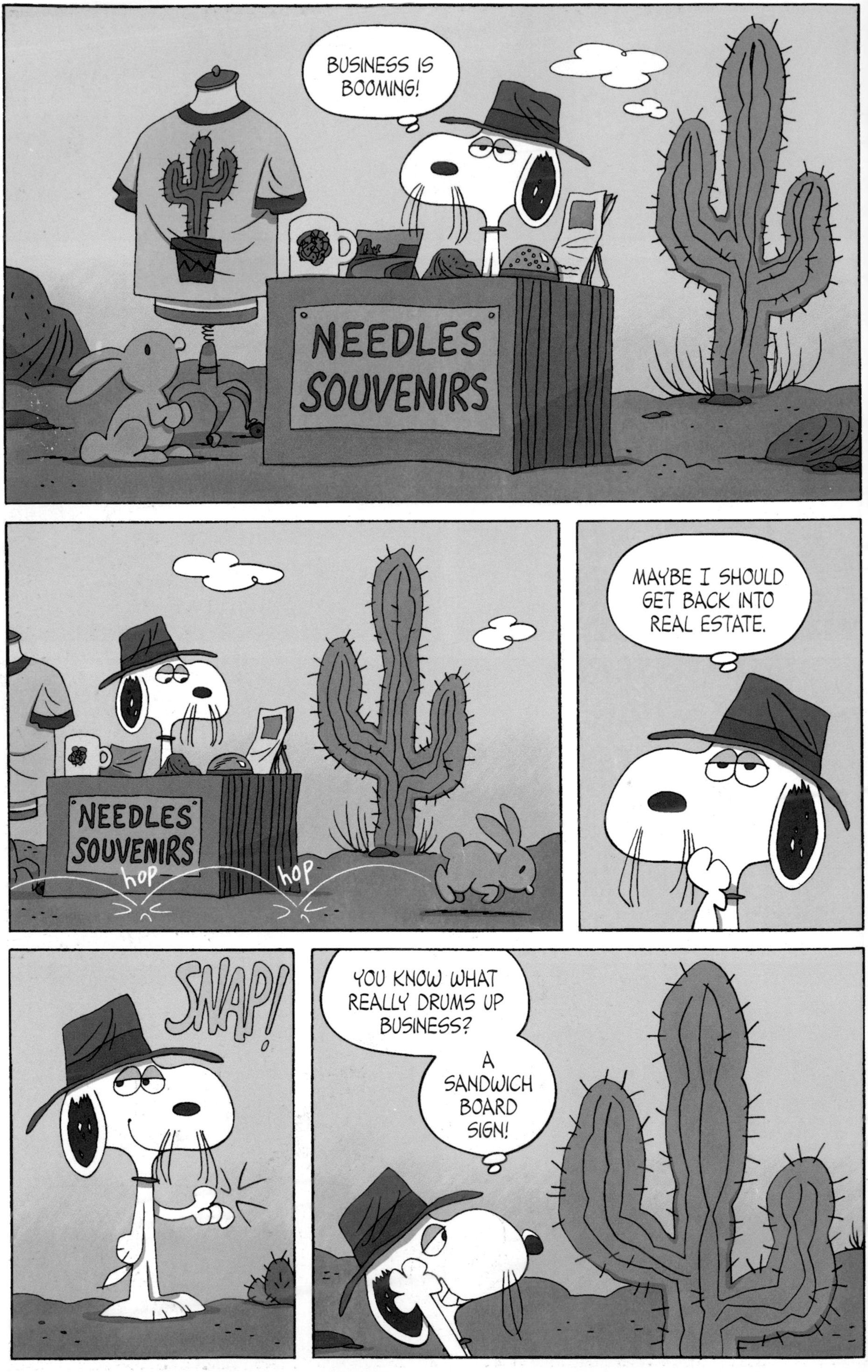
BUSINESS IS BOOMING!
NEEDLES SOUVENIRS
NEEDLES SOUVENIRS
hop
hop
MAYBE I SHOULD GET BACK INTO REAL ESTATE.
SNAP!
YOU KNOW WHAT REALLY DRUMS UP BUSINESS?
A SANDWICH BOARD SIGN!

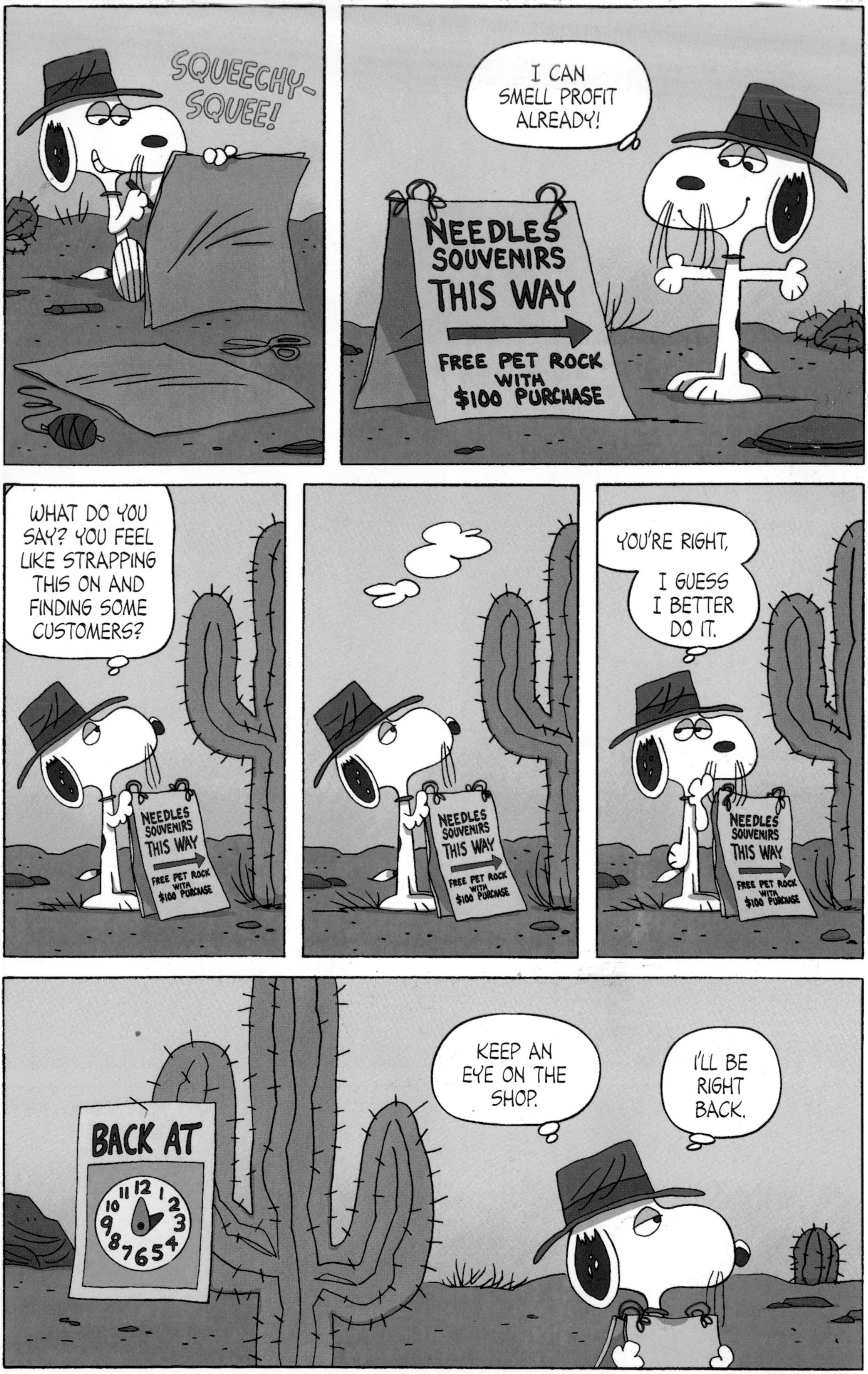
SQUEECHY-SQUEE!
I CAN SMELL PROFIT ALREADY!
NEEDLES SOUVENIRS THIS WAY
FREE PET ROCK WITH $100 PURCHASE
WHAT DO YOU SAY? YOU FEEL LIKE STRAPPING THIS ON AND FINDING SOME CUSTOMERS?
YOU'RE RIGHT,
I GUESS I BETTER DO IT.
BACK AT
KEEP AN EYE ON THE SHOP.
I'LL BE RIGHT BACK.

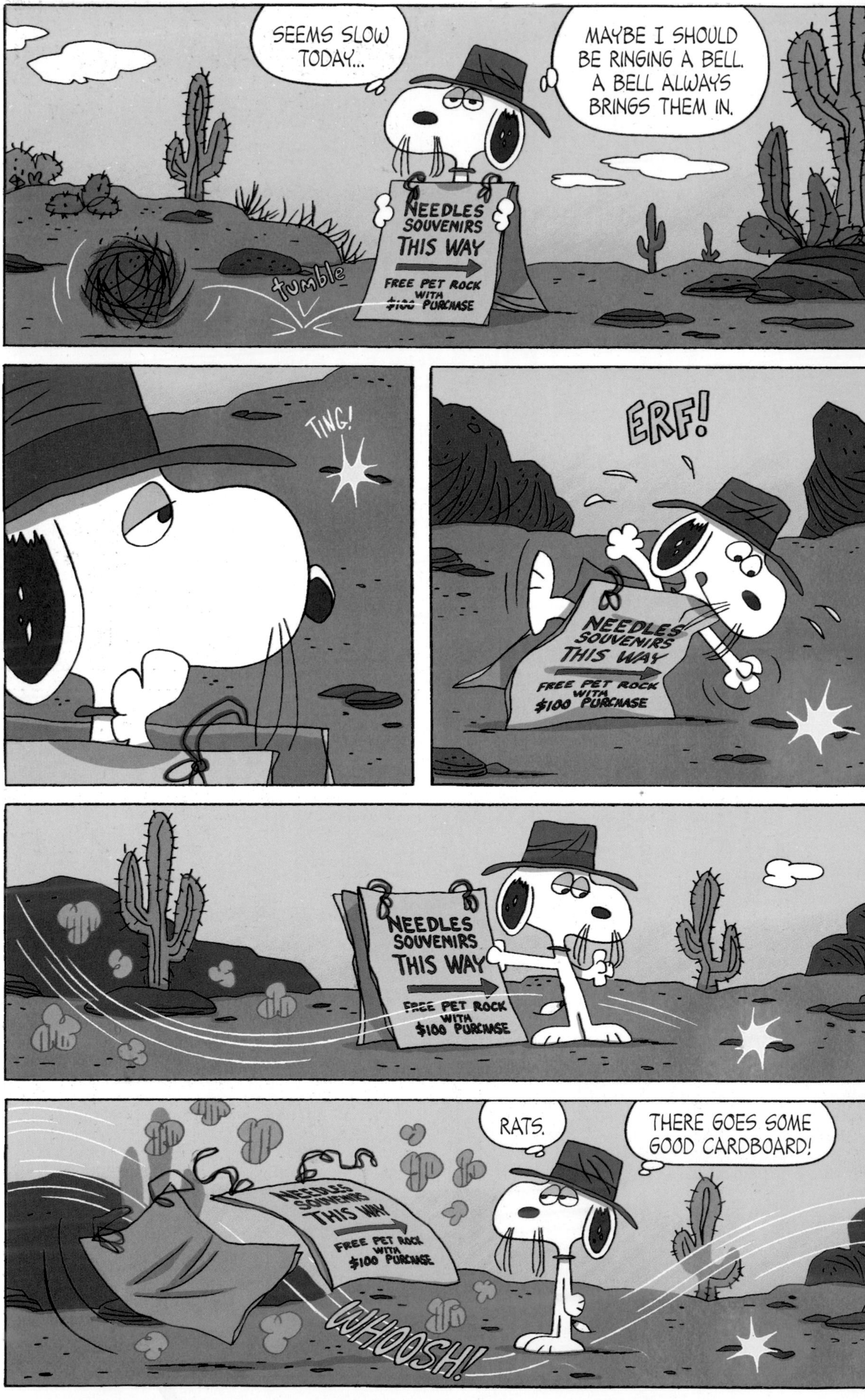
SEEMS SLOW TODAY...
MAYBE I SHOULD BE RINGING A BELL. A BELL ALWAYS BRINGS THEM IN.
NEEDLES SOUVENIRS THIS WAY
FREE PET ROCK WITH $100 PURCHASE
tumble
TING!
ERF!
NEEDLES SOUVENIRS THIS WAY
FREE PET ROCK WITH $100 PURCHASE
NEEDLES SOUVENIRS THIS WAY
FREE PET ROCK WITH $100 PURCHASE
RATS.
THERE GOES SOME GOOD CARDBOARD!
NEEDLES SOUVENIRS THIS WAY
FREE PET ROCK WITH $100 PURCHASE
WHOOSH!

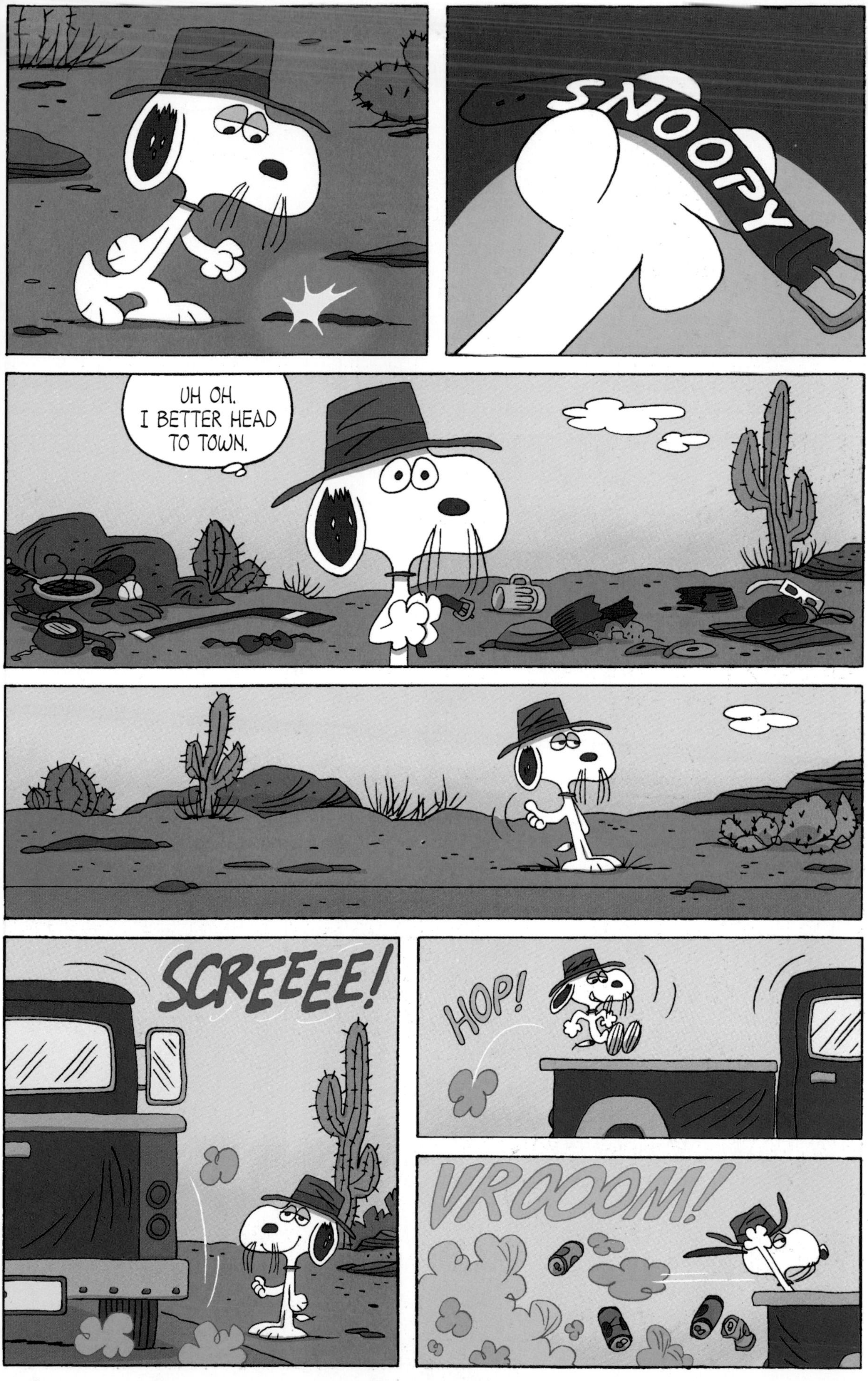
SNOOPY
UH OH. I BETTER HEAD TO TOWN.
SCREEEE!
HOP!
VROOOM!

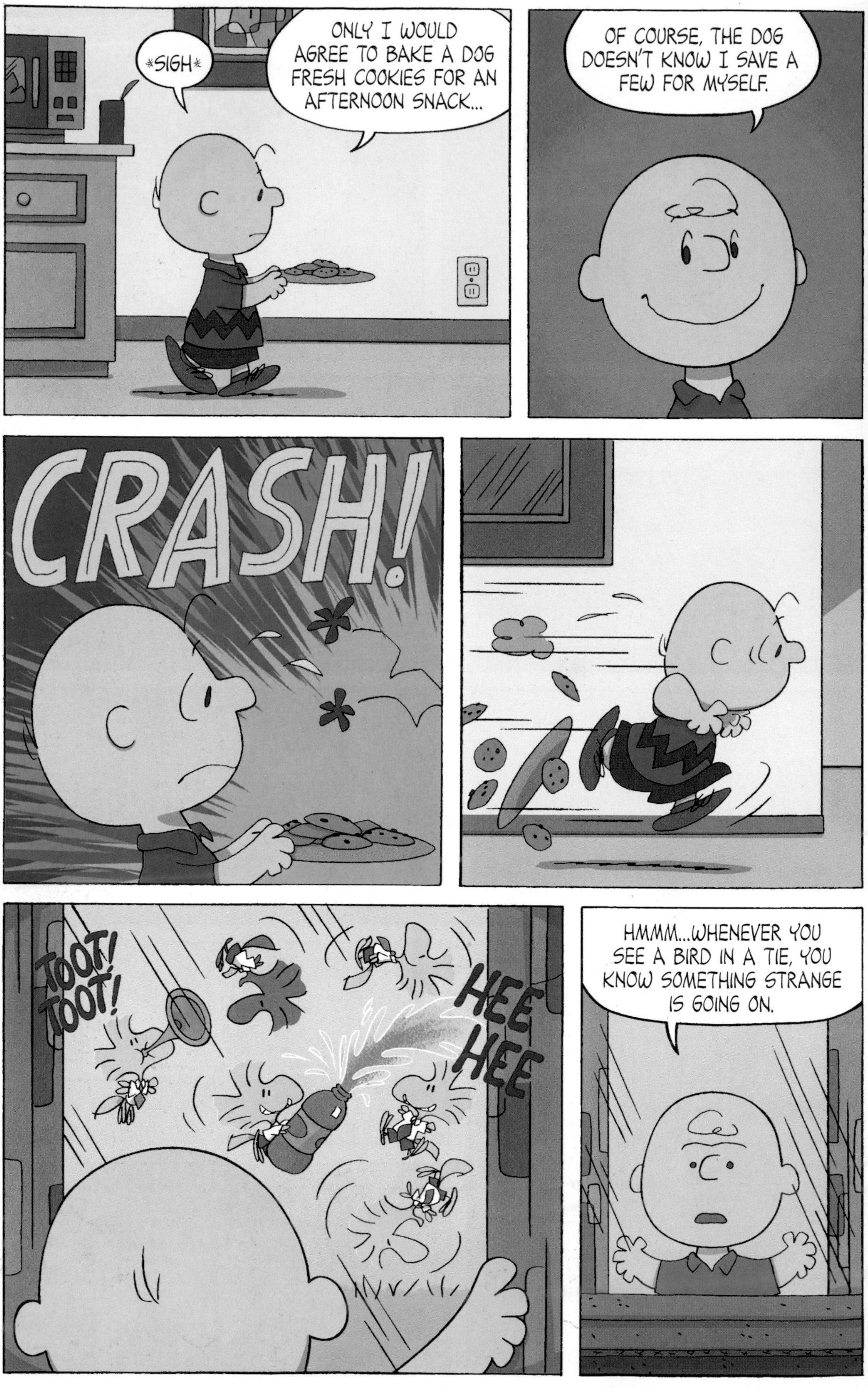
SIGH
ONLY I WOULD AGREE TO BAKE A DOG FRESH COOKIES FOR AN AFTERNOON SNACK...
OF COURSE, THE DOG DOESN'T KNOW I SAVE A FEW FOR MYSELF.
CRASH!
TOOT! TOOT!
HEE HEE
HMMM...WHENEVER YOU SEE A BIRD IN A TIE, YOU KNOW SOMETHING STRANGE IS GOING ON.

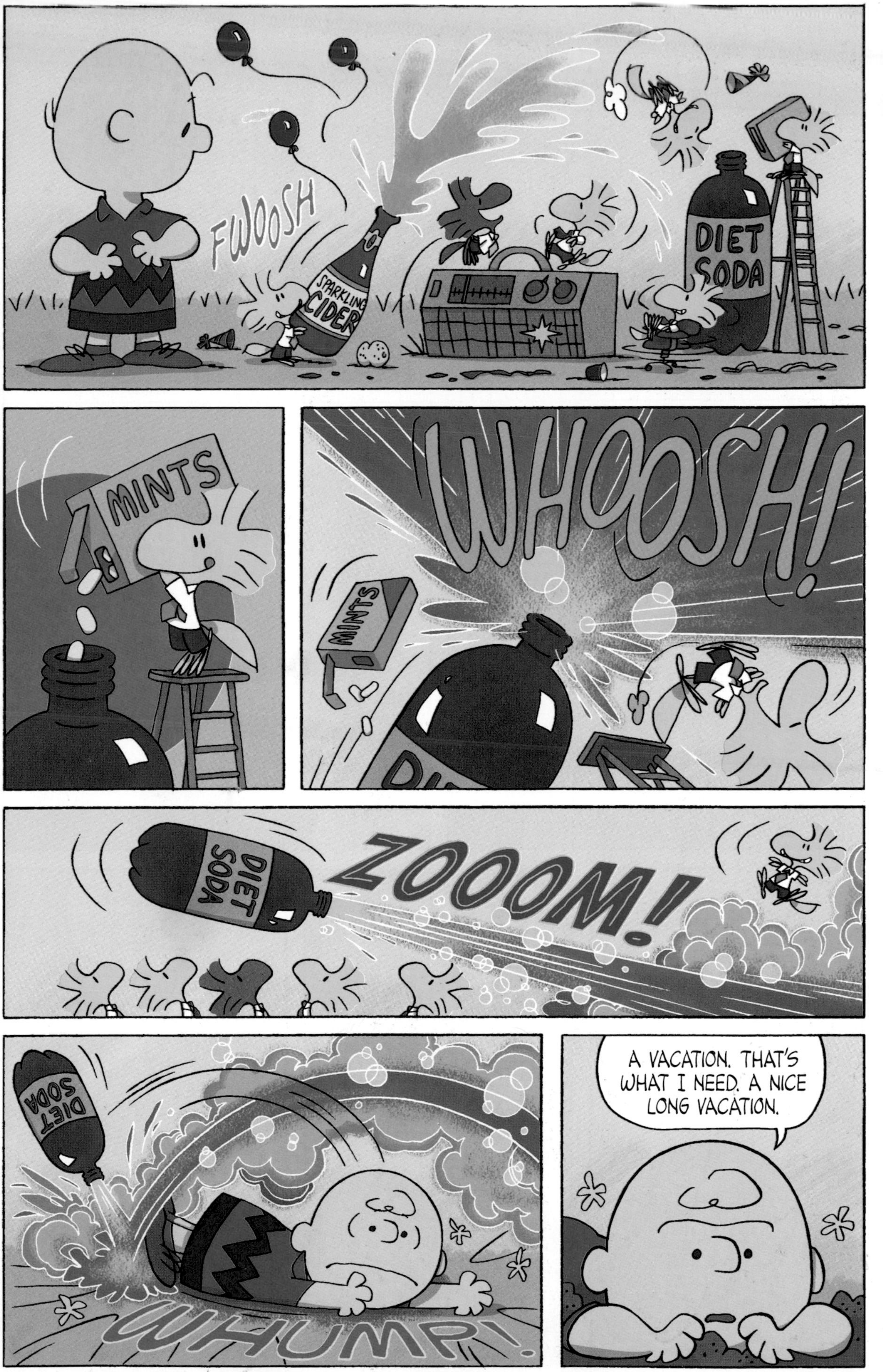
FWOOSH
SPARKLING CIDER
DIET SODA
MINTS
WHOOSH!
MINTS
DIET SODA
ZOOOM!
DIET SODA
WHUMP!
A VACATION. THAT'S WHAT I NEED. A NICE LONG VACATION.

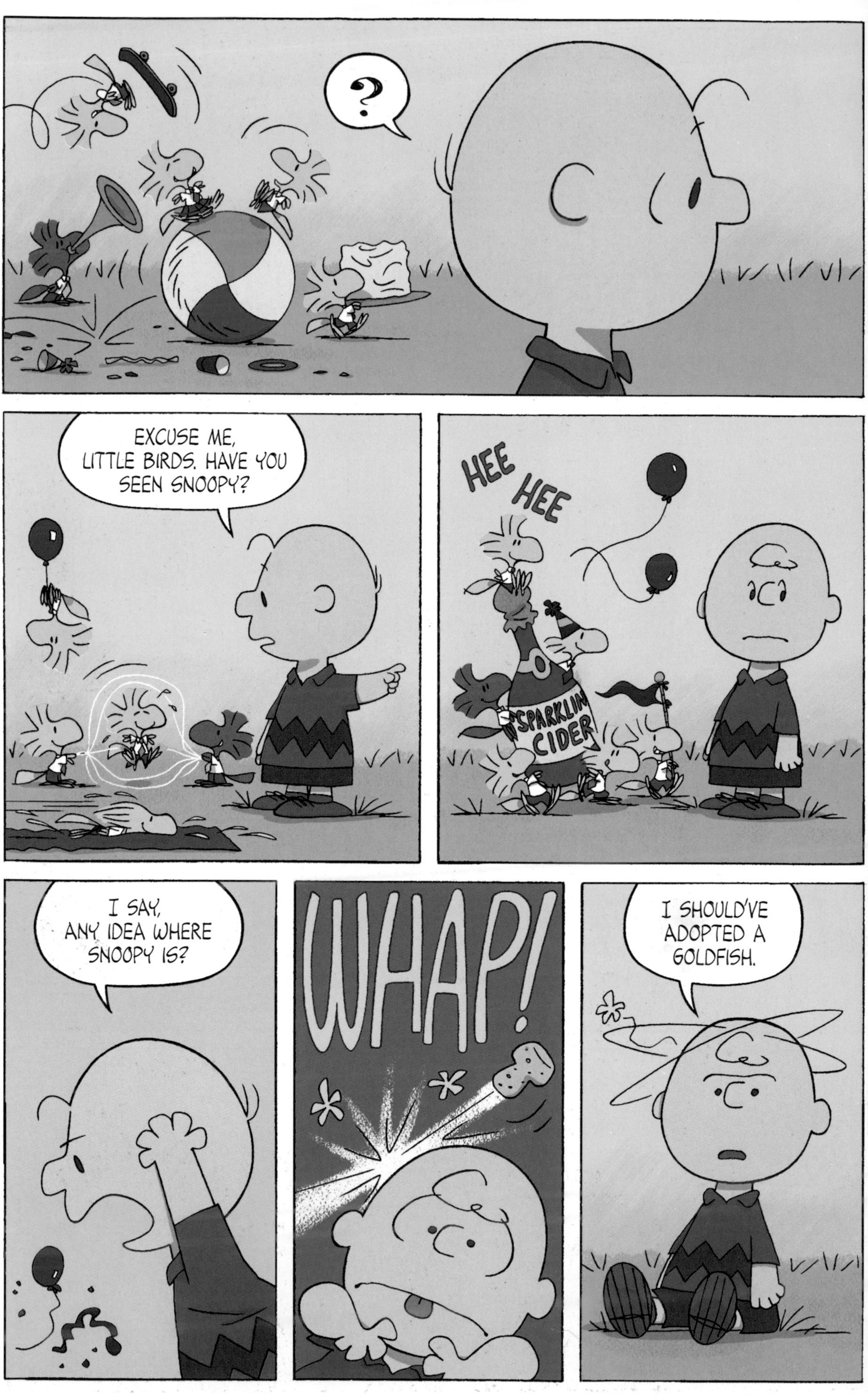
?
EXCUSE ME, LITTLE BIRDS. HAVE YOU SEEN SNOOPY?
HEE HEE
SPARKLIN CIDER
I SAY, ANY IDEA WHERE SNOOPY IS?
WHAP!
I SHOULD'VE ADOPTED A GOLDFISH.

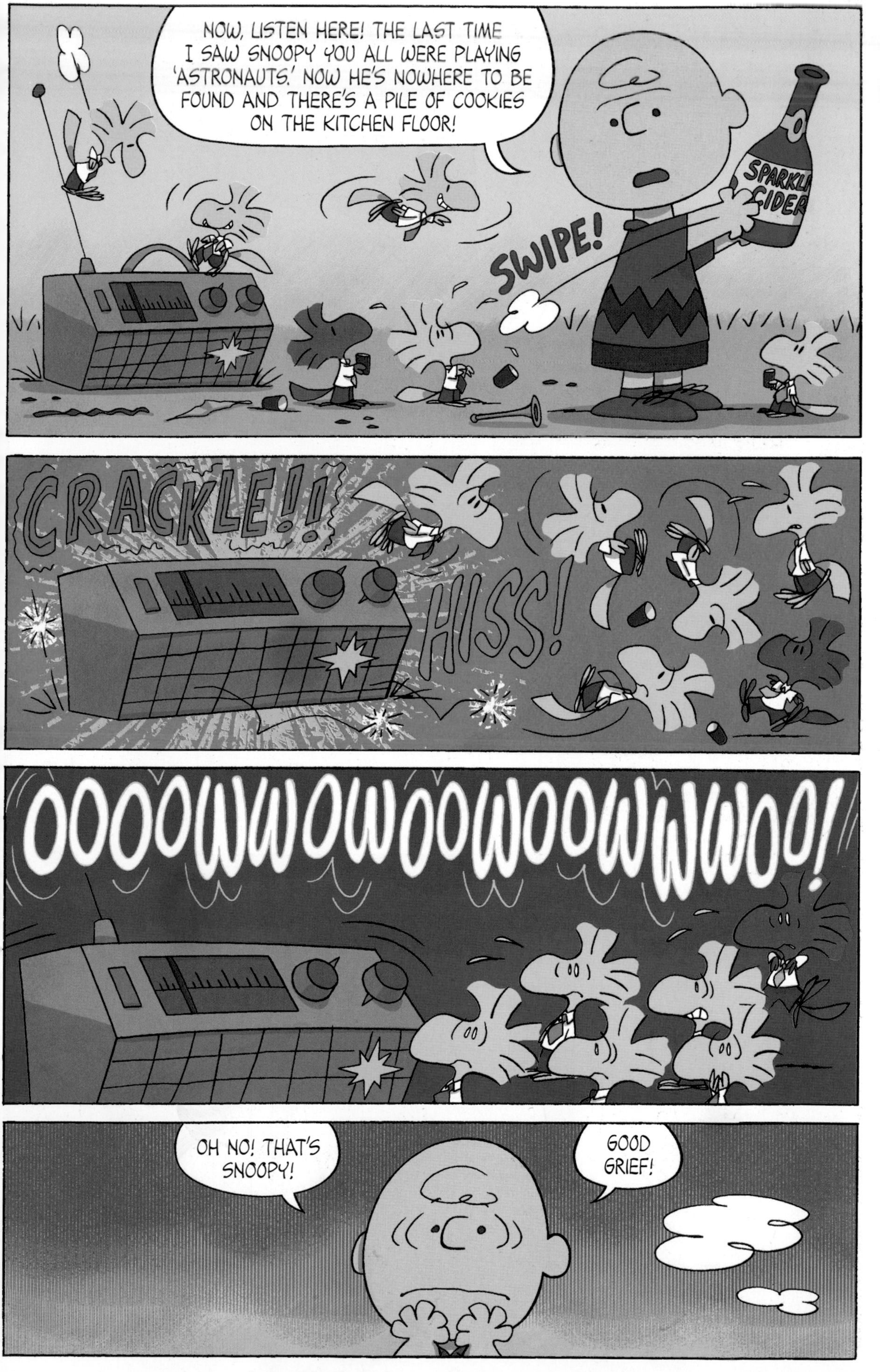
NOW, LISTEN HERE! THE LAST TIME I SAW SNOOPY YOU ALL WERE PLAYING 'ASTRONAUTS.' NOW HE'S NOWHERE TO BE FOUND AND THERE'S A PILE OF COOKIES ON THE KITCHEN FLOOR!
SPARKLI CIDER
SWIPE!
CRACKLE!!
HISS!
OOOOWWOWOOWOOWWWOO!
OH NO! THAT'S SNOOPY!
GOOD GRIEF!

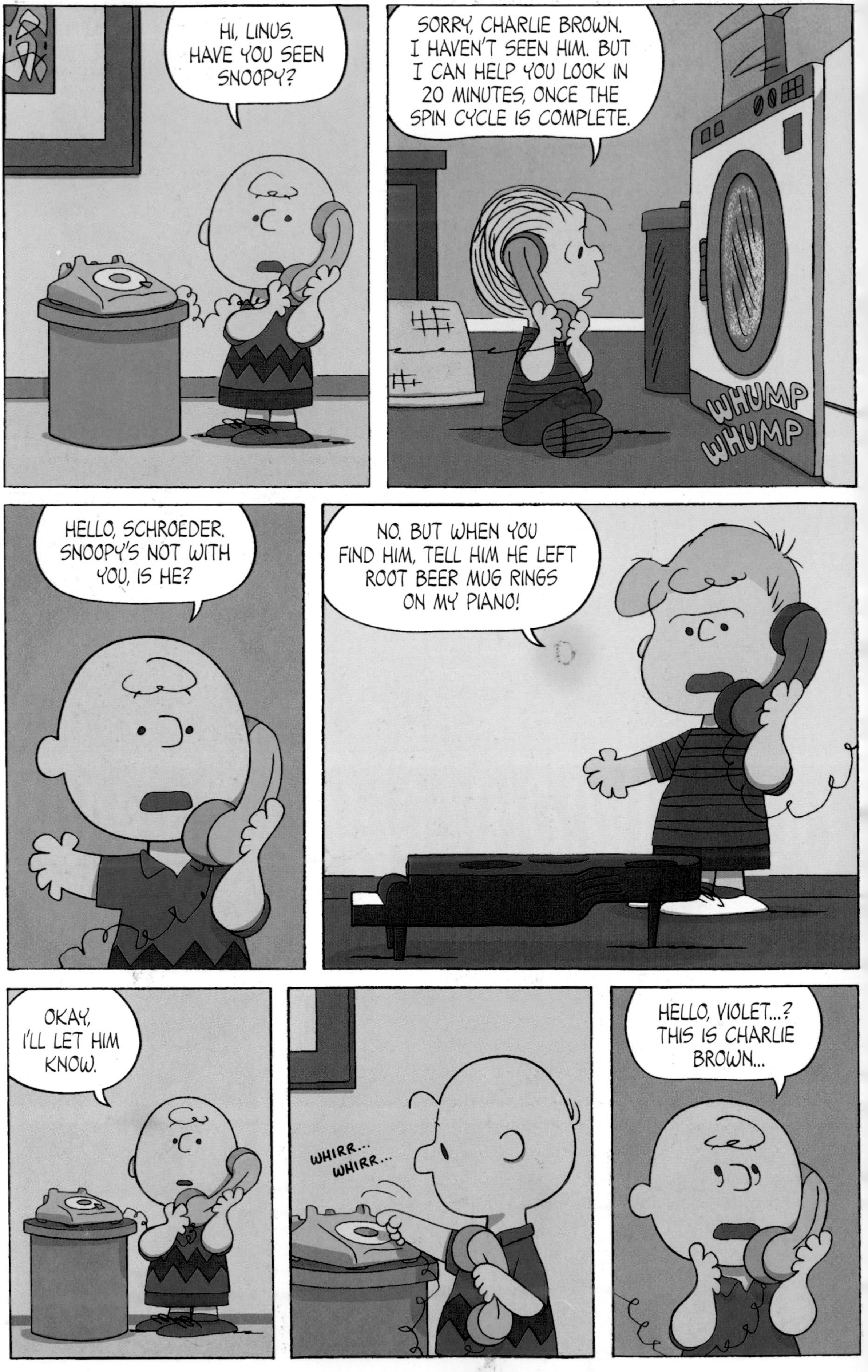

HI, LINUS. HAVE YOU SEEN SNOOPY?
SORRY, CHARLIE BROWN. I HAVEN'T SEEN HIM. BUT I CAN HELP YOU LOOK IN 20 MINUTES, ONCE THE SPIN CYCLE IS COMPLETE.
WHUMP WHUMP
HELLO, SCHROEDER. SNOOPY'S NOT WITH YOU, IS HE?
NO. BUT WHEN YOU FIND HIM, TELL HIM HE LEFT ROOT BEER MUG RINGS ON MY PIANO!
OKAY, I'LL LET HIM KNOW.
WHIRR... WHIRR...
HELLO, VIOLET...? THIS IS CHARLIE BROWN...

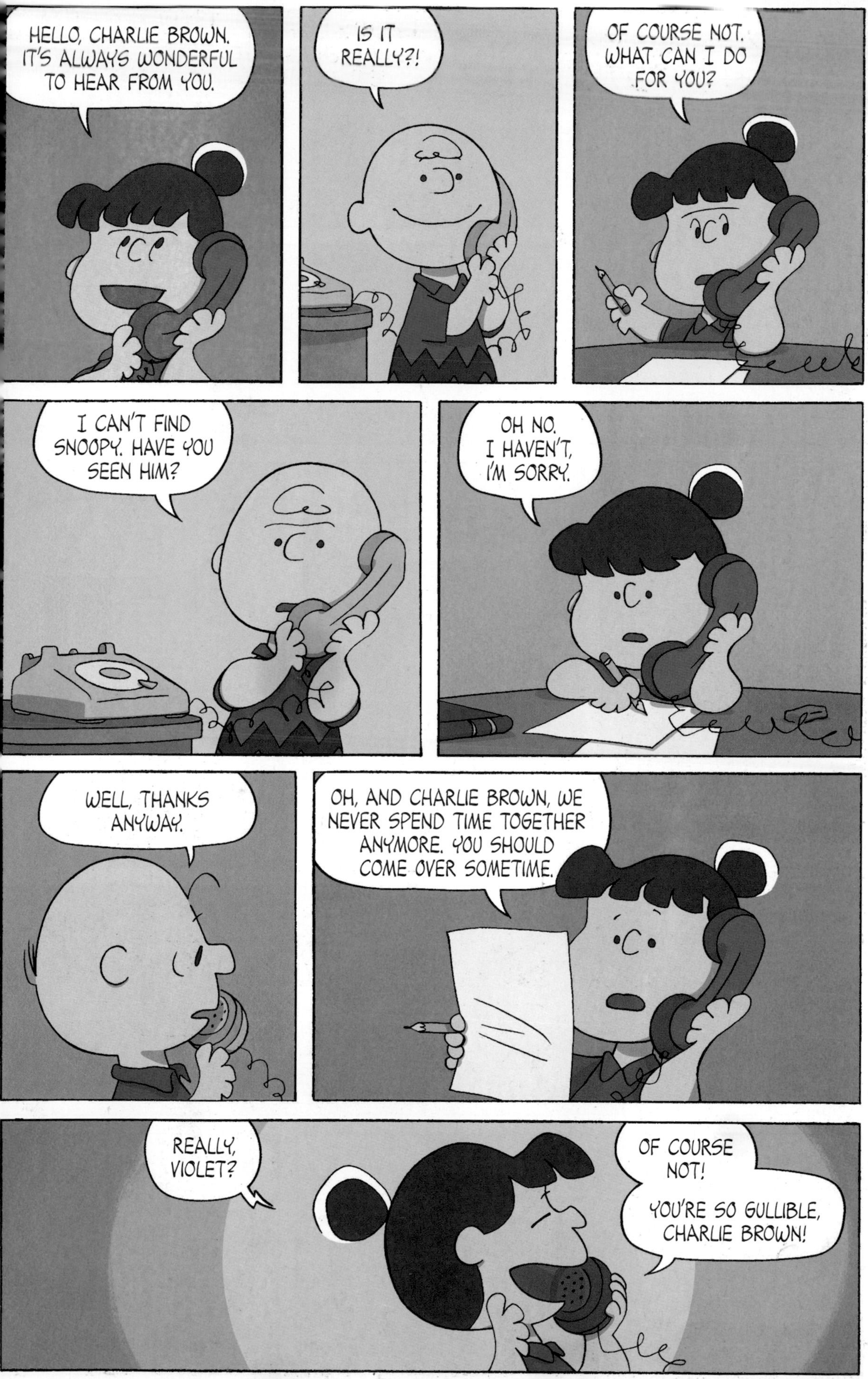
HELLO, CHARLIE BROWN. IT'S ALWAYS WONDERFUL TO HEAR FROM YOU.
IS IT REALLY?!
OF COURSE NOT. WHAT CAN I DO FOR YOU?
I CAN'T FIND SNOOPY. HAVE YOU SEEN HIM?
OH NO. I HAVEN'T, I'M SORRY.
WELL, THANKS ANYWAY.
OH, AND CHARLIE BROWN, WE NEVER SPEND TIME TOGETHER ANYMORE. YOU SHOULD COME OVER SOMETIME.
REALLY, VIOLET?
OF COURSE NOT!
YOU'RE SO GULLIBLE, CHARLIE BROWN!

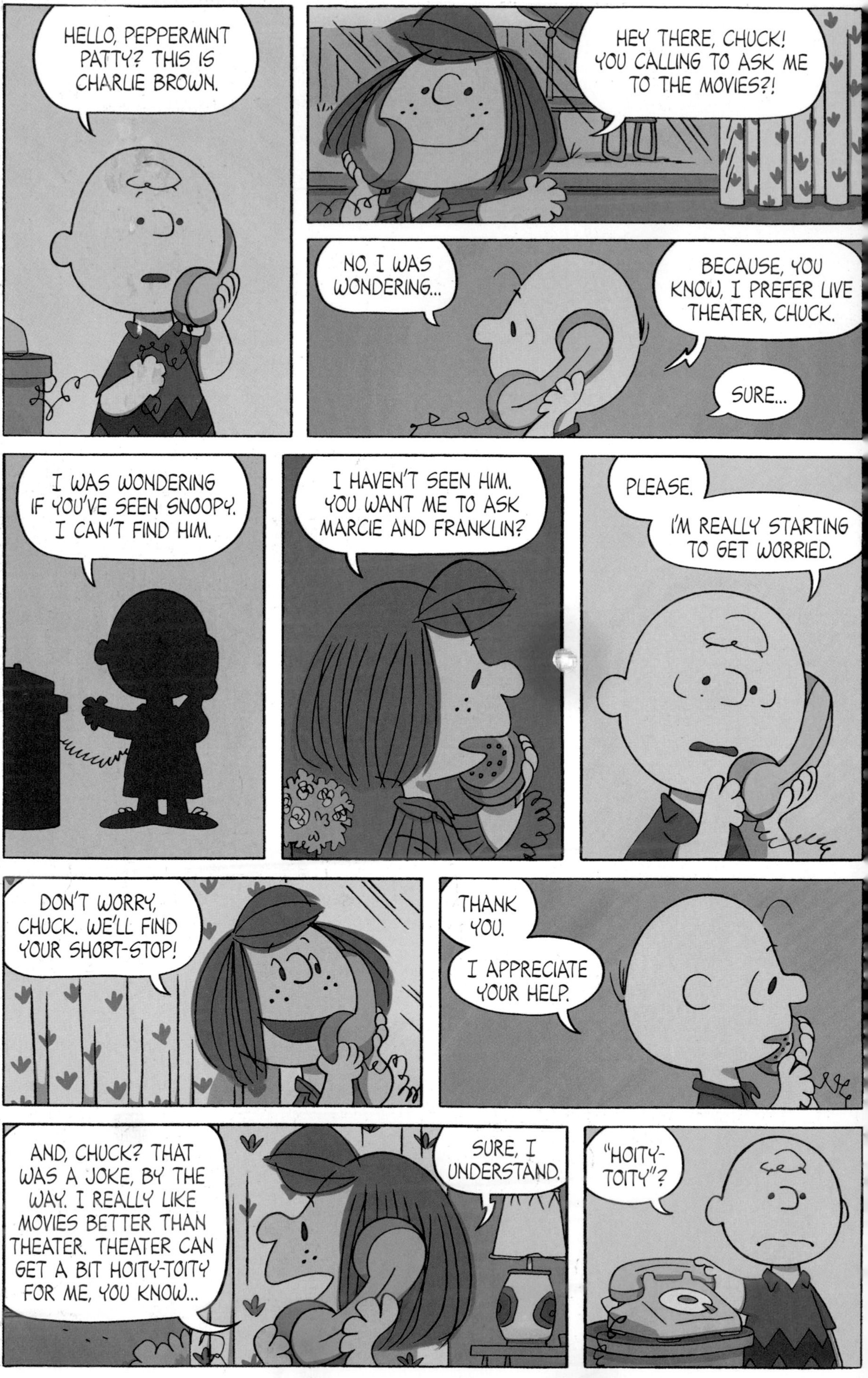
HELLO, PEPPERMINT PATTY? THIS IS CHARLIE BROWN.
HEY THERE, CHUCK! YOU CALLING TO ASK ME TO THE MOVIES?!
NO, I WAS WONDERING...
BECAUSE, YOU KNOW, I PREFER LIVE THEATER, CHUCK.
SURE...
I WAS WONDERING IF YOU'VE SEEN SNOOPY. I CAN'T FIND HIM.
I HAVEN'T SEEN HIM. YOU WANT ME TO ASK MARCIE AND FRANKLIN?
PLEASE.
I'M REALLY STARTING TO GET WORRIED.
DON'T WORRY, CHUCK. WE'LL FIND YOUR SHORT-STOP!
THANK YOU.
I APPRECIATE YOUR HELP.
AND, CHUCK? THAT WAS A JOKE, BY THE WAY. I REALLY LIKE MOVIES BETTER THAN THEATER. THEATER CAN GET A BIT HOITY-TOITY FOR ME, YOU KNOW...
SURE, I UNDERSTAND.
"HOITY-TOITY"?

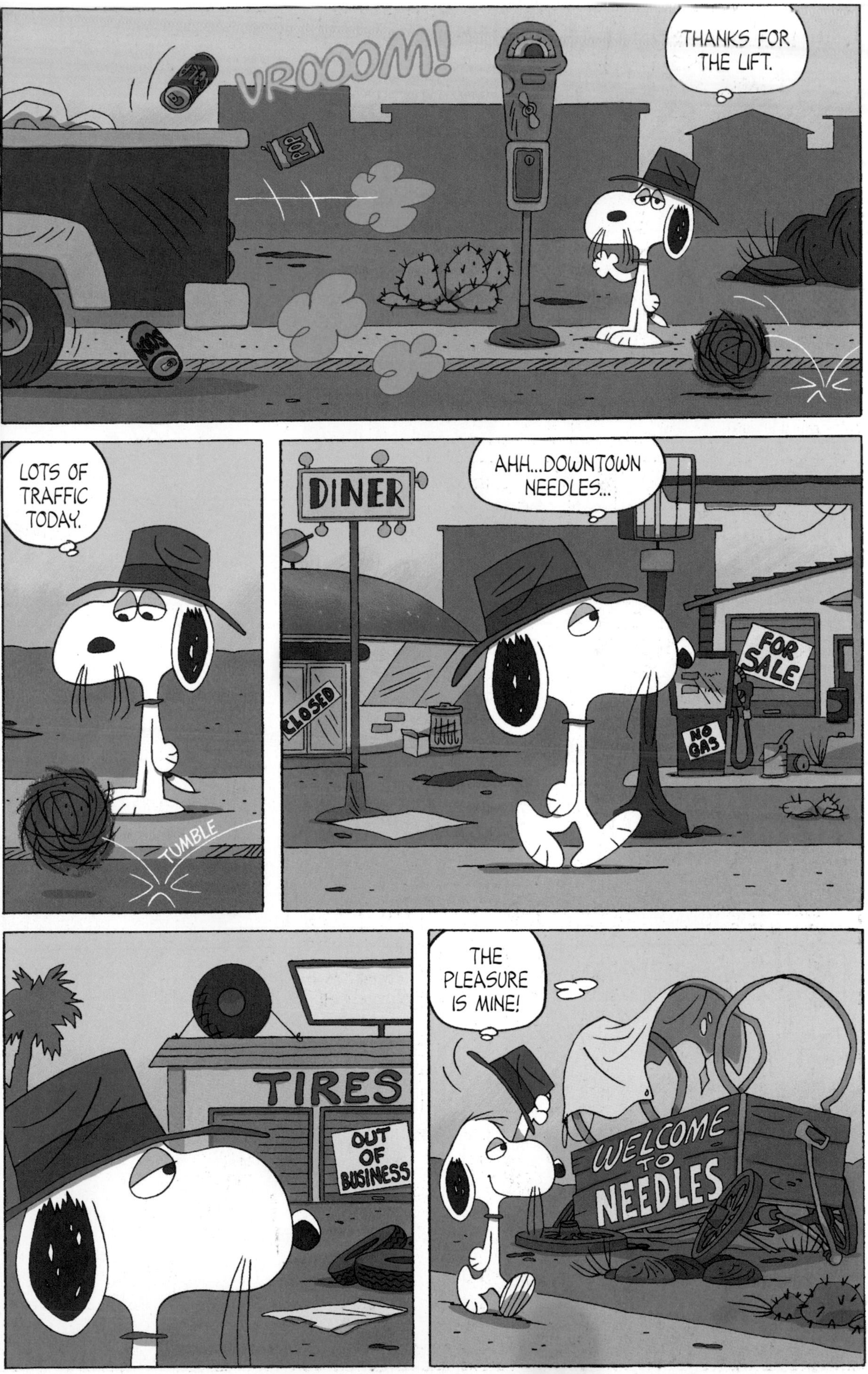
VROOOM!
POP
THANKS FOR THE LIFT.
LOTS OF TRAFFIC TODAY.
TUMBLE
DINER
AHH...DOWNTOWN NEEDLES...
CLOSED
FOR SALE
NO GAS
TIRES
OUT OF BUSINESS
THE PLEASURE IS MINE!
WELCOME TO NEEDLES

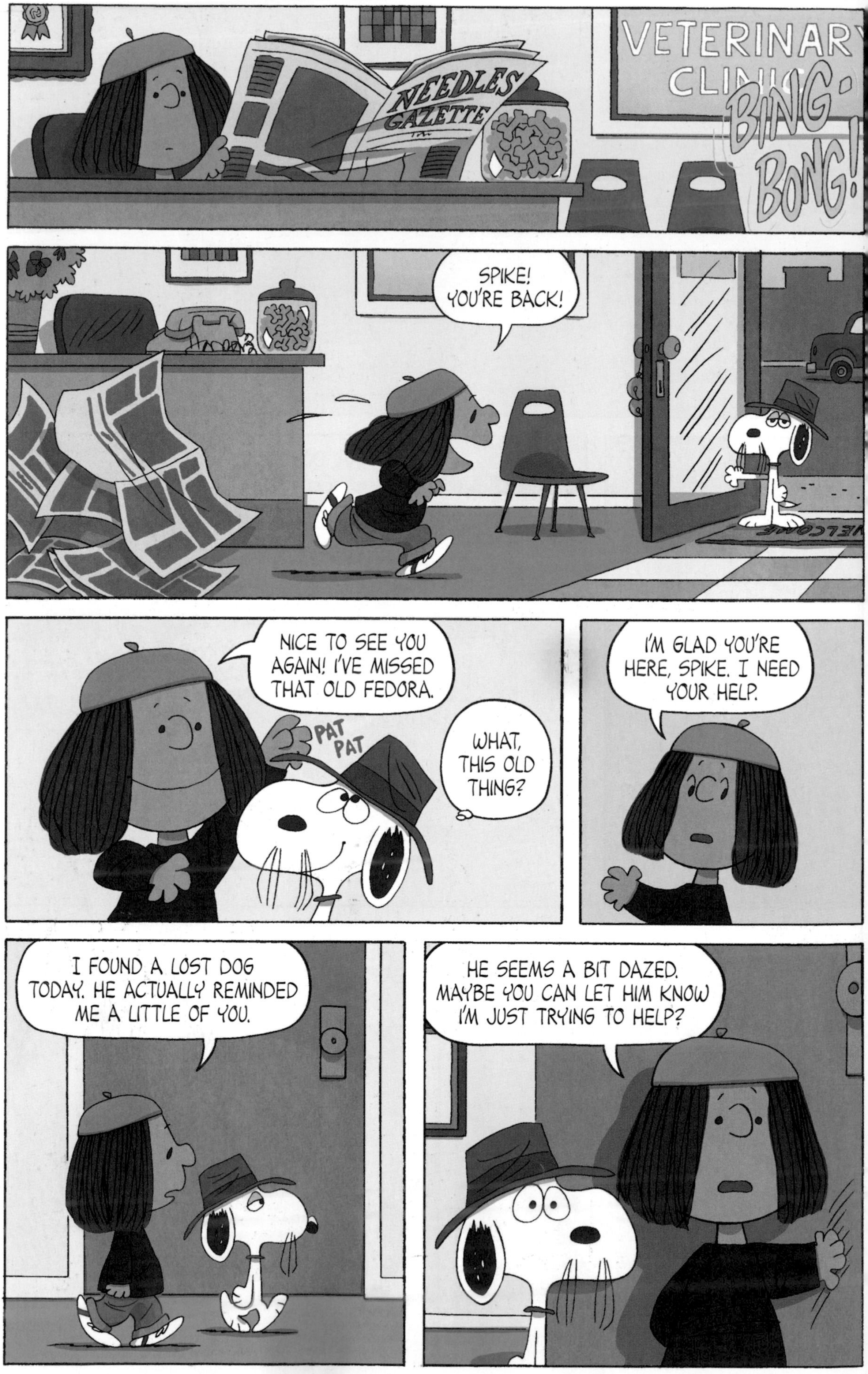
VETERINARY
CLINIC
NEEDLES GAZETTE
BING-BONG!
SPIKE! YOU'RE BACK!
NICE TO SEE YOU AGAIN! I'VE MISSED THAT OLD FEDORA.
PAT PAT
WHAT, THIS OLD THING?
I'M GLAD YOU'RE HERE, SPIKE. I NEED YOUR HELP.
I FOUND A LOST DOG TODAY. HE ACTUALLY REMINDED ME A LITTLE OF YOU.
HE SEEMS A BIT DAZED. MAYBE YOU CAN LET HIM KNOW I'M JUST TRYING TO HELP?

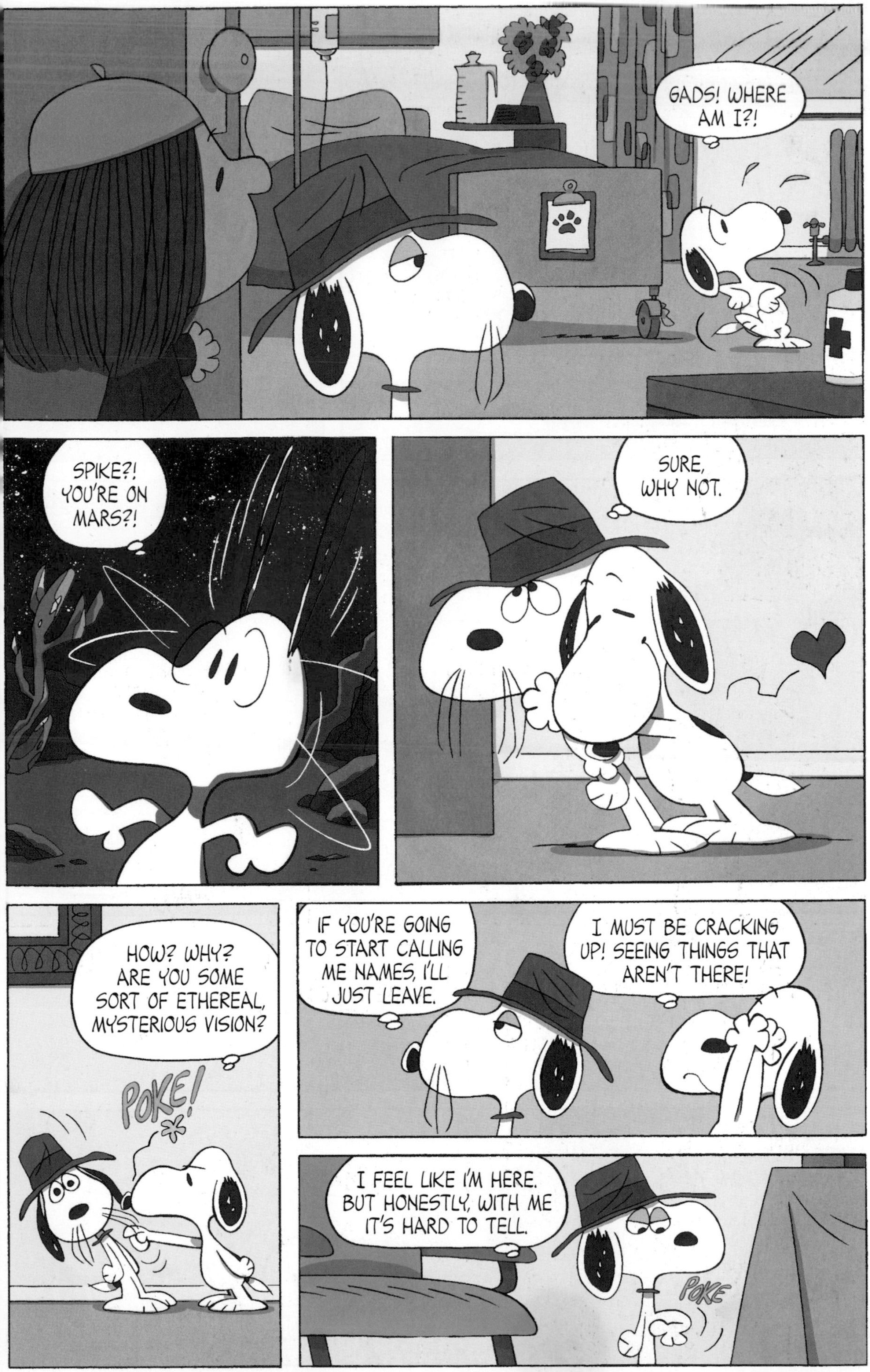
GADS! WHERE AM I?!
SPIKE?! YOU'RE ON MARS?!
SURE, WHY NOT.
HOW? WHY? ARE YOU SOME SORT OF ETHEREAL, MYSTERIOUS VISION?
POKE!
IF YOU'RE GOING TO START CALLING ME NAMES, I'LL JUST LEAVE.
I MUST BE CRACKING UP! SEEING THINGS THAT AREN'T THERE!
I FEEL LIKE I'M HERE. BUT HONESTLY, WITH ME IT'S HARD TO TELL.
POKE

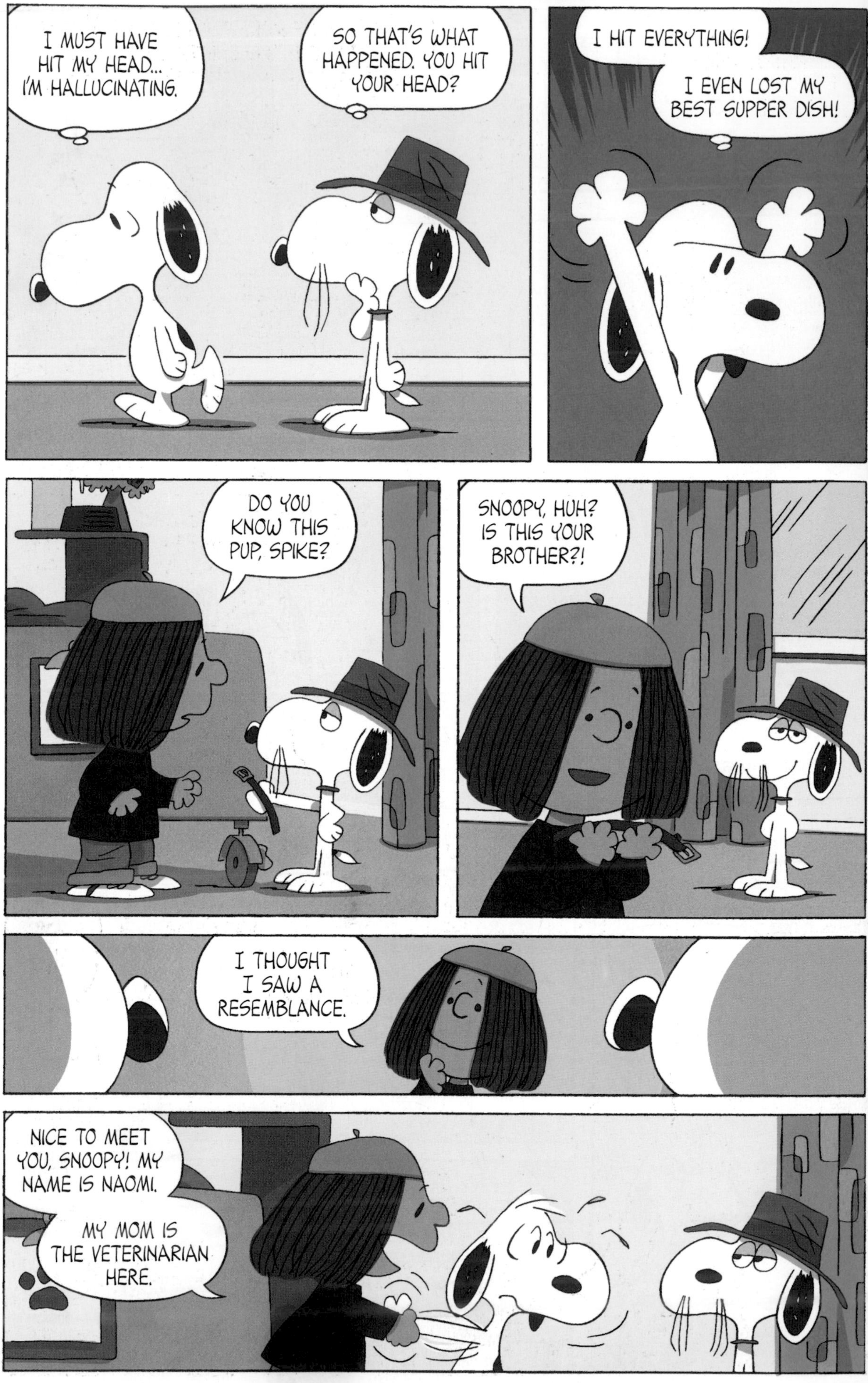
I MUST HAVE HIT MY HEAD... I'M HALLUCINATING.
SO THAT'S WHAT HAPPENED. YOU HIT YOUR HEAD?
I HIT EVERYTHING!
I EVEN LOST MY BEST SUPPER DISH!
DO YOU KNOW THIS PUP, SPIKE?
SNOOPY, HUH? IS THIS YOUR BROTHER?!
I THOUGHT I SAW A RESEMBLANCE.
NICE TO MEET YOU, SNOOPY! MY NAME IS NAOMI.
MY MOM IS THE VETERINARIAN HERE.

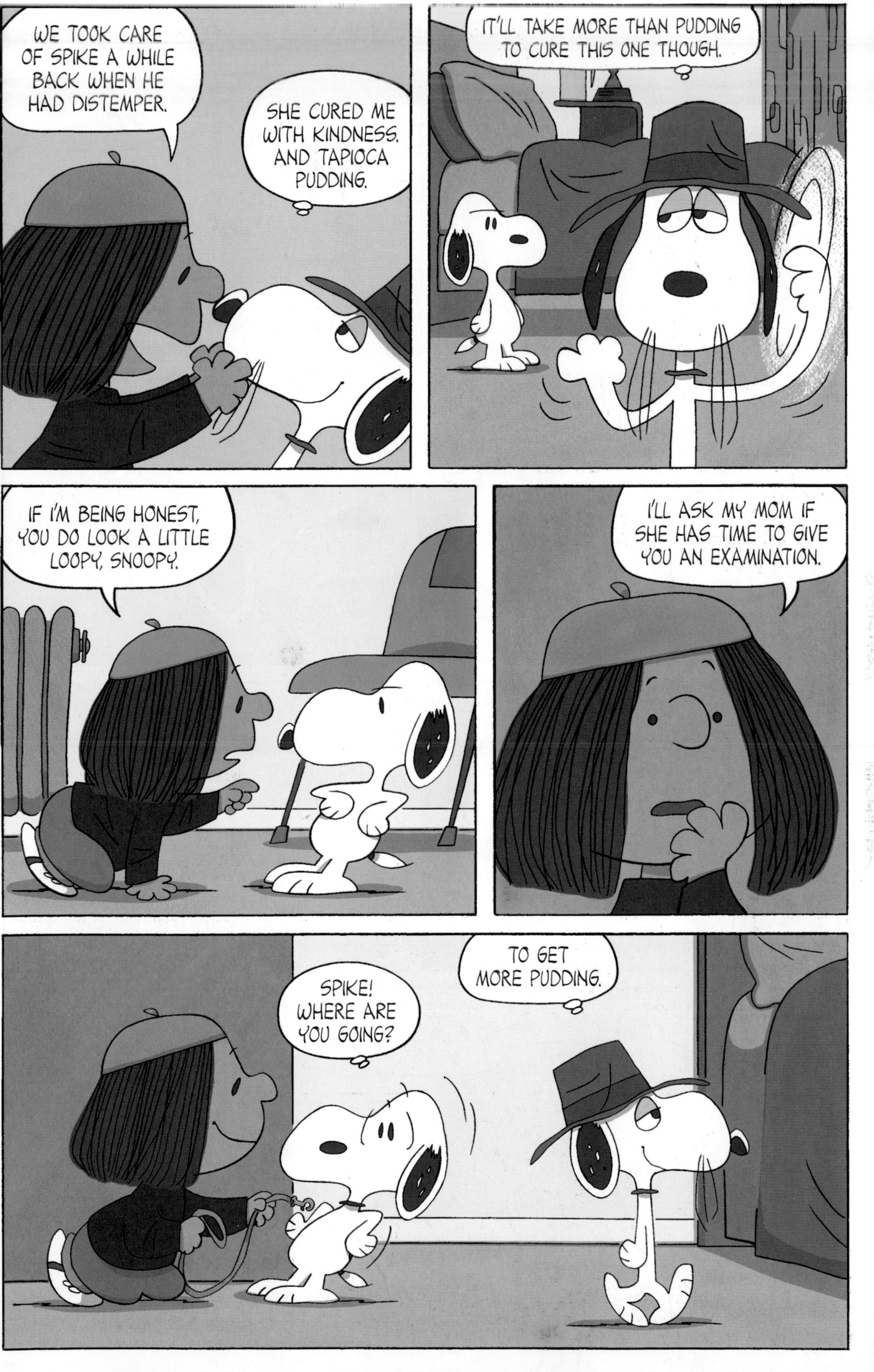
WE TOOK CARE OF SPIKE A WHILE BACK WHEN HE HAD DISTEMPER.
SHE CURED ME WITH KINDNESS. AND TAPIOCA PUDDING.
IT'LL TAKE MORE THAN PUDDING TO CURE THIS ONE THOUGH.
IF I'M BEING HONEST, YOU DO LOOK A LITTLE LOOPY, SNOOPY.
I'LL ASK MY MOM IF SHE HAS TIME TO GIVE YOU AN EXAMINATION.
SPIKE! WHERE ARE YOU GOING?
TO GET MORE PUDDING.

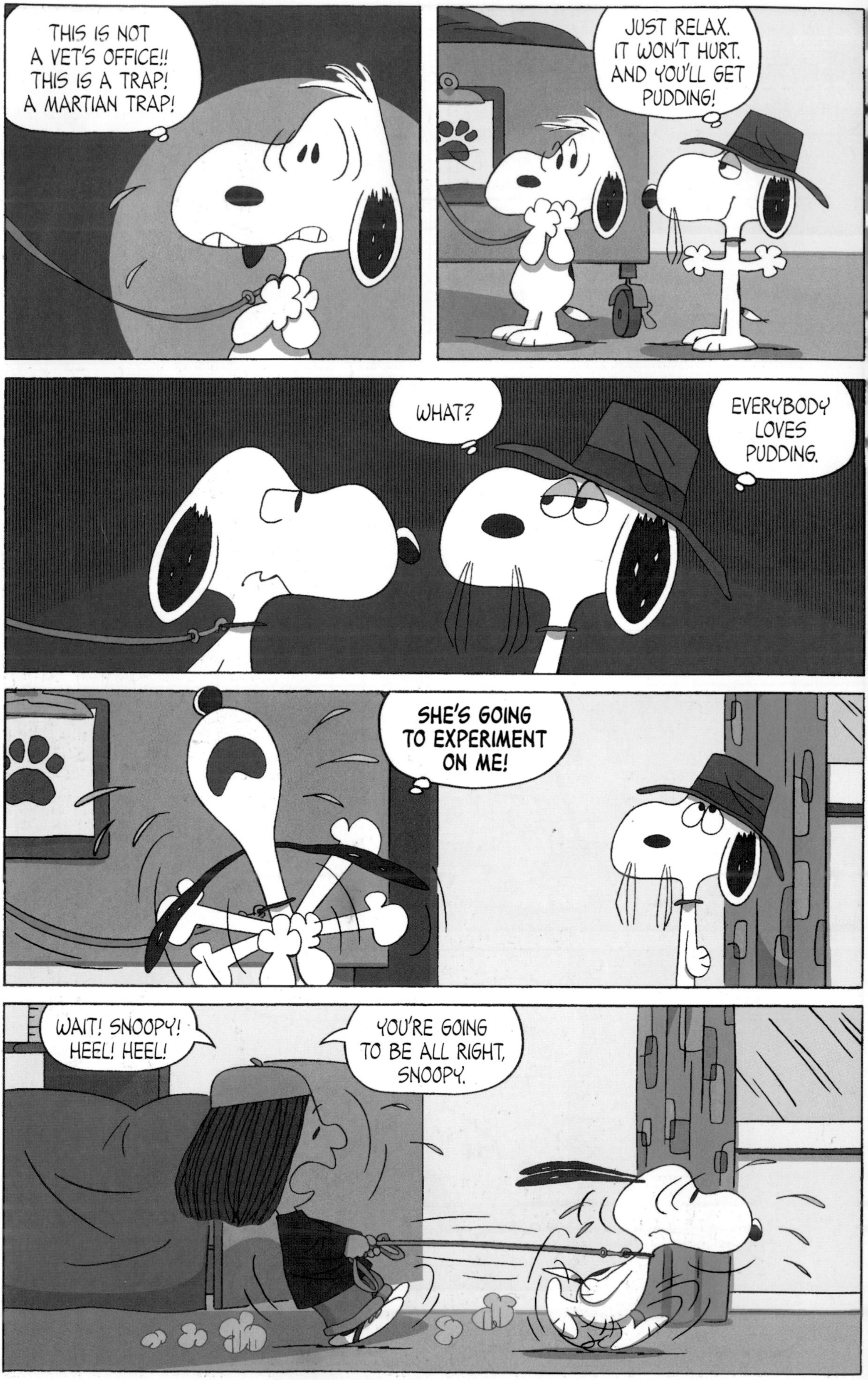
THIS IS NOT A VET'S OFFICE!! THIS IS A TRAP! A MARTIAN TRAP!
JUST RELAX. IT WON'T HURT. AND YOU'LL GET PUDDING!
WHAT?
EVERYBODY LOVES PUDDING.
SHE'S GOING TO EXPERIMENT ON ME!
WAIT! SNOOPY! HEEL! HEEL!
YOU'RE GOING TO BE ALL RIGHT, SNOOPY.

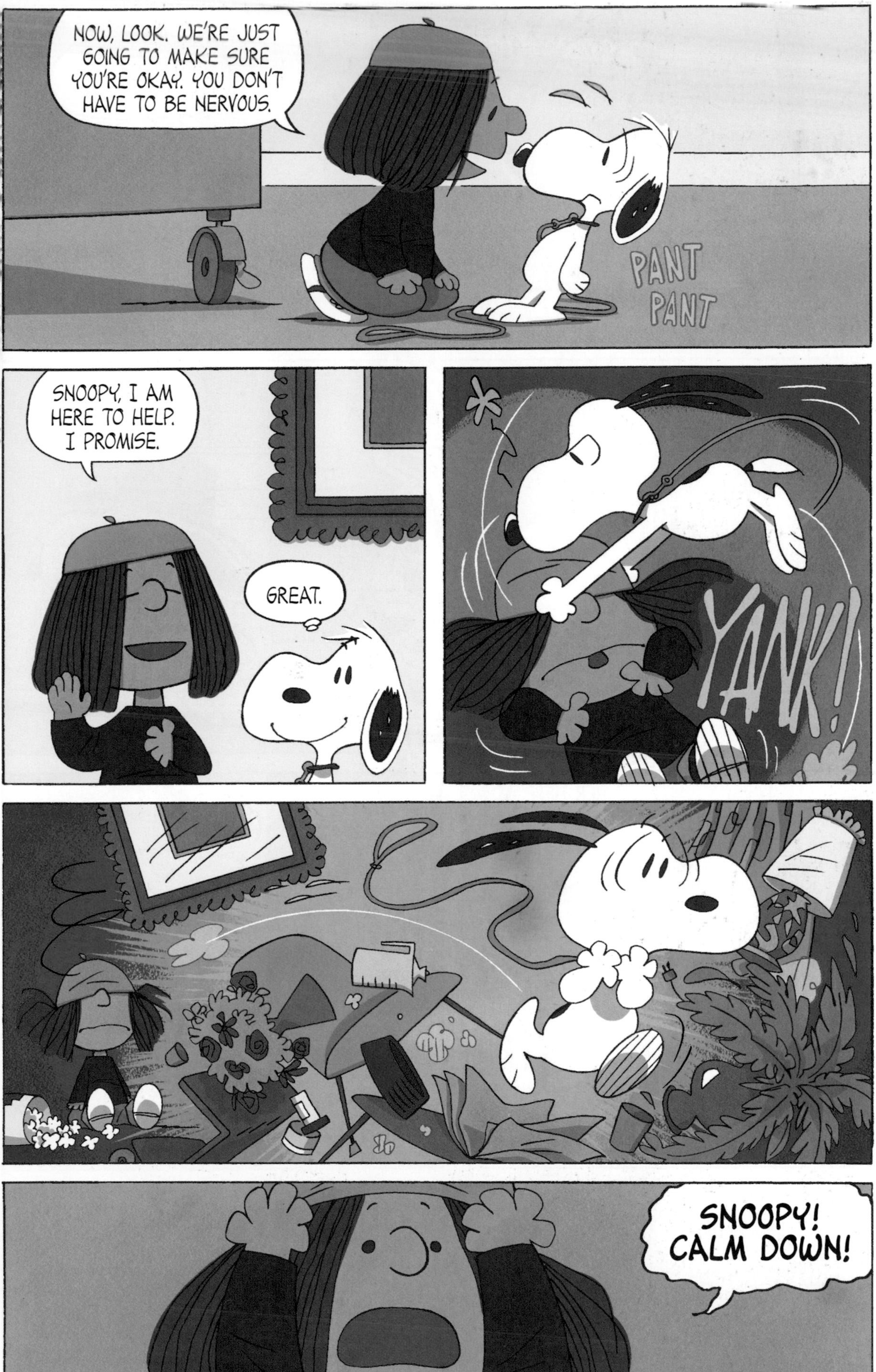
NOW, LOOK. WE'RE JUST GOING TO MAKE SURE YOU'RE OKAY. YOU DON'T HAVE TO BE NERVOUS.
PANT PANT
SNOOPY, I AM HERE TO HELP. I PROMISE.
GREAT.
YANK!
SNOOPY! CALM DOWN!

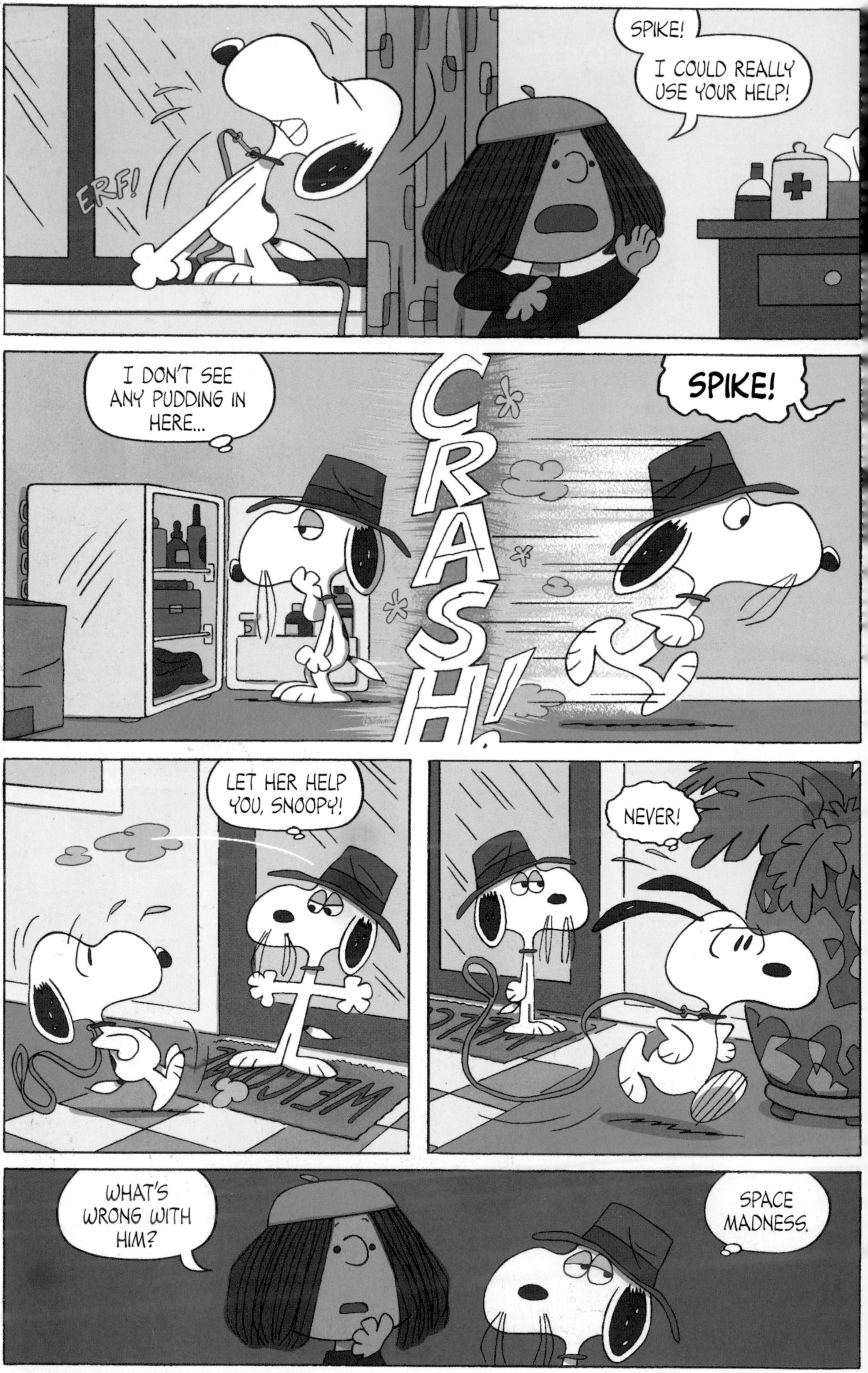
SPIKE!
I COULD REALLY USE YOUR HELP!
ERF!
I DON'T SEE ANY PUDDING IN HERE...
CRASH!
SPIKE!
LET HER HELP YOU, SNOOPY!
WELCOME
NEVER!
WHAT'S WRONG WITH HIM?
SPACE MADNESS.

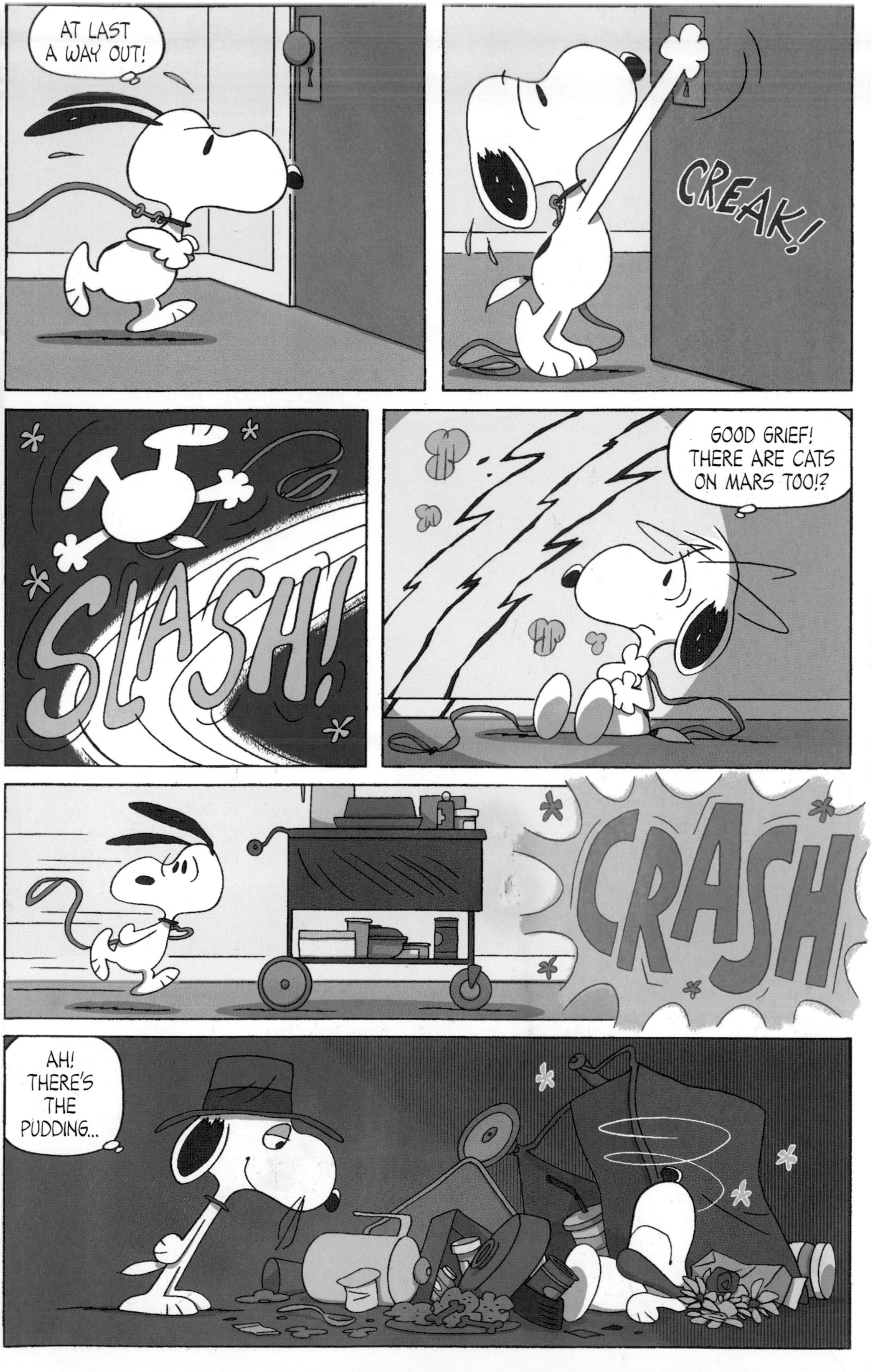

AT LAST A WAY OUT!
CREAK!
SLASH!
GOOD GRIEF! THERE ARE CATS ON MARS TOO!?
CRASH
AH! THERE'S THE PUDDING...

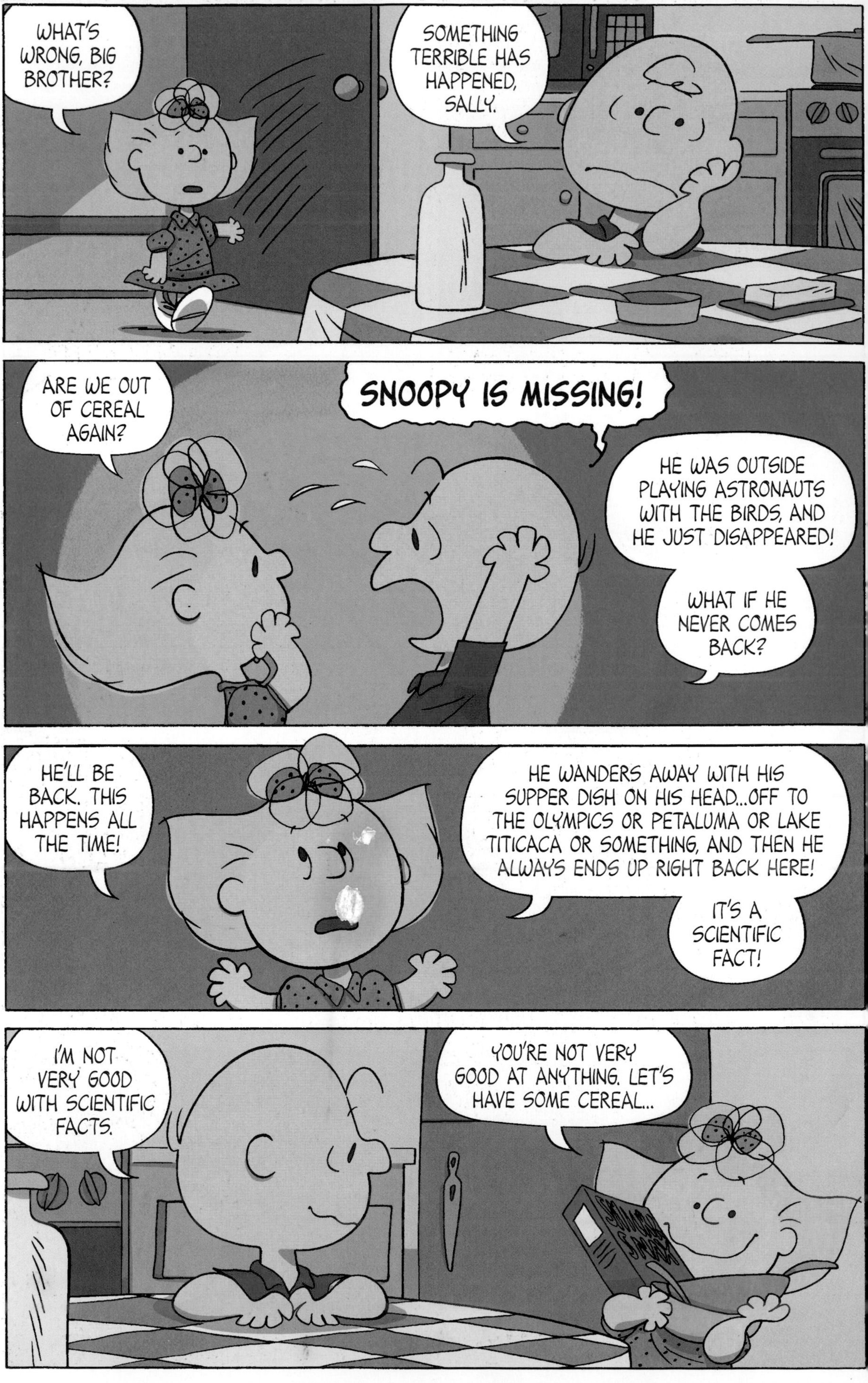
WHAT'S WRONG, BIG BROTHER?
SOMETHING TERRIBLE HAS HAPPENED, SALLY.
ARE WE OUT OF CEREAL AGAIN?
SNOOPY IS MISSING!
HE WAS OUTSIDE PLAYING ASTRONAUTS WITH THE BIRDS, AND HE JUST DISAPPEARED!
WHAT IF HE NEVER COMES BACK?
HE'LL BE BACK. THIS HAPPENS ALL THE TIME!
HE WANDERS AWAY WITH HIS SUPPER DISH ON HIS HEAD...OFF TO THE OLYMPICS OR PETALUMA OR LAKE TITICACA OR SOMETHING, AND THEN HE ALWAYS ENDS UP RIGHT BACK HERE!
IT'S A SCIENTIFIC FACT!
I'M NOT VERY GOOD WITH SCIENTIFIC FACTS.
YOU'RE NOT VERY GOOD AT ANYTHING. LET'S HAVE SOME CEREAL...

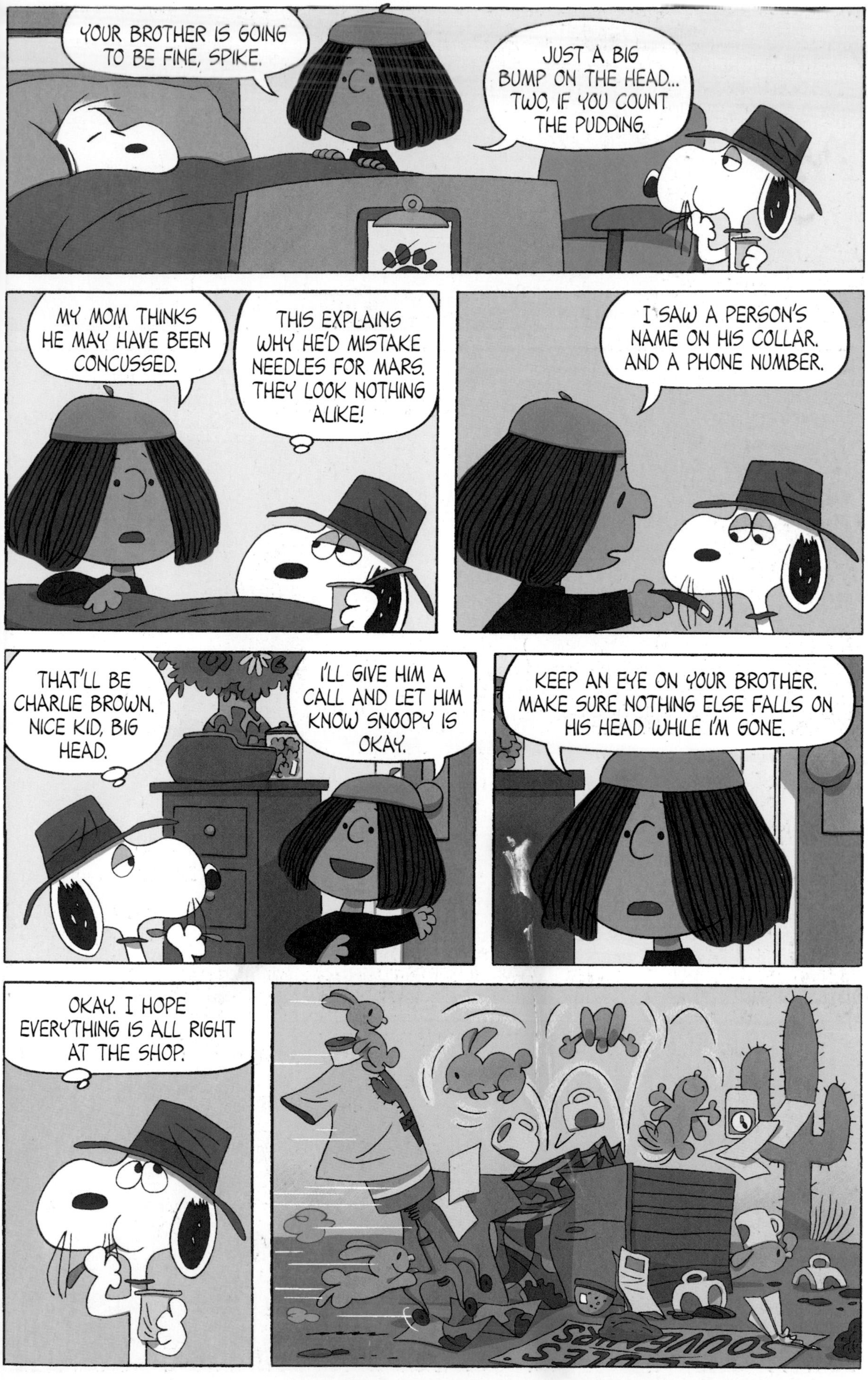
YOUR BROTHER IS GOING TO BE FINE, SPIKE.
JUST A BIG BUMP ON THE HEAD... TWO, IF YOU COUNT THE PUDDING.
MY MOM THINKS HE MAY HAVE BEEN CONCUSSED.
THIS EXPLAINS WHY HE'D MISTAKE NEEDLES FOR MARS. THEY LOOK NOTHING ALIKE!
I SAW A PERSON'S NAME ON HIS COLLAR. AND A PHONE NUMBER.
THAT'LL BE CHARLIE BROWN. NICE KID, BIG HEAD.
I'LL GIVE HIM A CALL AND LET HIM KNOW SNOOPY IS OKAY.
KEEP AN EYE ON YOUR BROTHER. MAKE SURE NOTHING ELSE FALLS ON HIS HEAD WHILE I'M GONE.
OKAY. I HOPE EVERYTHING IS ALL RIGHT AT THE SHOP.

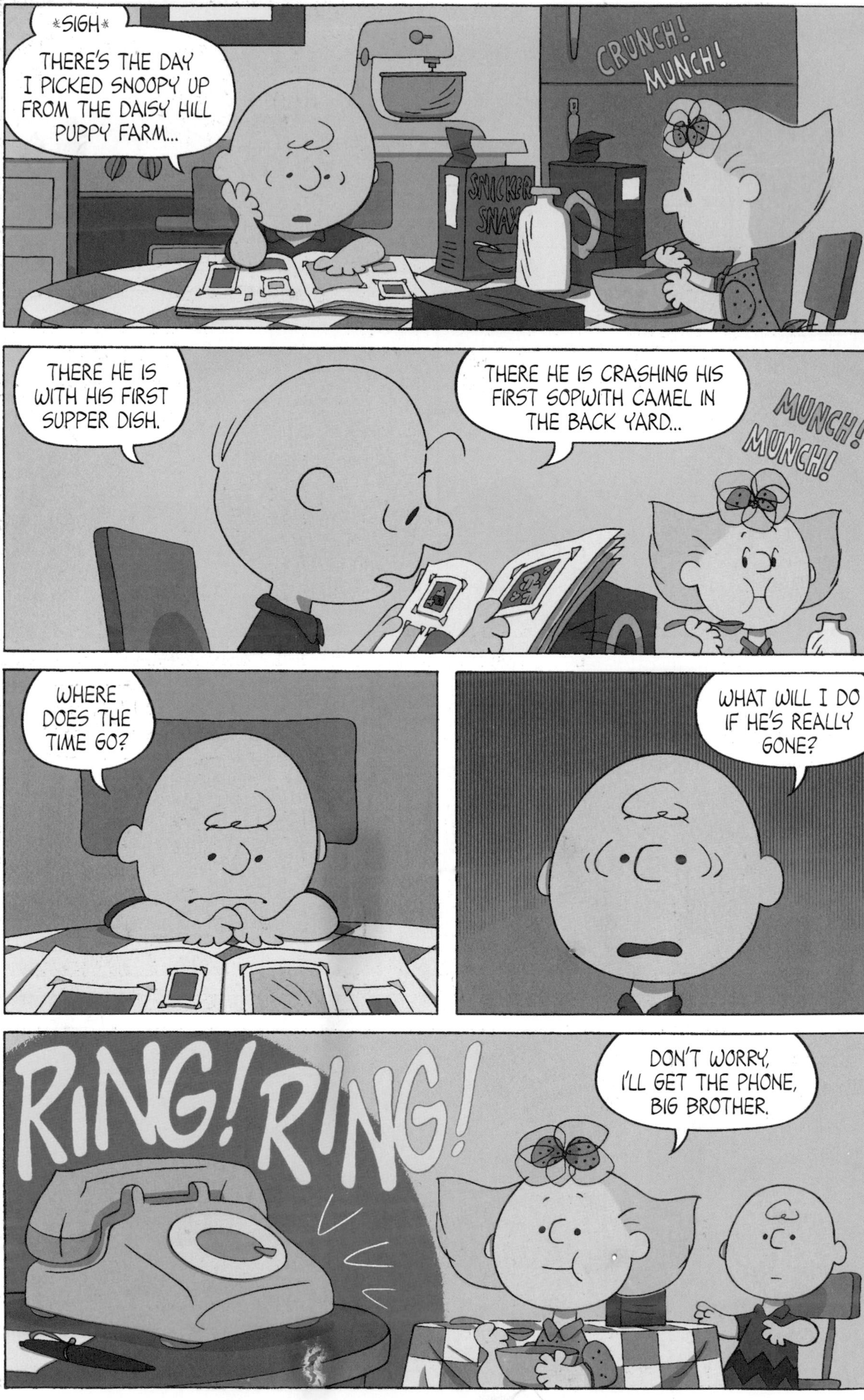
SIGH
THERE'S THE DAY I PICKED SNOOPY UP FROM THE DAISY HILL PUPPY FARM...
CRUNCH! MUNCH!
SNICKER SNAX
THERE HE IS WITH HIS FIRST SUPPER DISH.
THERE HE IS CRASHING HIS FIRST SOPWITH CAMEL IN THE BACK YARD...
MUNCH! MUNCH!
WHERE DOES THE TIME GO?
WHAT WILL I DO IF HE'S REALLY GONE?
RING! RING!
DON'T WORRY, I'LL GET THE PHONE, BIG BROTHER.

HELLO?!

NO. I'M HIS SISTER. HE'S SULKING RIGHT NOW. EVEN THOUGH WE STILL HAVE PLENTY OF CEREAL!

IT'S FOR YOU. SOME GIRL.

HELLO?

HELLO. IS THIS CHARLES BROWN?

YES, THIS IS CHARLES BROWN.

MAY I CALL YOU CHARLIE BROWN?

YES, THAT'S FINE.

I'M GLAD TO KNOW YOU HAVE PLENTY OF CEREAL.

THANK YOU.

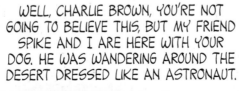

WELL, CHARLIE BROWN, YOU'RE NOT GOING TO BELIEVE THIS, BUT MY FRIEND SPIKE AND I ARE HERE WITH YOUR DOG. HE WAS WANDERING AROUND THE DESERT DRESSED LIKE AN ASTRONAUT.

ACTUALLY, THAT SOUNDS ABOUT RIGHT...

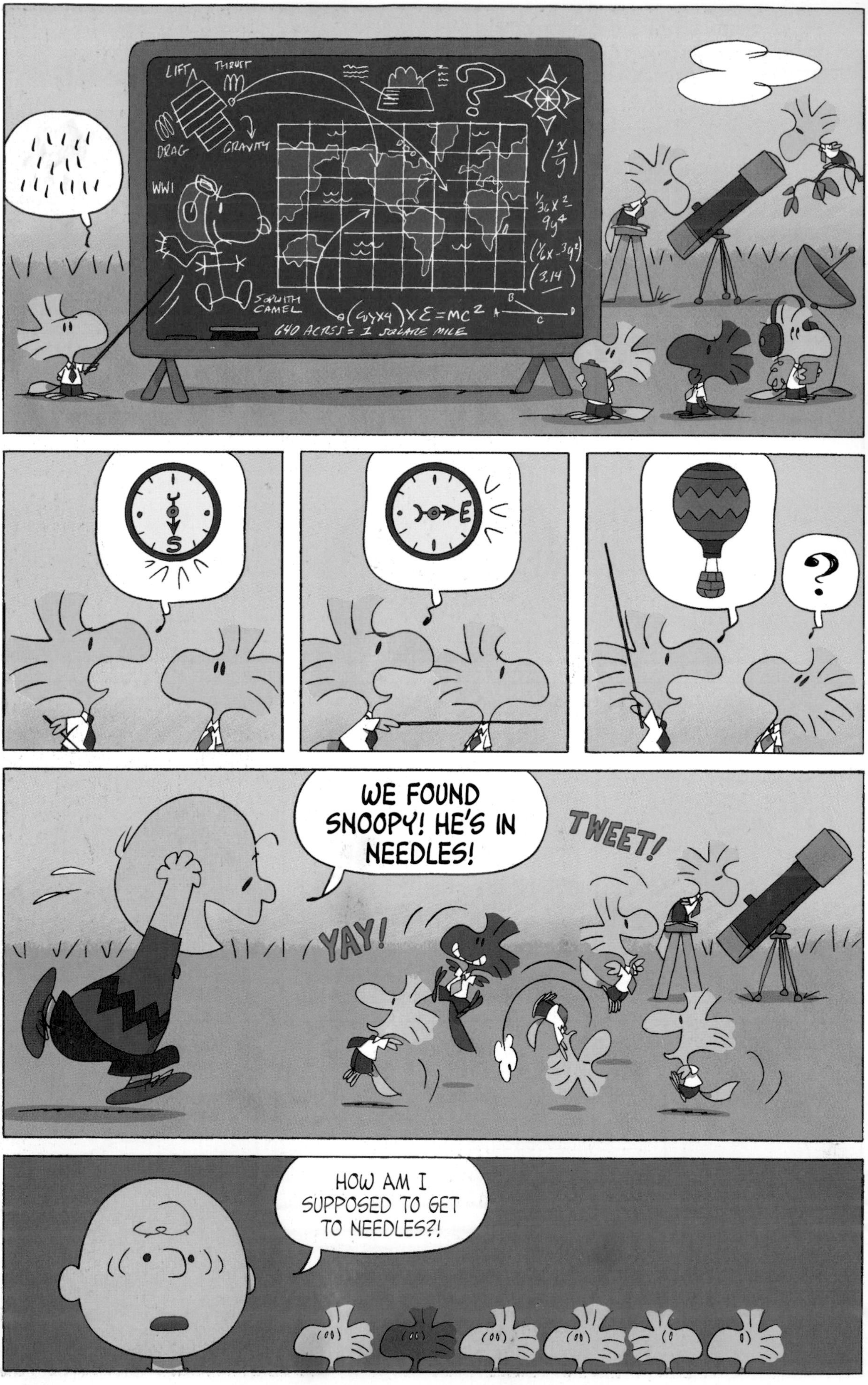

LIFT
THRUST
DRAG
GRAVITY
WWI
SOPWITH CAMEL
640 ACRES = 1 SQUARE MILE
(3.14)
S
E
?
WE FOUND SNOOPY! HE'S IN NEEDLES!
TWEET!
YAY!
HOW AM I SUPPOSED TO GET TO NEEDLES?!

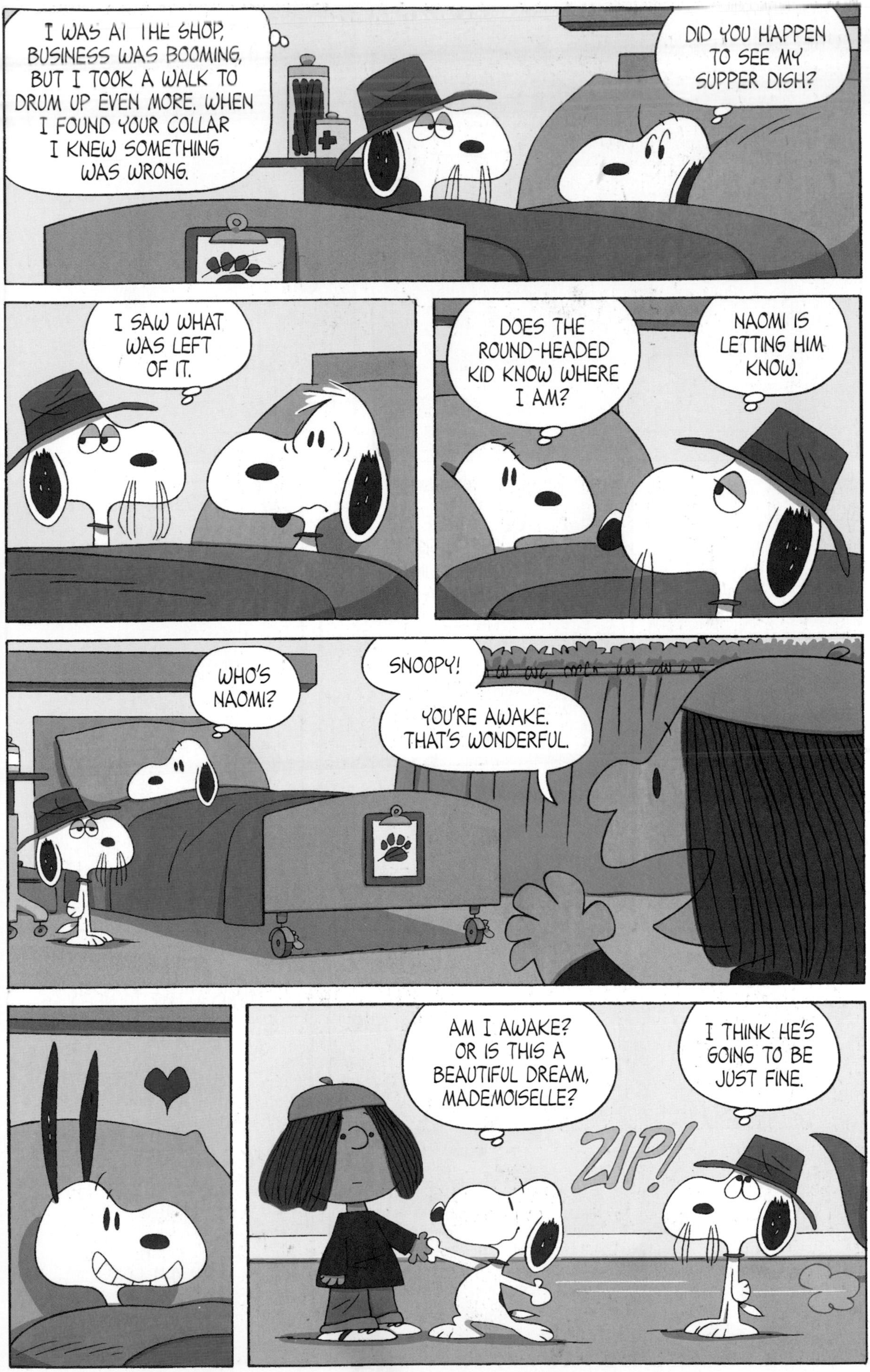
I WAS AT THE SHOP, BUSINESS WAS BOOMING, BUT I TOOK A WALK TO DRUM UP EVEN MORE. WHEN I FOUND YOUR COLLAR I KNEW SOMETHING WAS WRONG.
DID YOU HAPPEN TO SEE MY SUPPER DISH?
I SAW WHAT WAS LEFT OF IT.
DOES THE ROUND-HEADED KID KNOW WHERE I AM?
NAOMI IS LETTING HIM KNOW.
WHO'S NAOMI?
SNOOPY!
YOU'RE AWAKE. THAT'S WONDERFUL.
AM I AWAKE? OR IS THIS A BEAUTIFUL DREAM, MADEMOISELLE?
I THINK HE'S GOING TO BE JUST FINE.
ZIP!

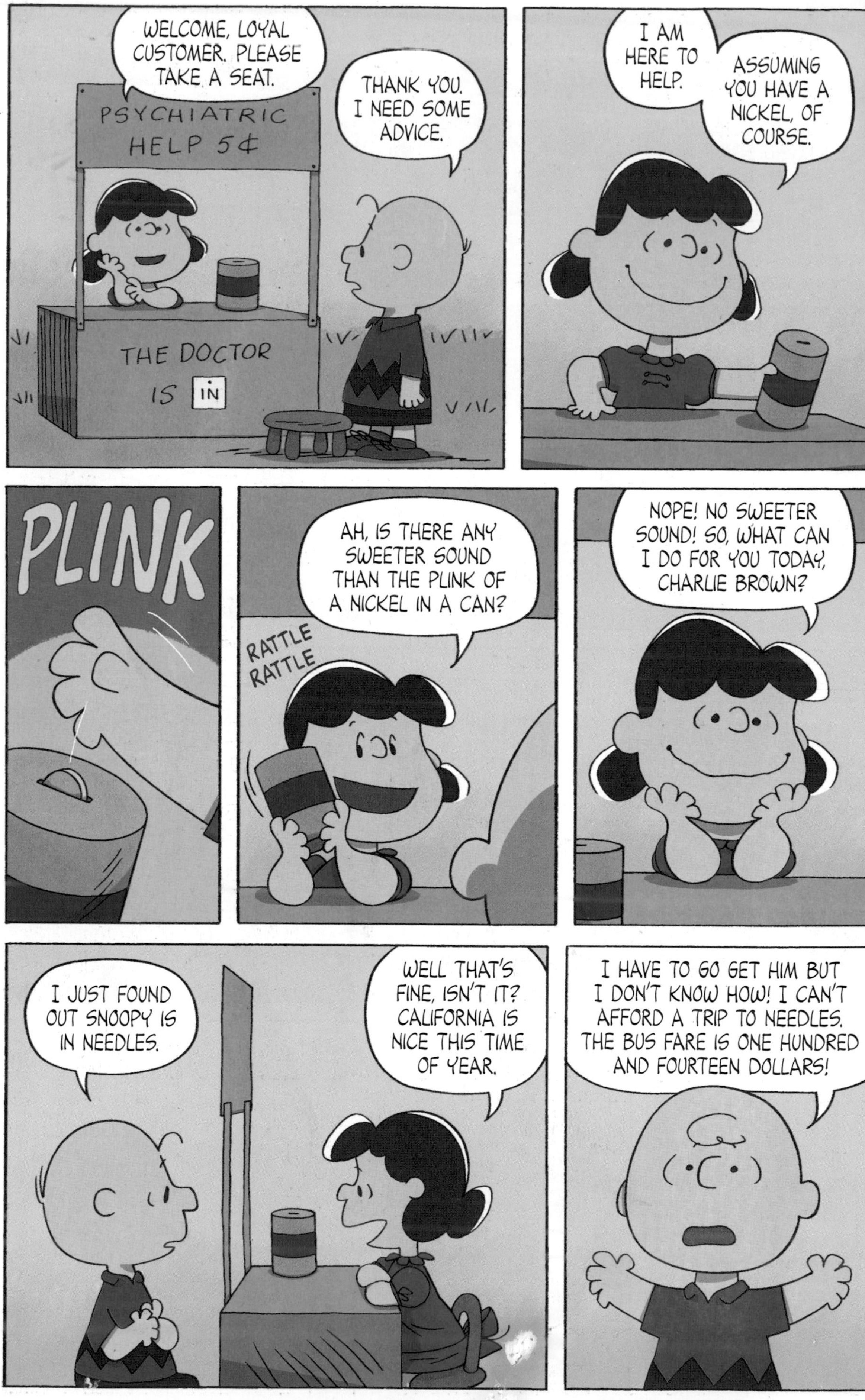
WELCOME, LOYAL CUSTOMER. PLEASE TAKE A SEAT.
PSYCHIATRIC HELP 5¢
THE DOCTOR IS IN
THANK YOU. I NEED SOME ADVICE.
I AM HERE TO HELP.
ASSUMING YOU HAVE A NICKEL, OF COURSE.
PLINK
RATTLE RATTLE
AH, IS THERE ANY SWEETER SOUND THAN THE PLINK OF A NICKEL IN A CAN?
NOPE! NO SWEETER SOUND! SO, WHAT CAN I DO FOR YOU TODAY, CHARLIE BROWN?
I JUST FOUND OUT SNOOPY IS IN NEEDLES.
WELL THAT'S FINE, ISN'T IT? CALIFORNIA IS NICE THIS TIME OF YEAR.
I HAVE TO GO GET HIM BUT I DON'T KNOW HOW! I CAN'T AFFORD A TRIP TO NEEDLES. THE BUS FARE IS ONE HUNDRED AND FOURTEEN DOLLARS!

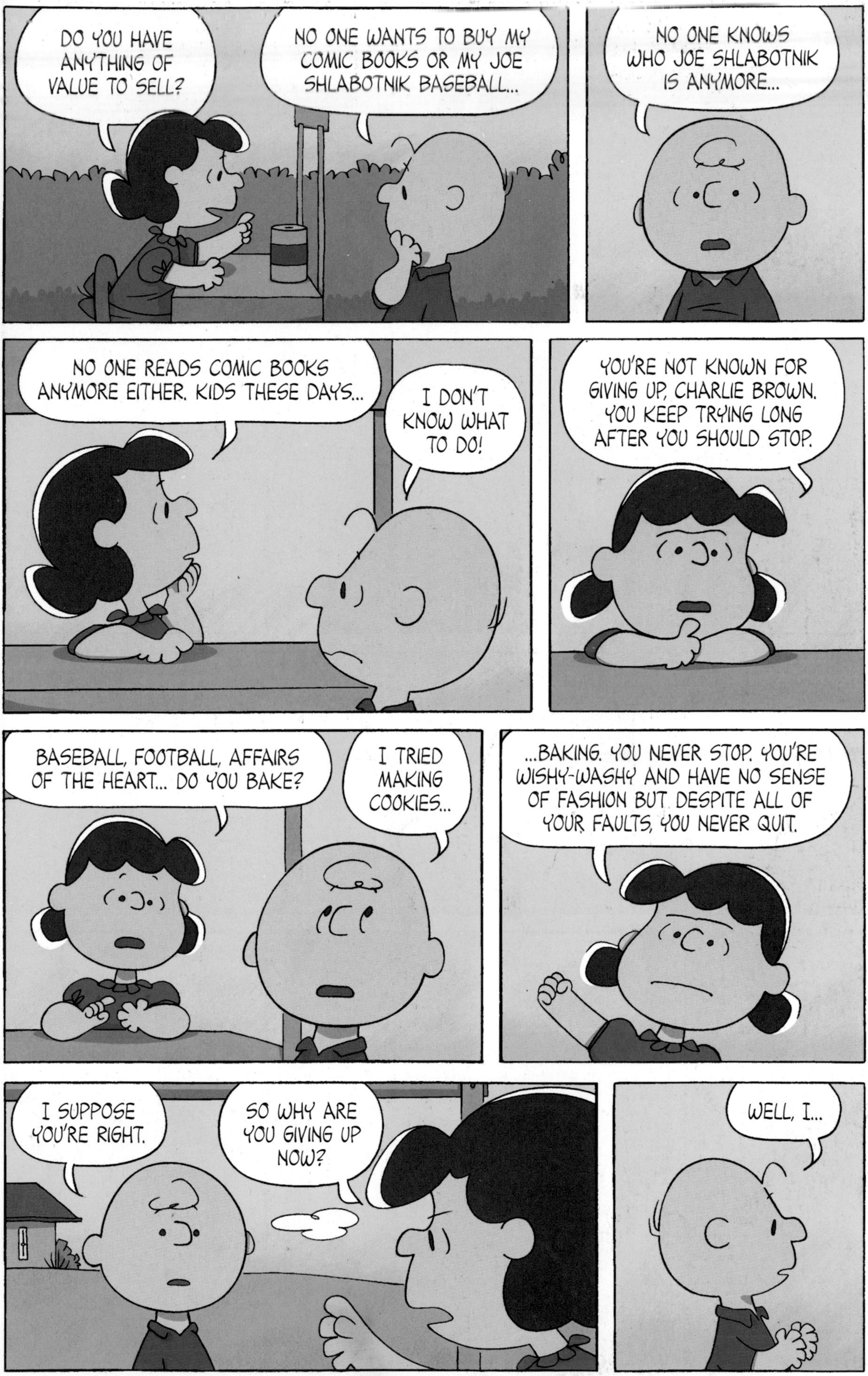
DO YOU HAVE ANYTHING OF VALUE TO SELL?
NO ONE WANTS TO BUY MY COMIC BOOKS OR MY JOE SHLABOTNIK BASEBALL...
NO ONE KNOWS WHO JOE SHLABOTNIK IS ANYMORE...
NO ONE READS COMIC BOOKS ANYMORE EITHER. KIDS THESE DAYS...
I DON'T KNOW WHAT TO DO!
YOU'RE NOT KNOWN FOR GIVING UP, CHARLIE BROWN. YOU KEEP TRYING LONG AFTER YOU SHOULD STOP.
BASEBALL, FOOTBALL, AFFAIRS OF THE HEART... DO YOU BAKE?
I TRIED MAKING COOKIES...
...BAKING. YOU NEVER STOP. YOU'RE WISHY-WASHY AND HAVE NO SENSE OF FASHION BUT DESPITE ALL OF YOUR FAULTS, YOU NEVER QUIT.
I SUPPOSE YOU'RE RIGHT.
SO WHY ARE YOU GIVING UP NOW?
WELL, I...

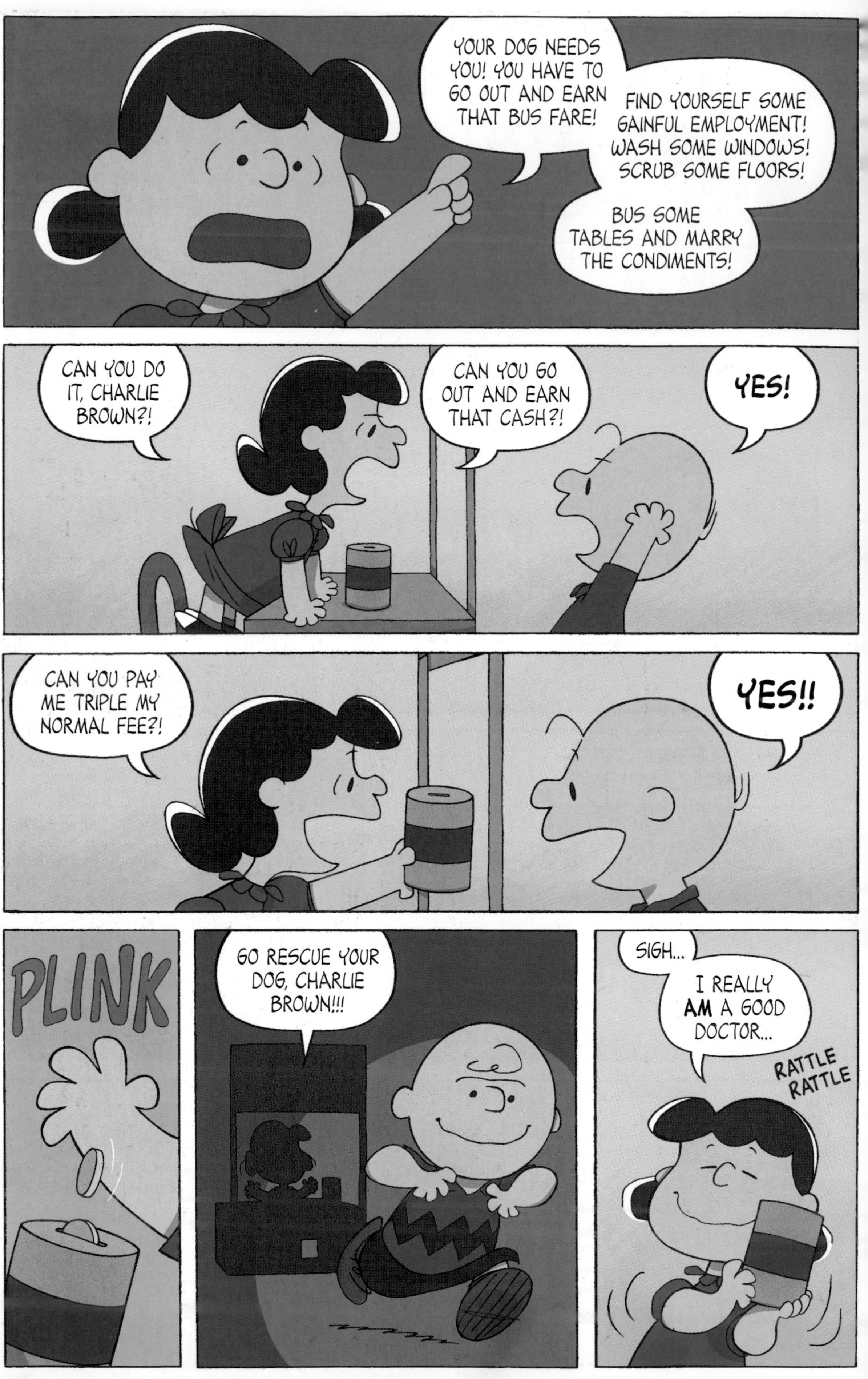
YOUR DOG NEEDS YOU! YOU HAVE TO GO OUT AND EARN THAT BUS FARE!
FIND YOURSELF SOME GAINFUL EMPLOYMENT! WASH SOME WINDOWS! SCRUB SOME FLOORS!
BUS SOME TABLES AND MARRY THE CONDIMENTS!
CAN YOU DO IT, CHARLIE BROWN?!
CAN YOU GO OUT AND EARN THAT CASH?!
YES!
CAN YOU PAY ME TRIPLE MY NORMAL FEE?!
YES!!
PLINK
GO RESCUE YOUR DOG, CHARLIE BROWN!!!
SIGH...
I REALLY **AM** A GOOD DOCTOR...
RATTLE RATTLE

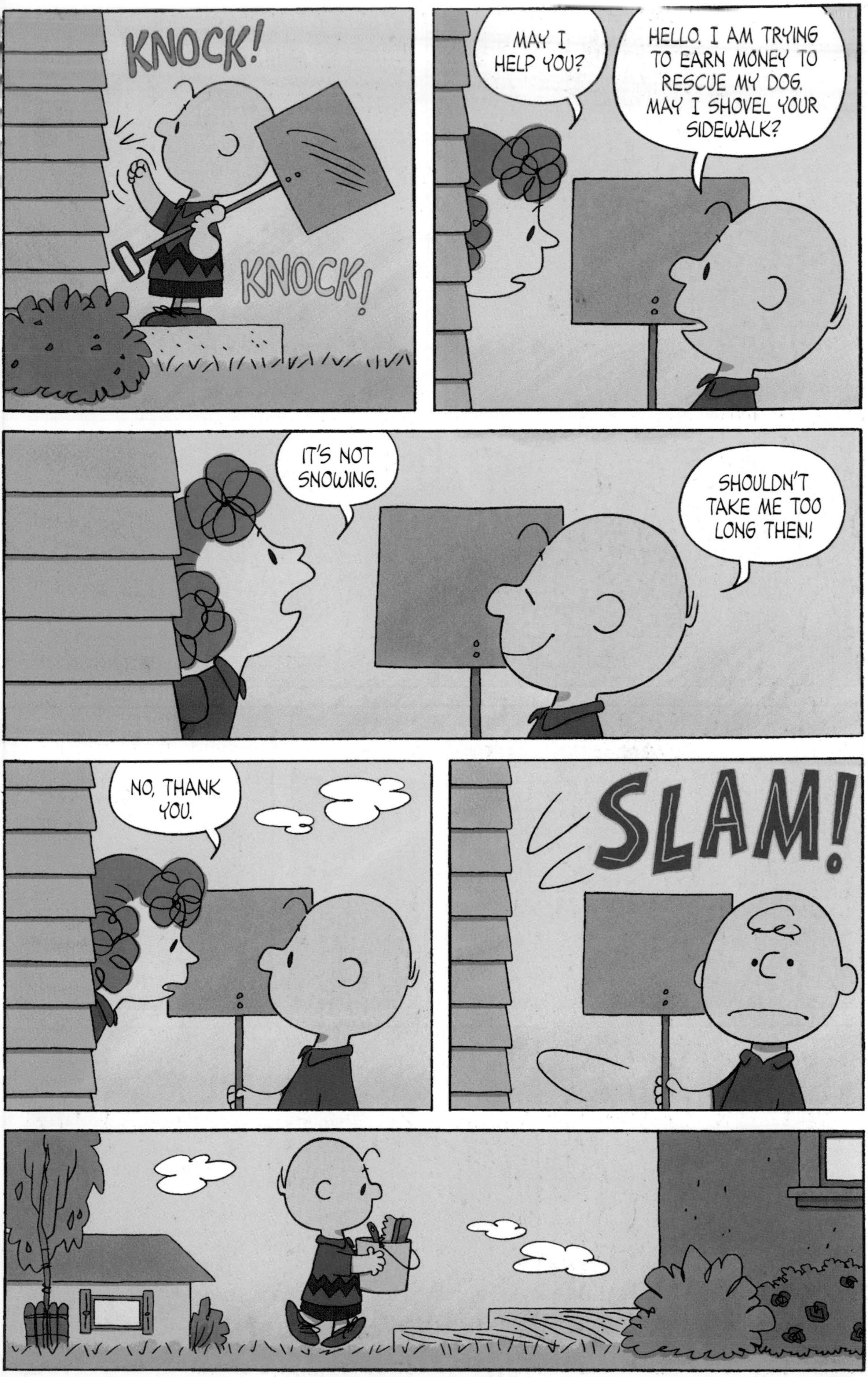
KNOCK!
KNOCK!
MAY I HELP YOU?
HELLO. I AM TRYING TO EARN MONEY TO RESCUE MY DOG. MAY I SHOVEL YOUR SIDEWALK?
IT'S NOT SNOWING.
SHOULDN'T TAKE ME TOO LONG THEN!
NO, THANK YOU.
SLAM!

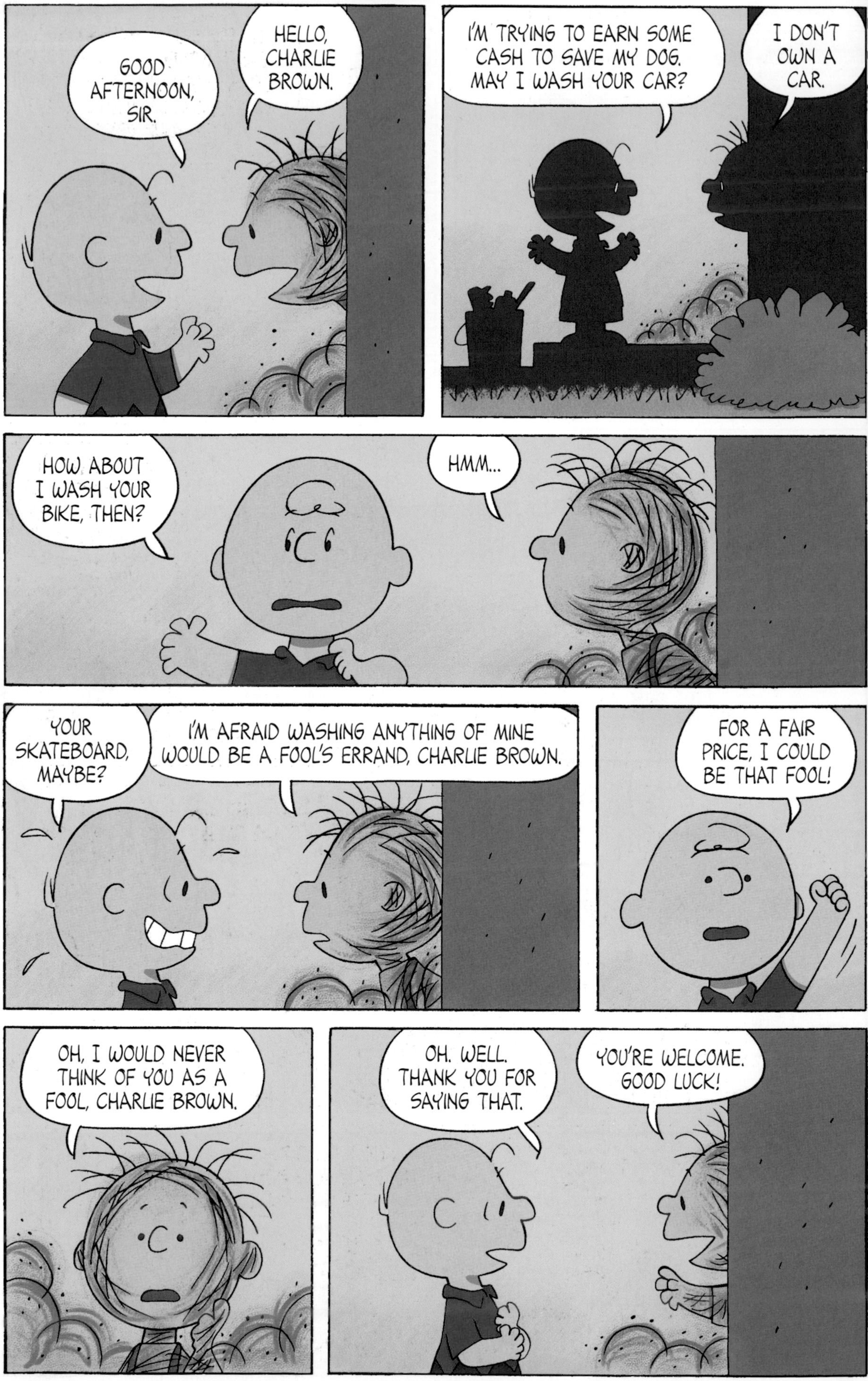
GOOD AFTERNOON, SIR.
HELLO, CHARLIE BROWN.
I'M TRYING TO EARN SOME CASH TO SAVE MY DOG. MAY I WASH YOUR CAR?
I DON'T OWN A CAR.
HOW ABOUT I WASH YOUR BIKE, THEN?
HMM...
YOUR SKATEBOARD, MAYBE?
I'M AFRAID WASHING ANYTHING OF MINE WOULD BE A FOOL'S ERRAND, CHARLIE BROWN.
FOR A FAIR PRICE, I COULD BE THAT FOOL!
OH, I WOULD NEVER THINK OF YOU AS A FOOL, CHARLIE BROWN.
OH. WELL. THANK YOU FOR SAYING THAT.
YOU'RE WELCOME. GOOD LUCK!

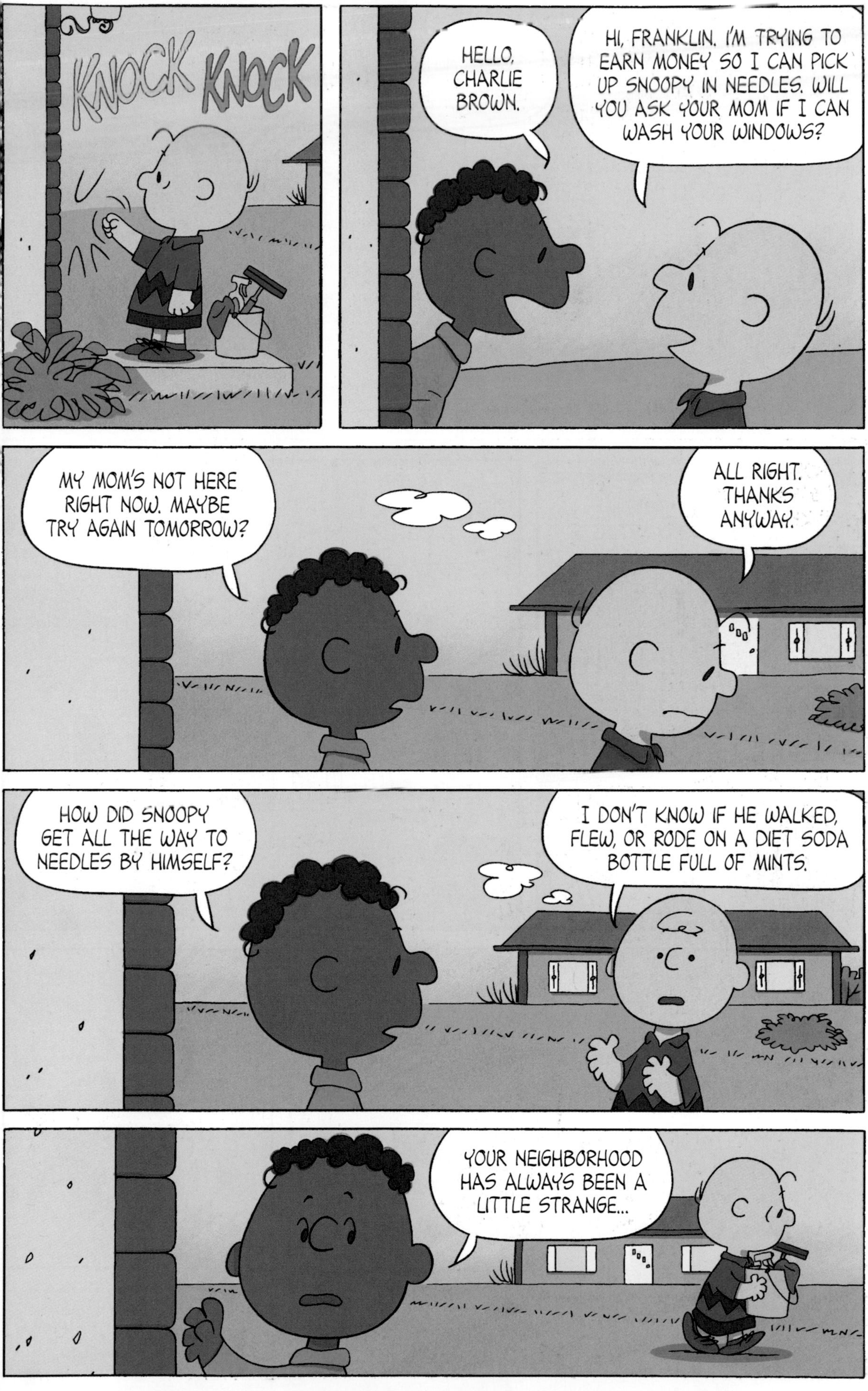
KNOCK KNOCK
HELLO, CHARLIE BROWN.
HI, FRANKLIN. I'M TRYING TO EARN MONEY SO I CAN PICK UP SNOOPY IN NEEDLES. WILL YOU ASK YOUR MOM IF I CAN WASH YOUR WINDOWS?
MY MOM'S NOT HERE RIGHT NOW. MAYBE TRY AGAIN TOMORROW?
ALL RIGHT. THANKS ANYWAY.
HOW DID SNOOPY GET ALL THE WAY TO NEEDLES BY HIMSELF?
I DON'T KNOW IF HE WALKED, FLEW, OR RODE ON A DIET SODA BOTTLE FULL OF MINTS.
YOUR NEIGHBORHOOD HAS ALWAYS BEEN A LITTLE STRANGE...

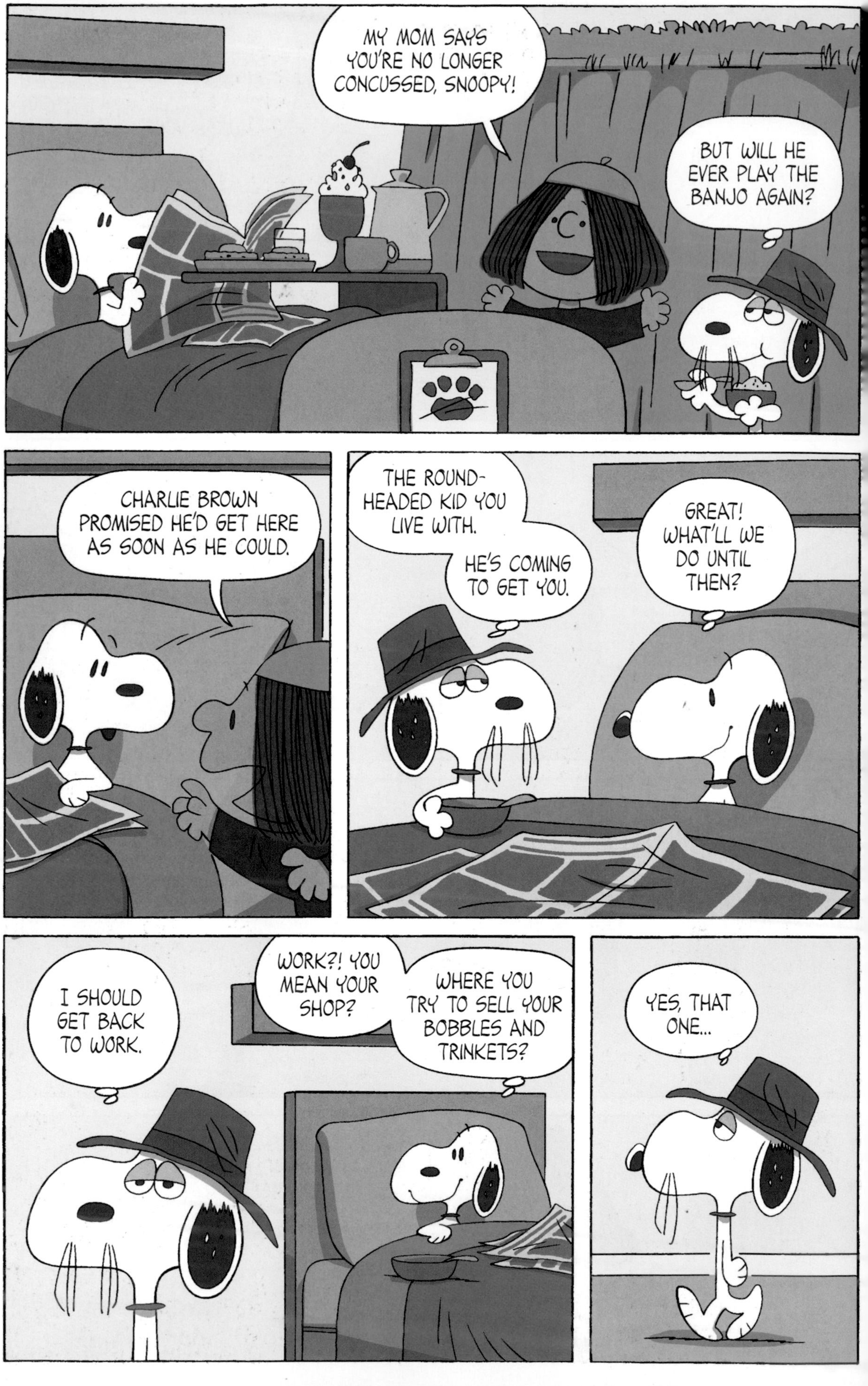

MY MOM SAYS YOU'RE NO LONGER CONCUSSED, SNOOPY!
BUT WILL HE EVER PLAY THE BANJO AGAIN?
CHARLIE BROWN PROMISED HE'D GET HERE AS SOON AS HE COULD.
THE ROUND-HEADED KID YOU LIVE WITH.
HE'S COMING TO GET YOU.
GREAT! WHAT'LL WE DO UNTIL THEN?
I SHOULD GET BACK TO WORK.
WORK?! YOU MEAN YOUR SHOP?
WHERE YOU TRY TO SELL YOUR BOBBLES AND TRINKETS?
YES, THAT ONE...

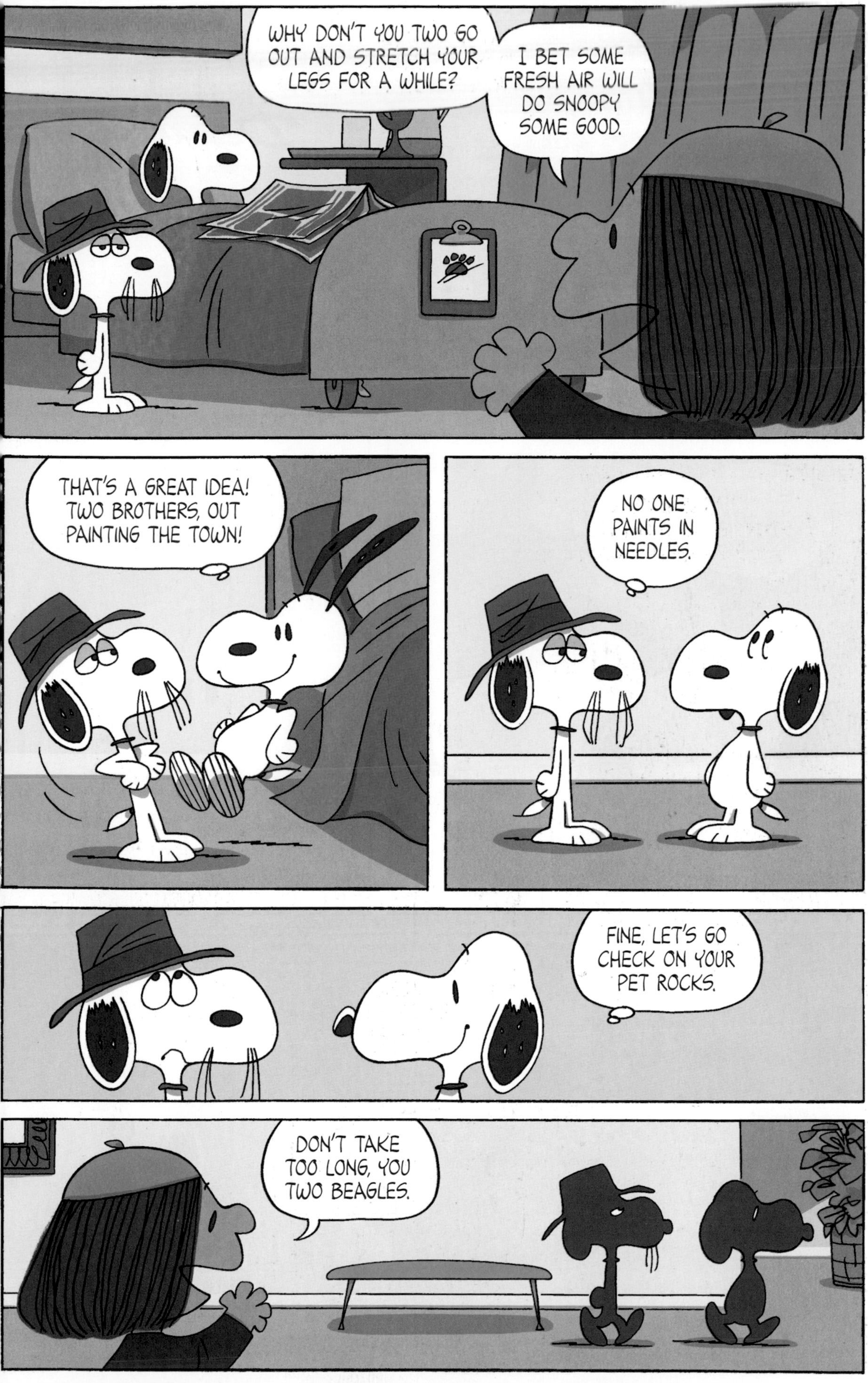
WHY DON'T YOU TWO GO OUT AND STRETCH YOUR LEGS FOR A WHILE?
I BET SOME FRESH AIR WILL DO SNOOPY SOME GOOD.
THAT'S A GREAT IDEA! TWO BROTHERS, OUT PAINTING THE TOWN!
NO ONE PAINTS IN NEEDLES.
FINE, LET'S GO CHECK ON YOUR PET ROCKS.
DON'T TAKE TOO LONG, YOU TWO BEAGLES.

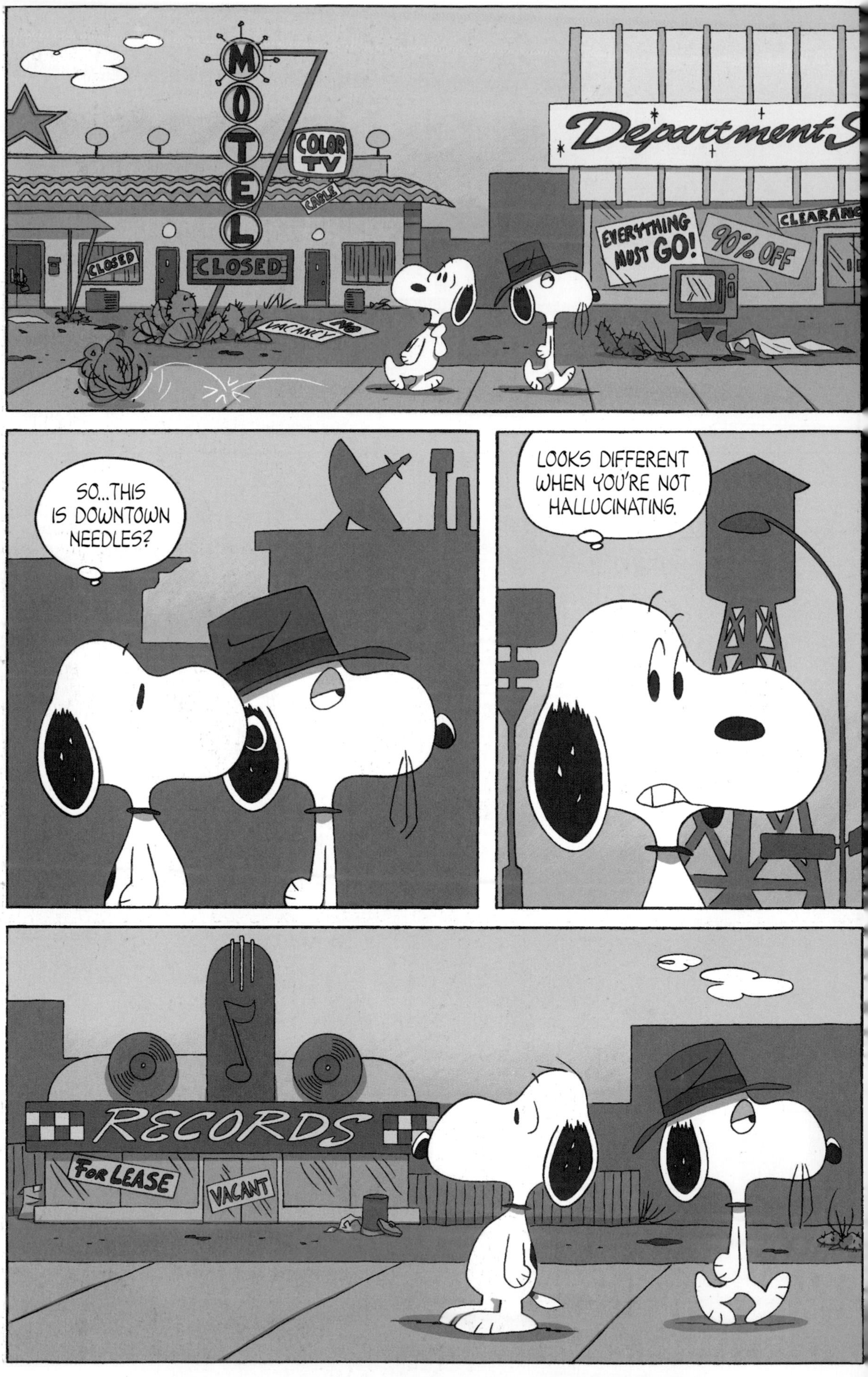
MOTEL
COLOR TV
CABLE
CLOSED
CLOSED
NO
VACANCY
EVERYTHING MUST GO!
90% OFF
SO...THIS IS DOWNTOWN NEEDLES?
LOOKS DIFFERENT WHEN YOU'RE NOT HALLUCINATING.
RECORDS
FOR LEASE
VACANT

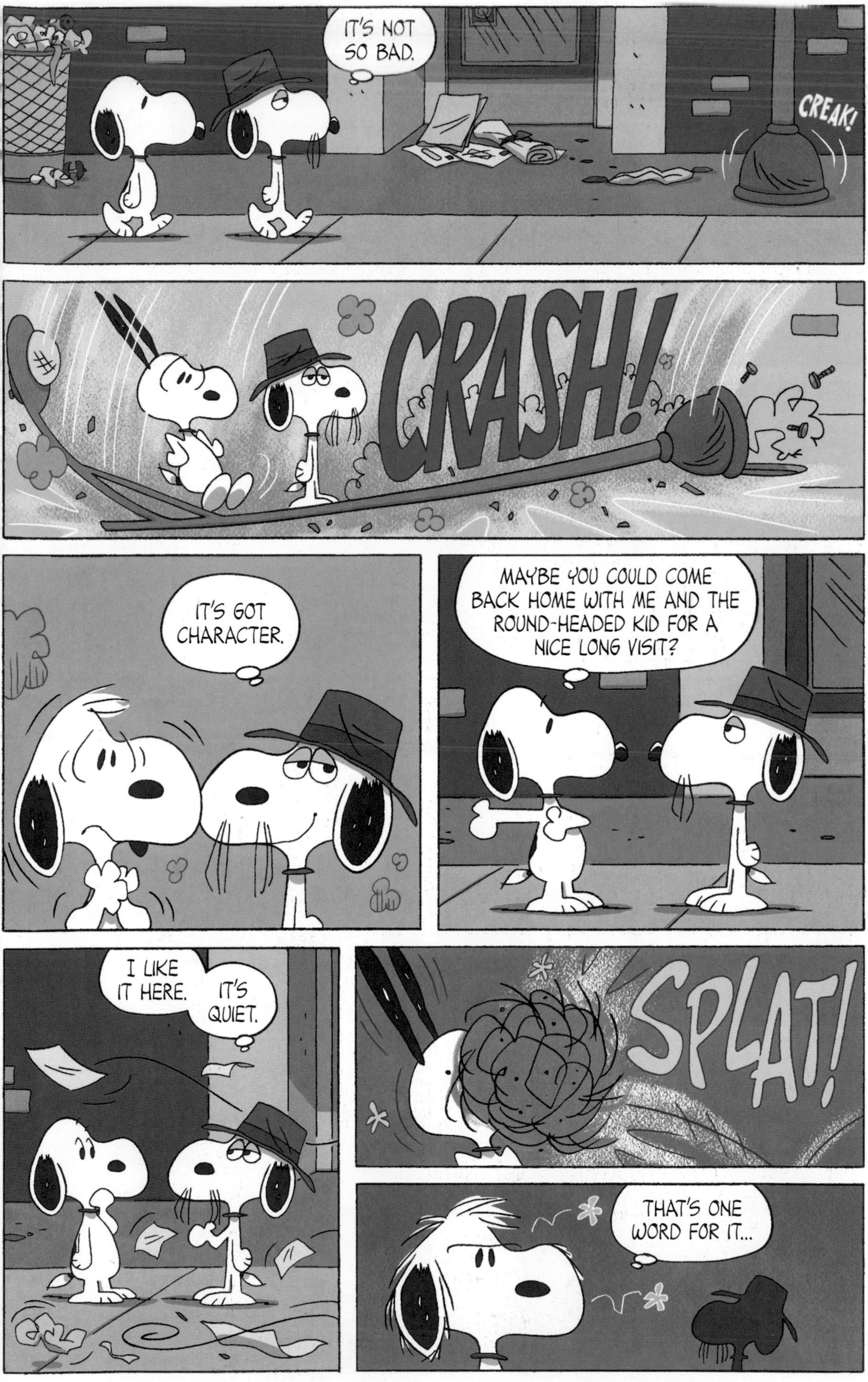
IT'S NOT SO BAD.
CREAK!
CRASH!
IT'S GOT CHARACTER.
MAYBE YOU COULD COME BACK HOME WITH ME AND THE ROUND-HEADED KID FOR A NICE LONG VISIT?
I LIKE IT HERE.
IT'S QUIET.
SPLAT!
THAT'S ONE WORD FOR IT...

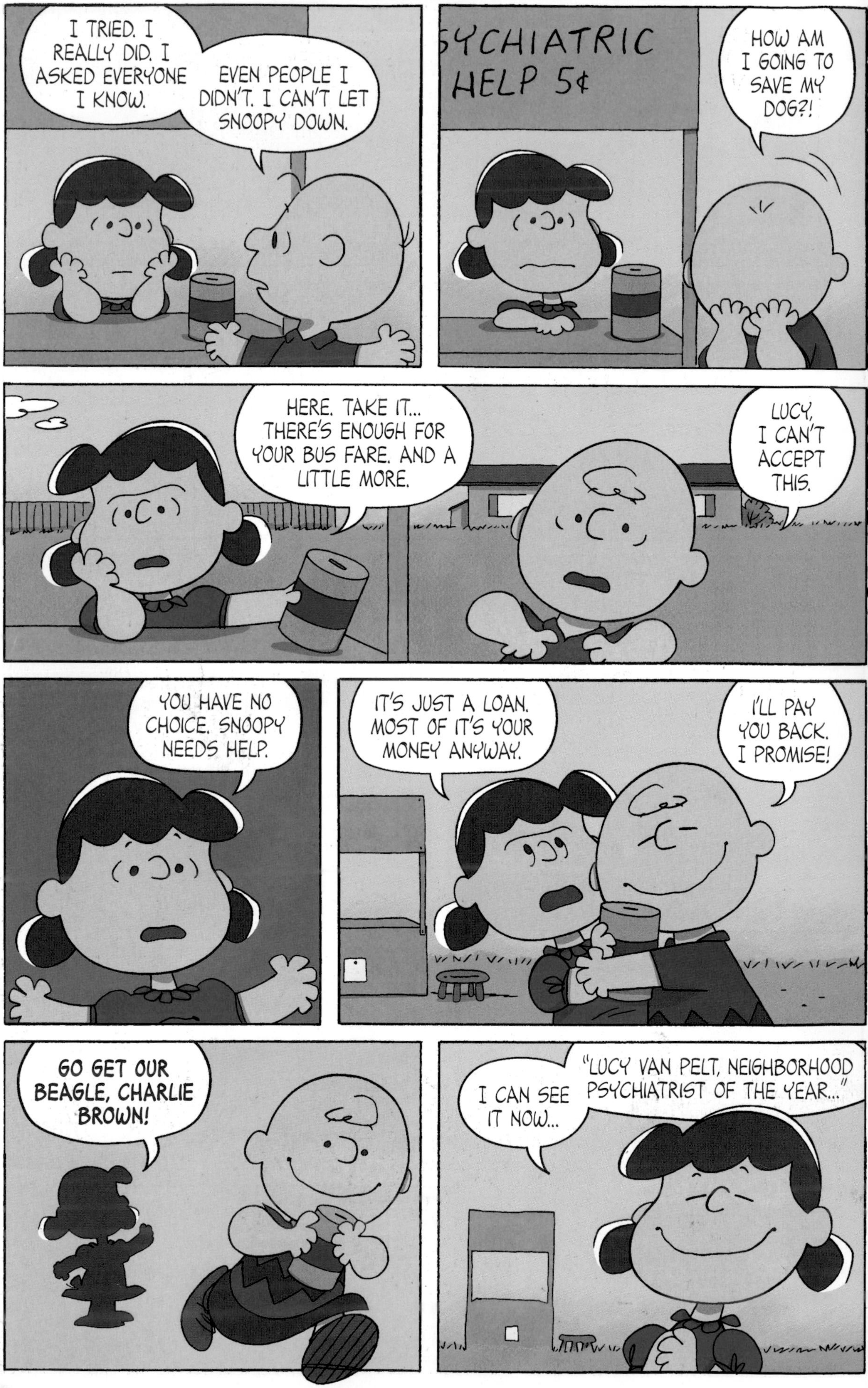
I TRIED. I REALLY DID. I ASKED EVERYONE I KNOW.
EVEN PEOPLE I DIDN'T. I CAN'T LET SNOOPY DOWN.
SYCHIATRIC HELP 5¢
HOW AM I GOING TO SAVE MY DOG?!
HERE. TAKE IT... THERE'S ENOUGH FOR YOUR BUS FARE. AND A LITTLE MORE.
LUCY, I CAN'T ACCEPT THIS.
YOU HAVE NO CHOICE. SNOOPY NEEDS HELP.
IT'S JUST A LOAN. MOST OF IT'S YOUR MONEY ANYWAY.
I'LL PAY YOU BACK. I PROMISE!
GO GET OUR BEAGLE, CHARLIE BROWN!
I CAN SEE IT NOW...
"LUCY VAN PELT, NEIGHBORHOOD PSYCHIATRIST OF THE YEAR..."

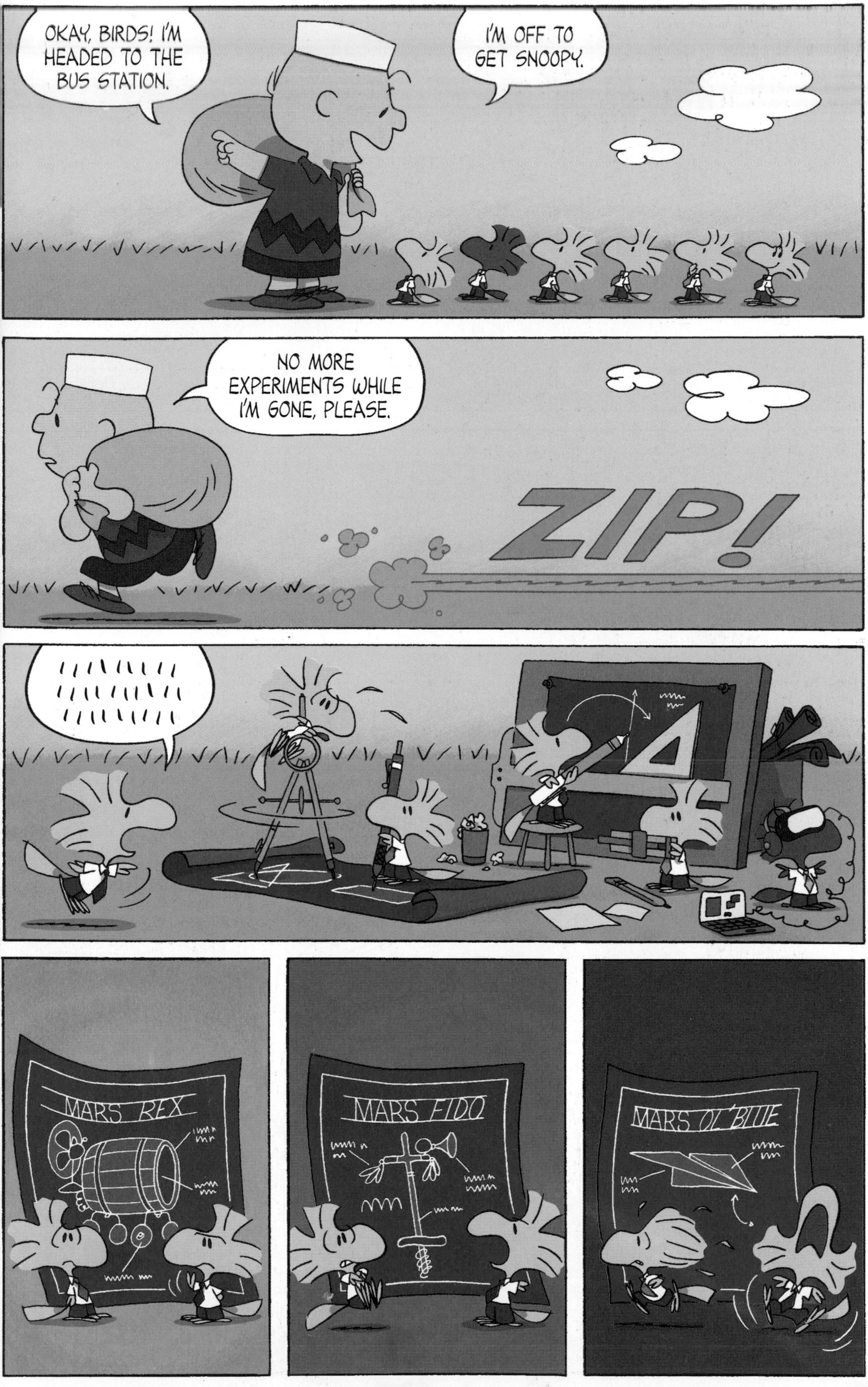
OKAY, BIRDS! I'M HEADED TO THE BUS STATION.
I'M OFF TO GET SNOOPY.
NO MORE EXPERIMENTS WHILE I'M GONE, PLEASE.
ZIP!
MARS REX
MARS FIDO
MARS OL' BLUE

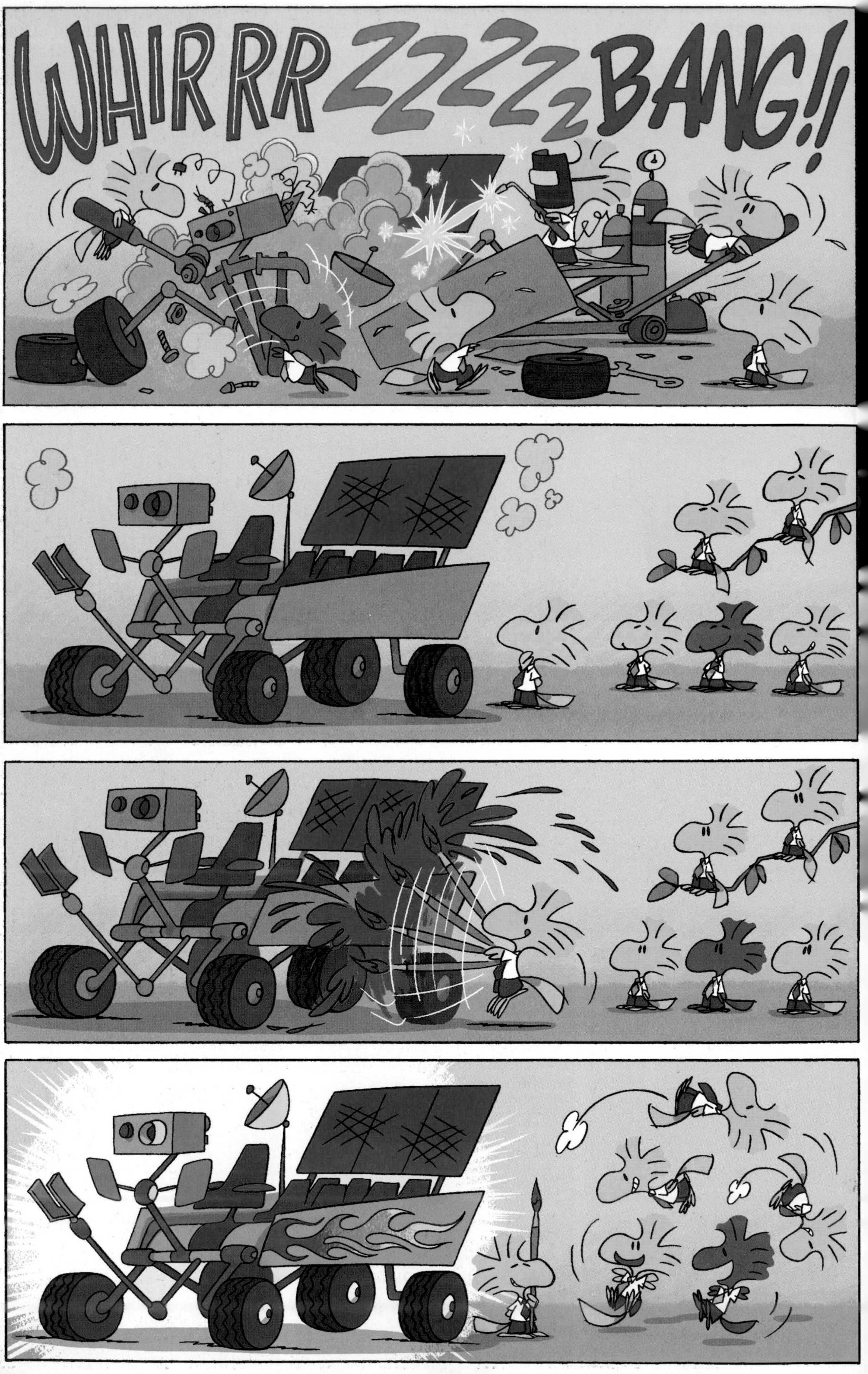
WHIRRR ZZZZz BANG!!

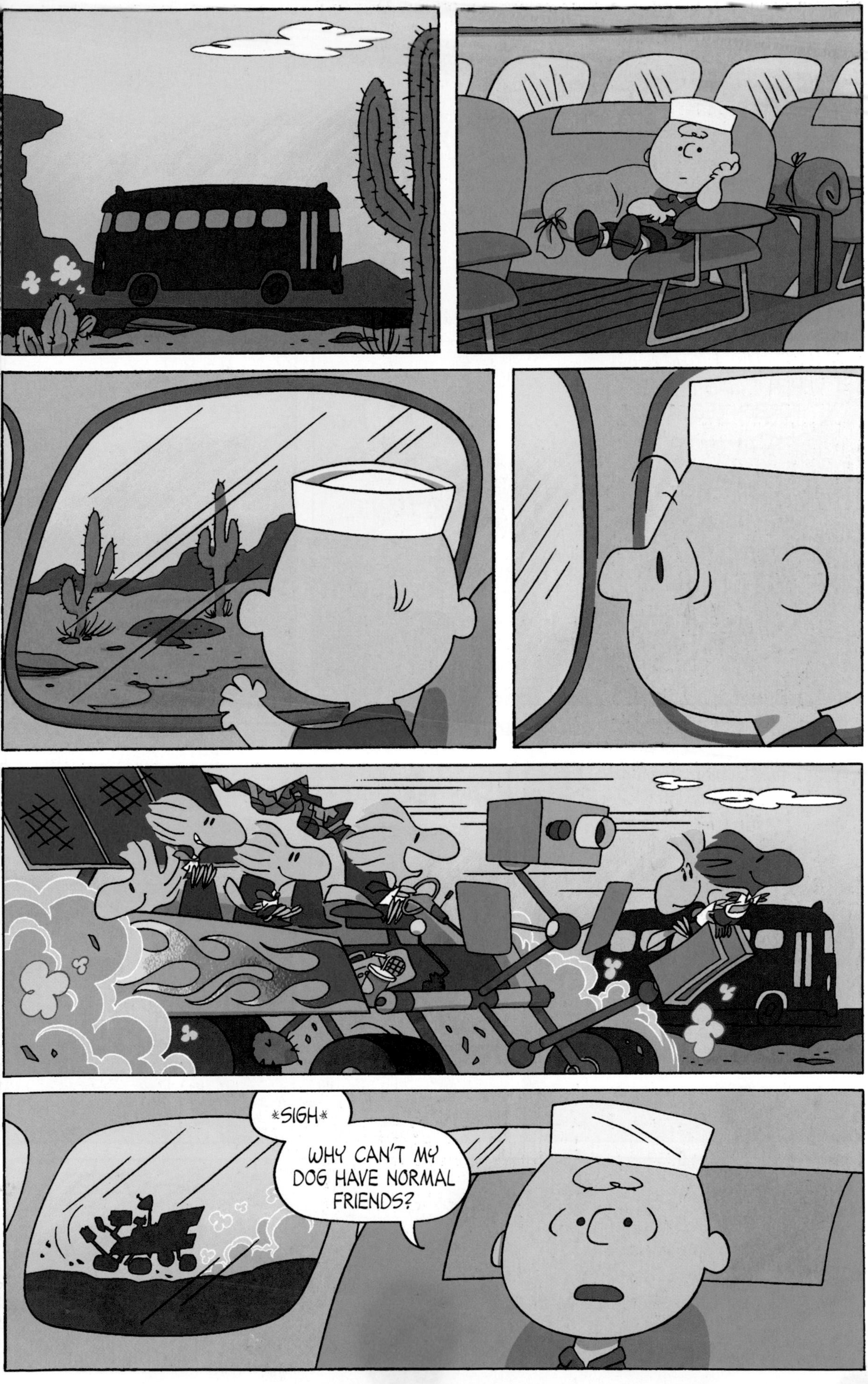
SIGH
WHY CAN'T MY DOG HAVE NORMAL FRIENDS?

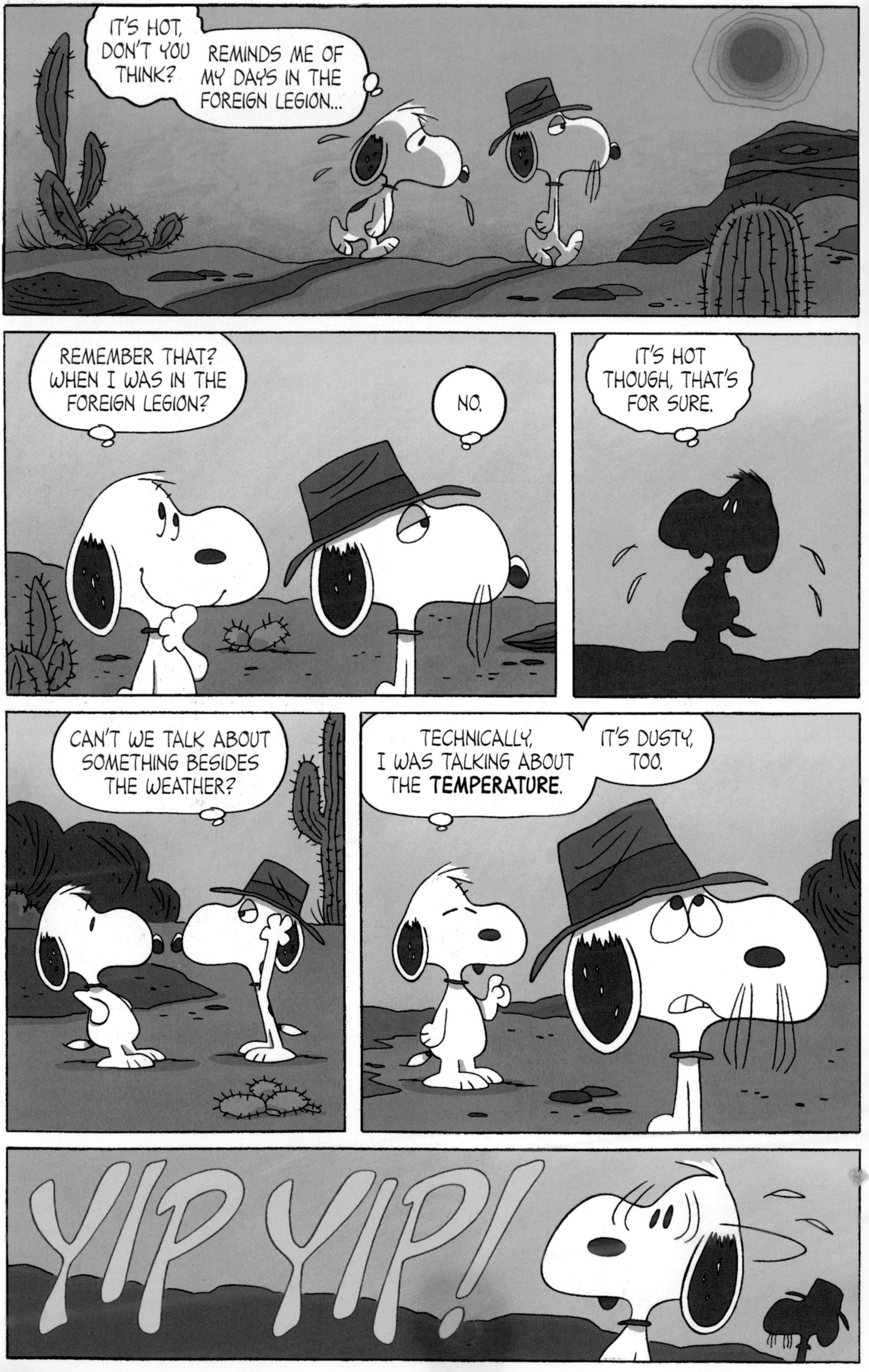

IT'S HOT, DON'T YOU THINK?
REMINDS ME OF MY DAYS IN THE FOREIGN LEGION...
REMEMBER THAT? WHEN I WAS IN THE FOREIGN LEGION?
NO.
IT'S HOT THOUGH, THAT'S FOR SURE.
CAN'T WE TALK ABOUT SOMETHING BESIDES THE WEATHER?
TECHNICALLY, I WAS TALKING ABOUT THE **TEMPERATURE**.
IT'S DUSTY, TOO.
YIP YIP!

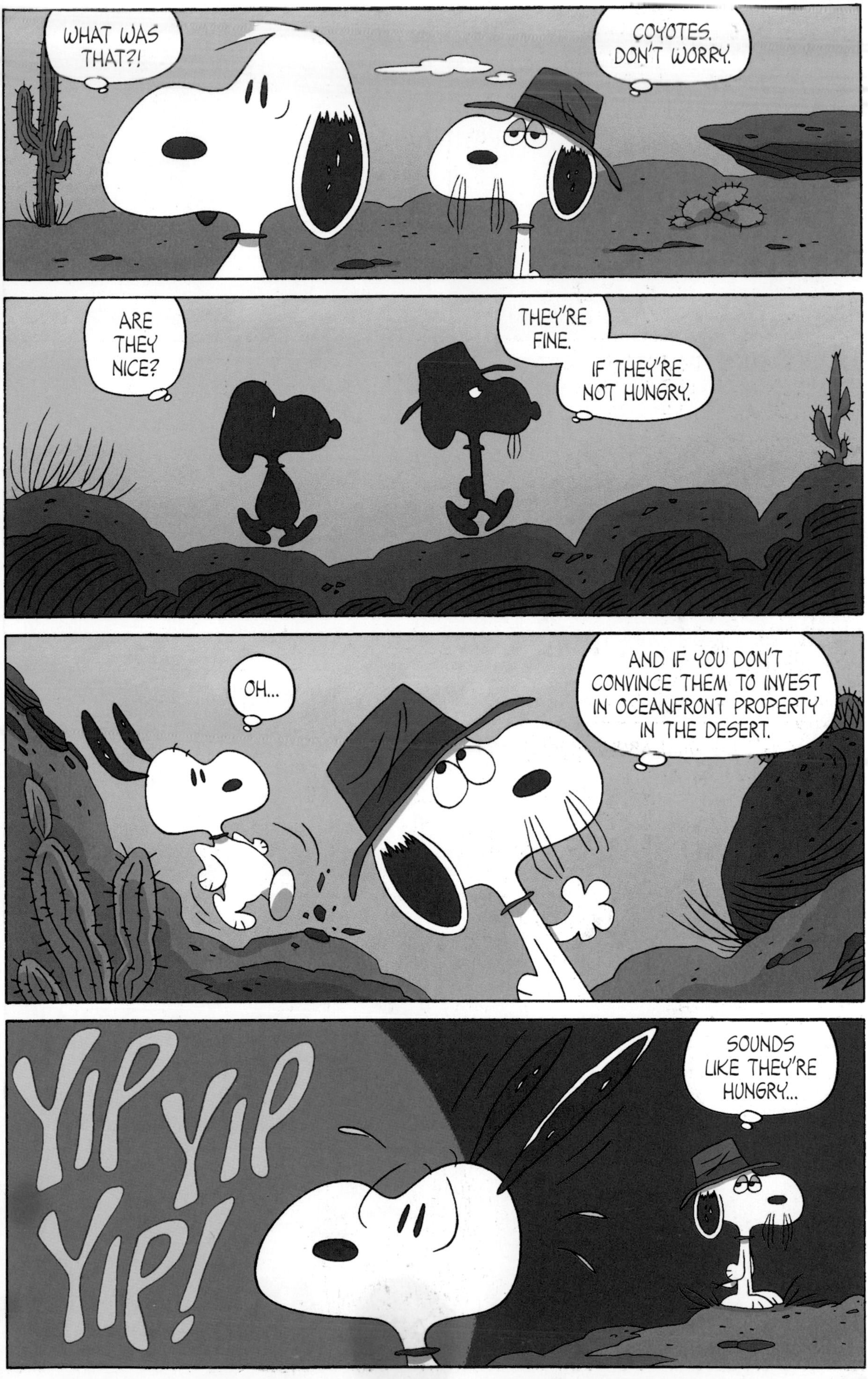
WHAT WAS THAT?!
COYOTES. DON'T WORRY.
ARE THEY NICE?
THEY'RE FINE.
IF THEY'RE NOT HUNGRY.
OH...
AND IF YOU DON'T CONVINCE THEM TO INVEST IN OCEANFRONT PROPERTY IN THE DESERT.
YIP YIP YIP!
SOUNDS LIKE THEY'RE HUNGRY...

ARE YOU SURE YOU KNOW WHERE YOUR SHOP IS?

OF COURSE.

I SAW A SCORPION BACK THERE.

NO, YOU DIDN'T.

I KNOW A SCORPION WHEN I SEE ONE! AND I SAW ONE. AND HE LOOKED MAD.

SURE IS HOT.

WILL YOU STOP COMPLAINING?

I'M NOT COMPLAINING! I'M JUST TELLING YOU I SAW AN ANGRY BUG! AND IT'S TOO HOT!

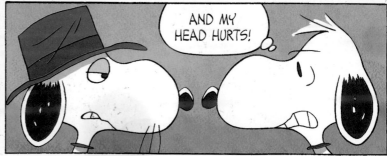

AND MY HEAD HURTS!

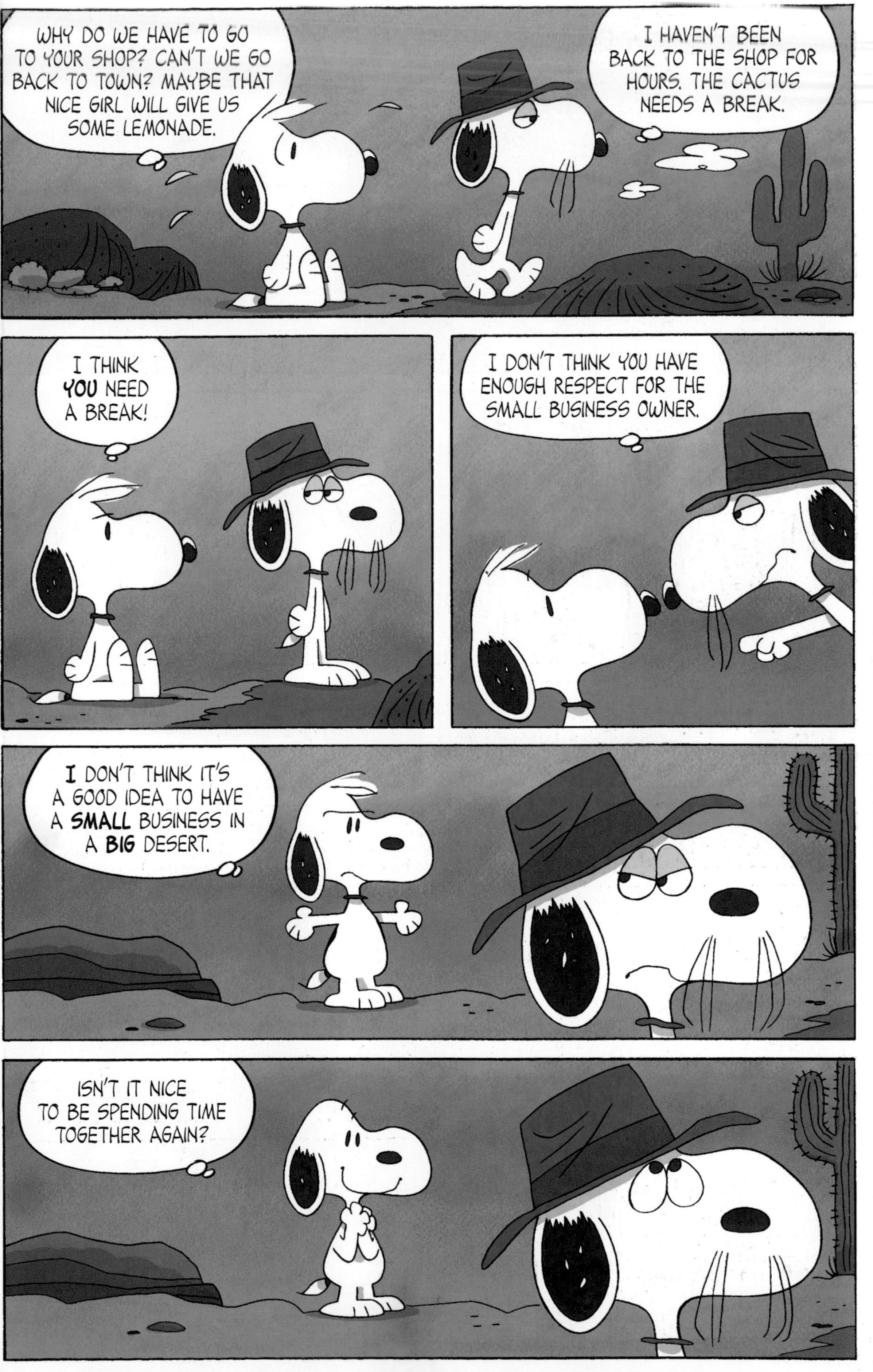
WHY DO WE HAVE TO GO TO YOUR SHOP? CAN'T WE GO BACK TO TOWN? MAYBE THAT NICE GIRL WILL GIVE US SOME LEMONADE.
I HAVEN'T BEEN BACK TO THE SHOP FOR HOURS. THE CACTUS NEEDS A BREAK.
I THINK **YOU** NEED A BREAK!
I DON'T THINK YOU HAVE ENOUGH RESPECT FOR THE SMALL BUSINESS OWNER.
I DON'T THINK IT'S A GOOD IDEA TO HAVE A **SMALL** BUSINESS IN A **BIG** DESERT.
ISN'T IT NICE TO BE SPENDING TIME TOGETHER AGAIN?

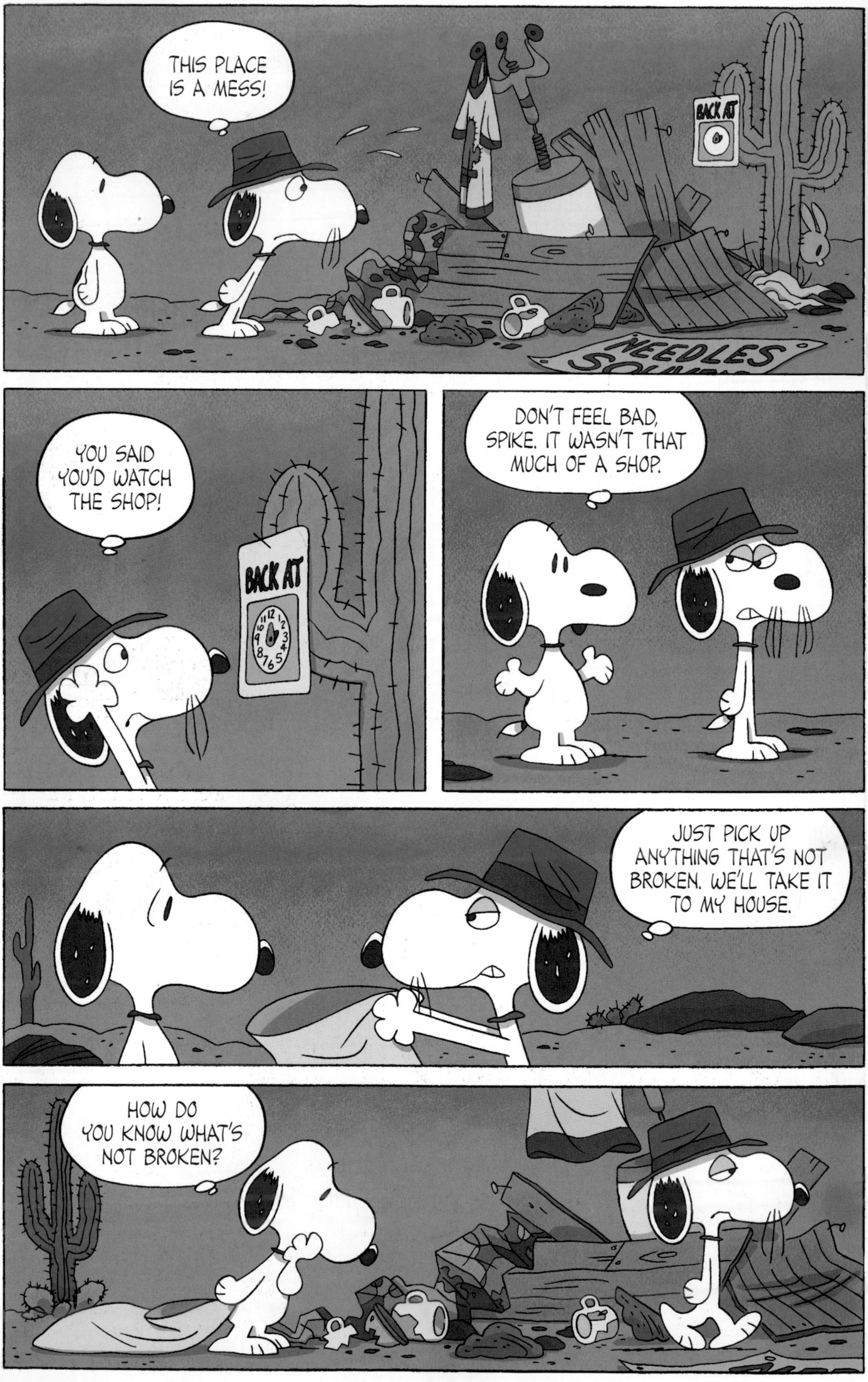
THIS PLACE IS A MESS!
BACK AT
NEEDLES
YOU SAID YOU'D WATCH THE SHOP!
BACK AT
DON'T FEEL BAD, SPIKE. IT WASN'T THAT MUCH OF A SHOP.
JUST PICK UP ANYTHING THAT'S NOT BROKEN. WE'LL TAKE IT TO MY HOUSE.
HOW DO YOU KNOW WHAT'S NOT BROKEN?

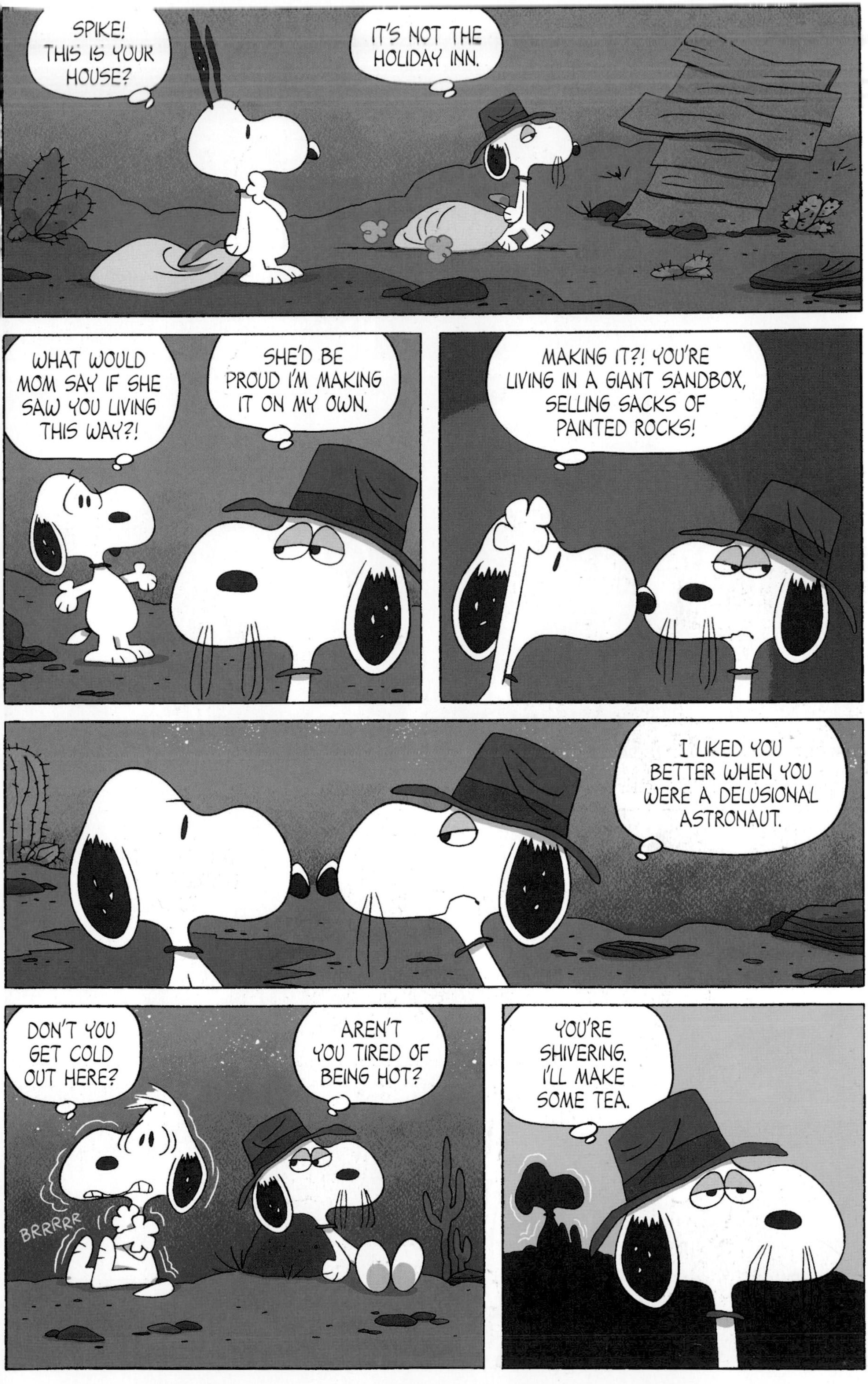
SPIKE! THIS IS YOUR HOUSE?
IT'S NOT THE HOLIDAY INN.
WHAT WOULD MOM SAY IF SHE SAW YOU LIVING THIS WAY?!
SHE'D BE PROUD I'M MAKING IT ON MY OWN.
MAKING IT?! YOU'RE LIVING IN A GIANT SANDBOX, SELLING SACKS OF PAINTED ROCKS!
I LIKED YOU BETTER WHEN YOU WERE A DELUSIONAL ASTRONAUT.
DON'T YOU GET COLD OUT HERE?
BRRRRR
AREN'T YOU TIRED OF BEING HOT?
YOU'RE SHIVERING. I'LL MAKE SOME TEA.

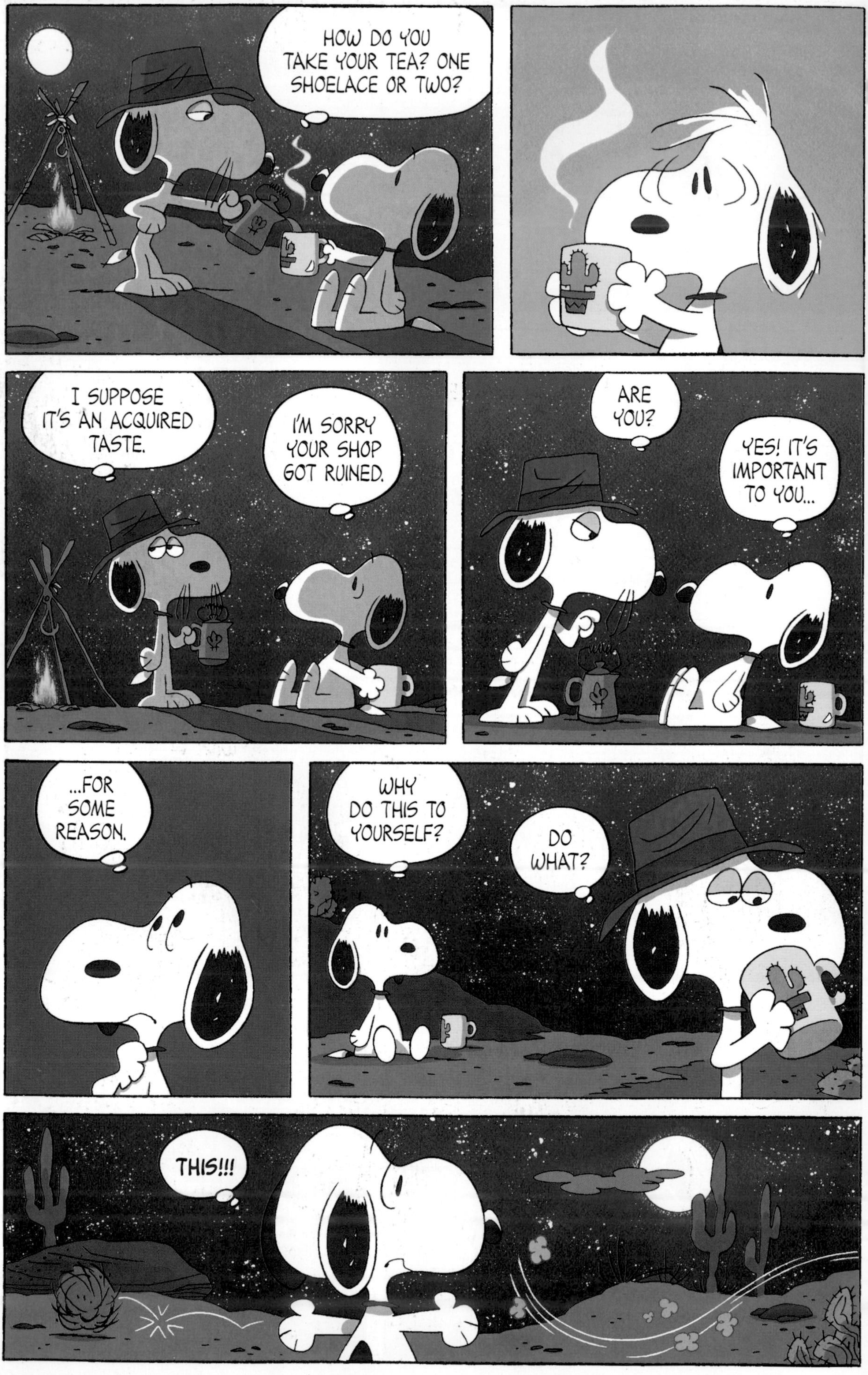
HOW DO YOU TAKE YOUR TEA? ONE SHOELACE OR TWO?
I SUPPOSE IT'S AN ACQUIRED TASTE.
I'M SORRY YOUR SHOP GOT RUINED.
ARE YOU?
YES! IT'S IMPORTANT TO YOU...
...FOR SOME REASON.
WHY DO THIS TO YOURSELF?
DO WHAT?
THIS!!!

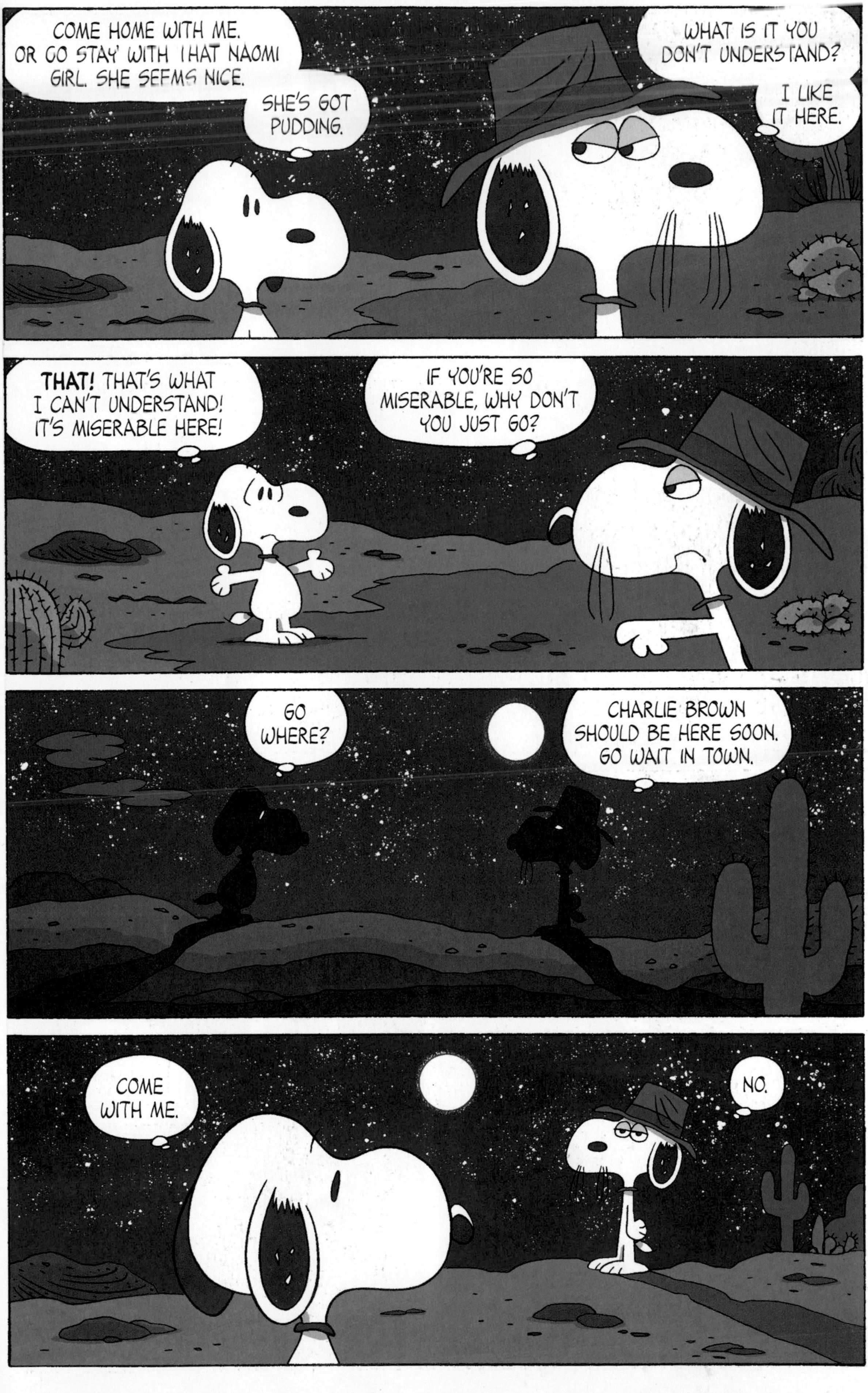
COME HOME WITH ME. OR GO STAY WITH THAT NAOMI GIRL. SHE SEEMS NICE.
SHE'S GOT PUDDING.
WHAT IS IT YOU DON'T UNDERSTAND?
I LIKE IT HERE.
THAT! THAT'S WHAT I CAN'T UNDERSTAND! IT'S MISERABLE HERE!
IF YOU'RE SO MISERABLE, WHY DON'T YOU JUST GO?
GO WHERE?
CHARLIE BROWN SHOULD BE HERE SOON. GO WAIT IN TOWN.
COME WITH ME.
NO.

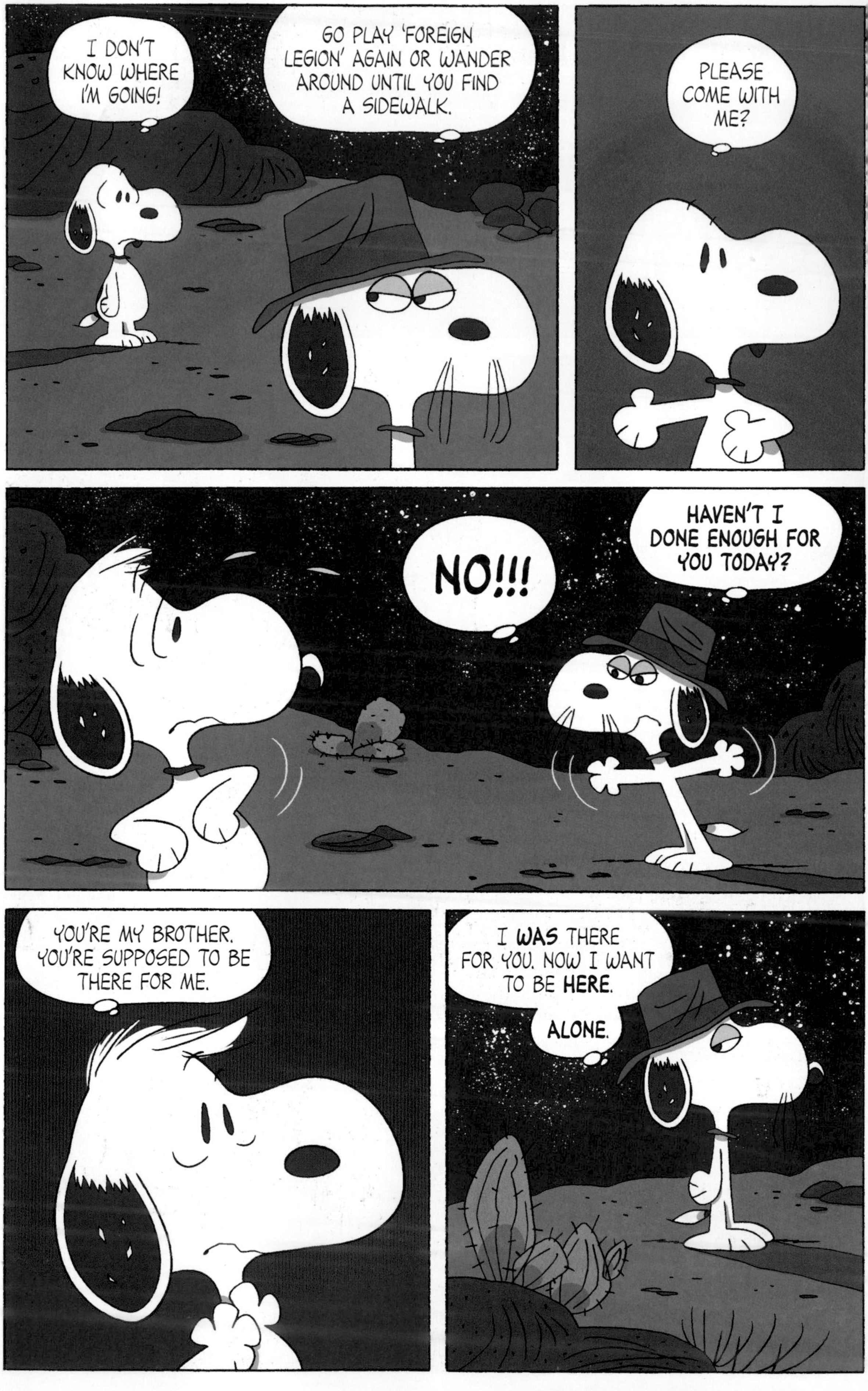
I DON'T KNOW WHERE I'M GOING!
GO PLAY 'FOREIGN LEGION' AGAIN OR WANDER AROUND UNTIL YOU FIND A SIDEWALK.
PLEASE COME WITH ME?
NO!!!
HAVEN'T I DONE ENOUGH FOR YOU TODAY?
YOU'RE MY BROTHER. YOU'RE SUPPOSED TO BE THERE FOR ME.
I **WAS** THERE FOR YOU. NOW I WANT TO BE **HERE**.
ALONE.

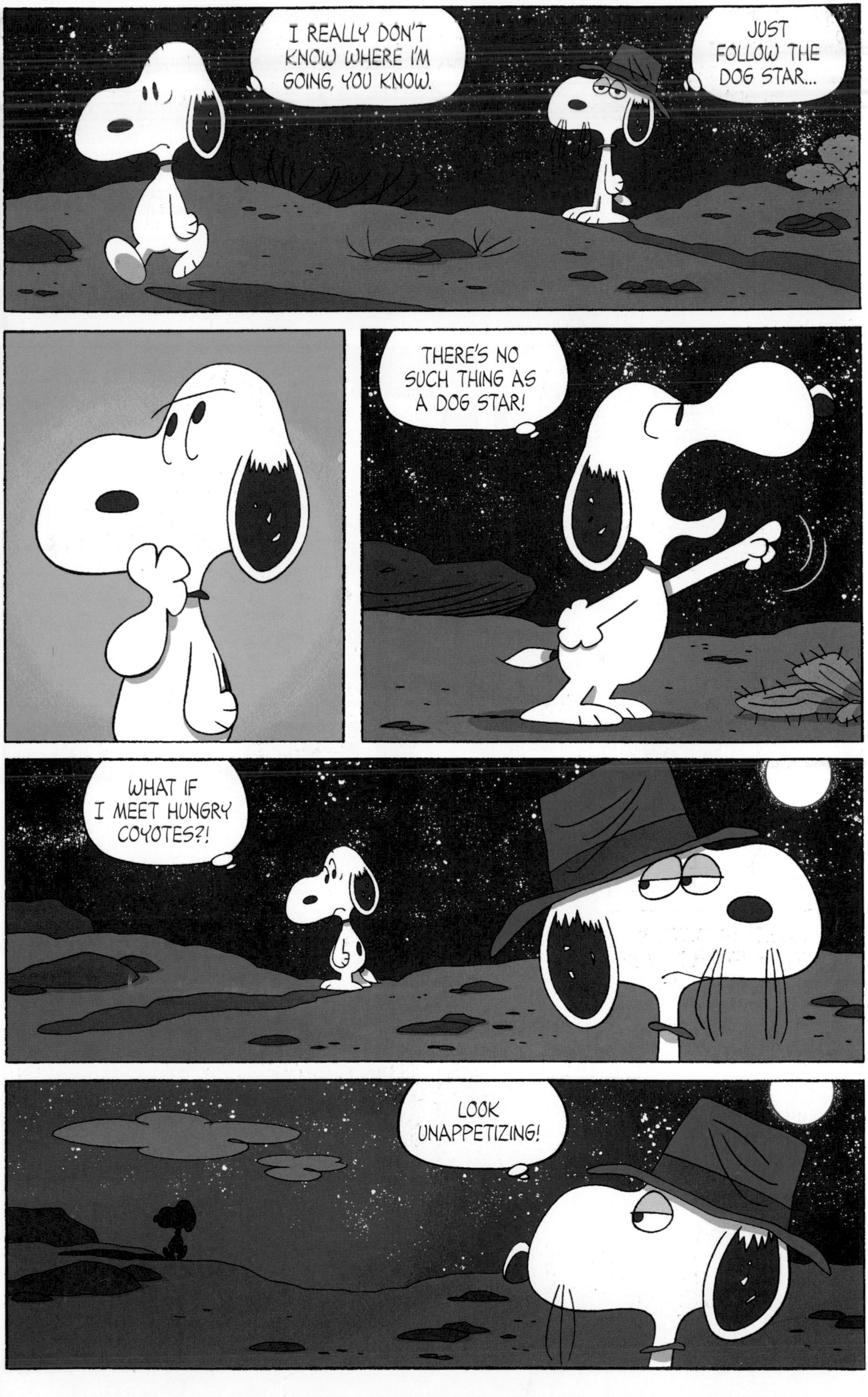
I REALLY DON'T KNOW WHERE I'M GOING, YOU KNOW.
JUST FOLLOW THE DOG STAR...
THERE'S NO SUCH THING AS A DOG STAR!
WHAT IF I MEET HUNGRY COYOTES?!
LOOK UNAPPETIZING!

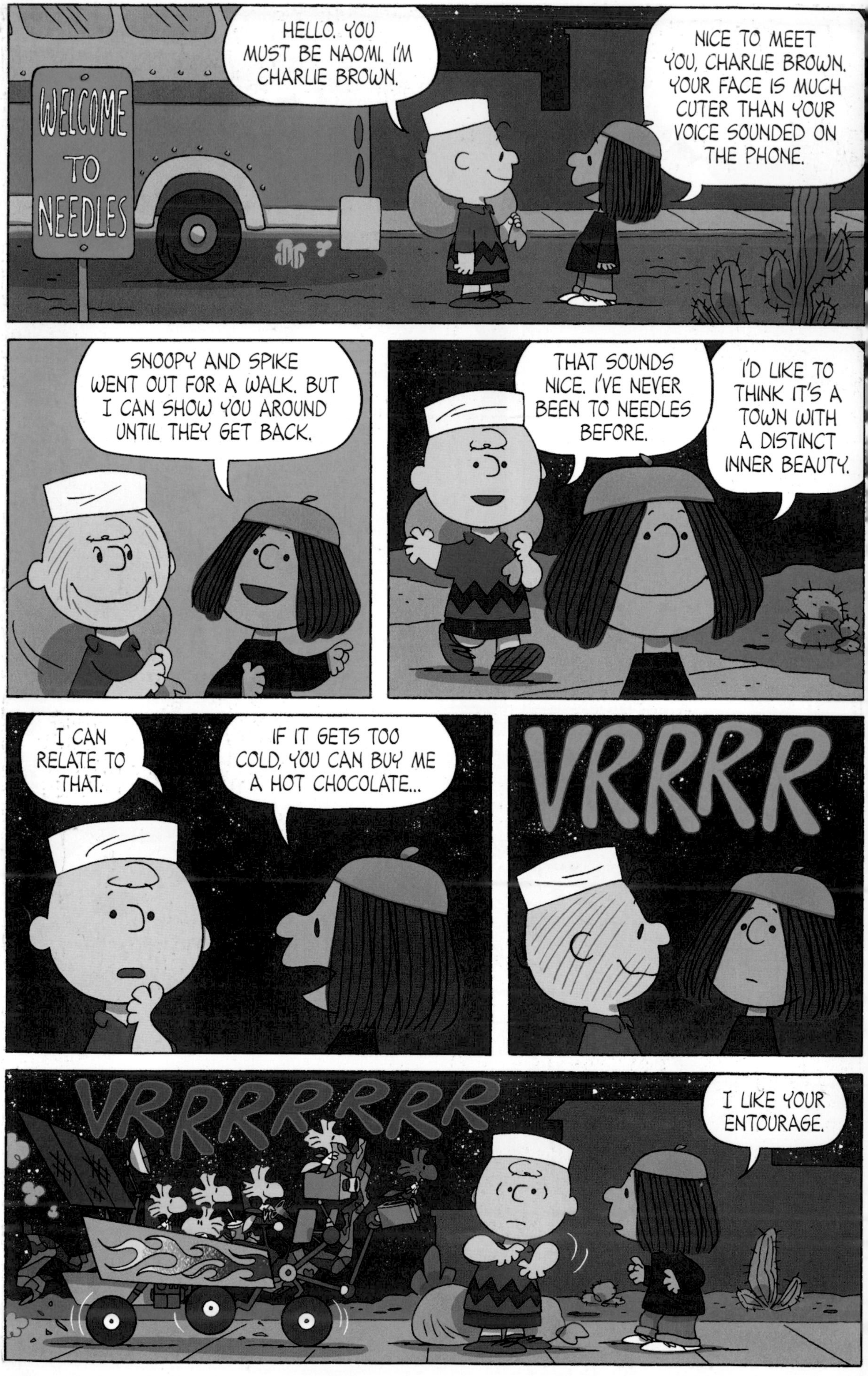
WELCOME TO NEEDLES
HELLO. YOU MUST BE NAOMI. I'M CHARLIE BROWN.
NICE TO MEET YOU, CHARLIE BROWN. YOUR FACE IS MUCH CUTER THAN YOUR VOICE SOUNDED ON THE PHONE.
SNOOPY AND SPIKE WENT OUT FOR A WALK. BUT I CAN SHOW YOU AROUND UNTIL THEY GET BACK.
THAT SOUNDS NICE. I'VE NEVER BEEN TO NEEDLES BEFORE.
I'D LIKE TO THINK IT'S A TOWN WITH A DISTINCT INNER BEAUTY.
I CAN RELATE TO THAT.
IF IT GETS TOO COLD, YOU CAN BUY ME A HOT CHOCOLATE...
VRRRR
VRRRRRRR
I LIKE YOUR ENTOURAGE.

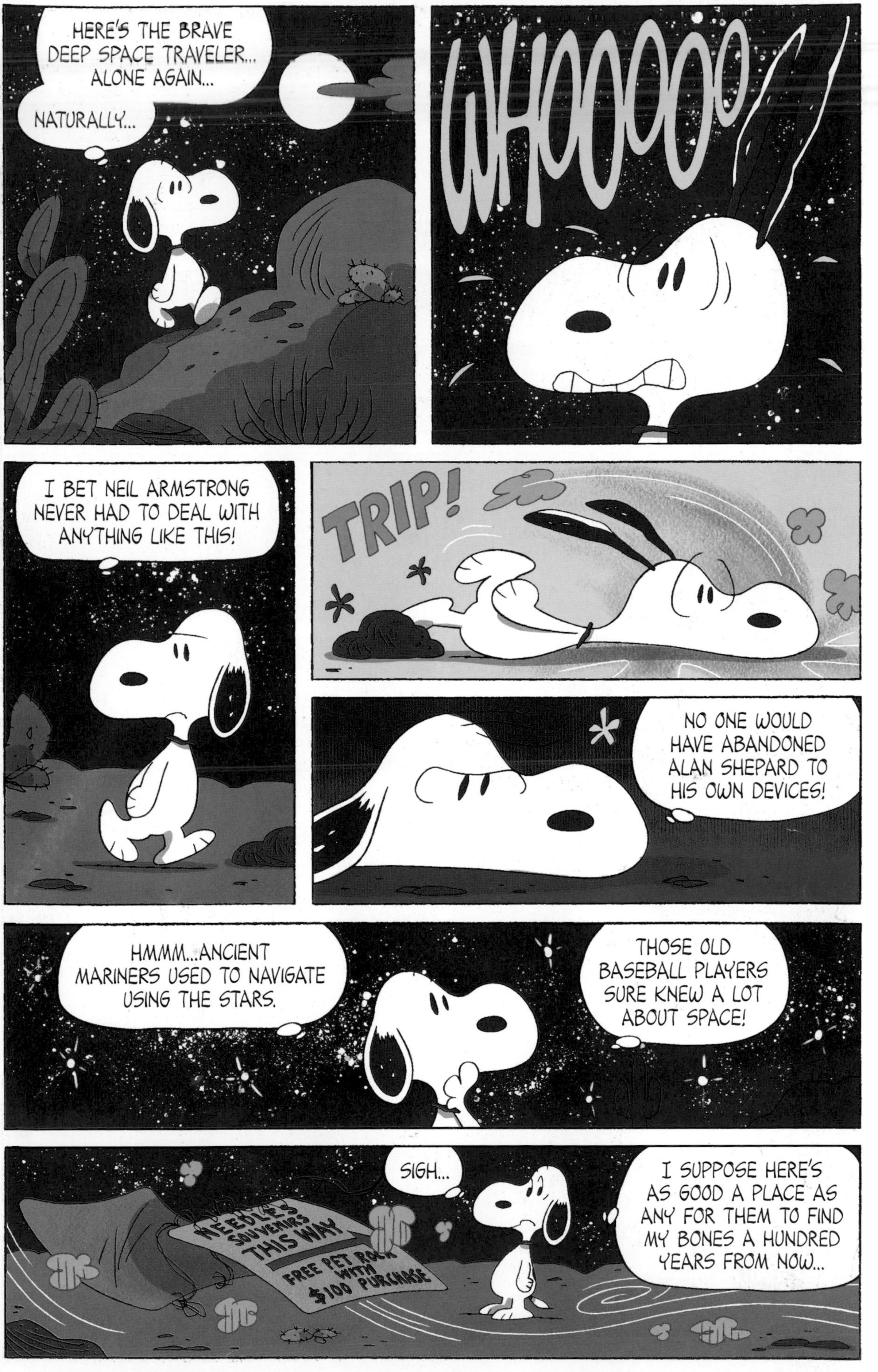
HERE'S THE BRAVE DEEP SPACE TRAVELER... ALONE AGAIN...
NATURALLY...
WHOOOOO
I BET NEIL ARMSTRONG NEVER HAD TO DEAL WITH ANYTHING LIKE THIS!
TRIP!
NO ONE WOULD HAVE ABANDONED ALAN SHEPARD TO HIS OWN DEVICES!
HMMM...ANCIENT MARINERS USED TO NAVIGATE USING THE STARS.
THOSE OLD BASEBALL PLAYERS SURE KNEW A LOT ABOUT SPACE!
NEEDLES SOUVENIRS THIS WAY
FREE PET ROCK WITH $100 PURCHASE
SIGH...
I SUPPOSE HERE'S AS GOOD A PLACE AS ANY FOR THEM TO FIND MY BONES A HUNDRED YEARS FROM NOW...

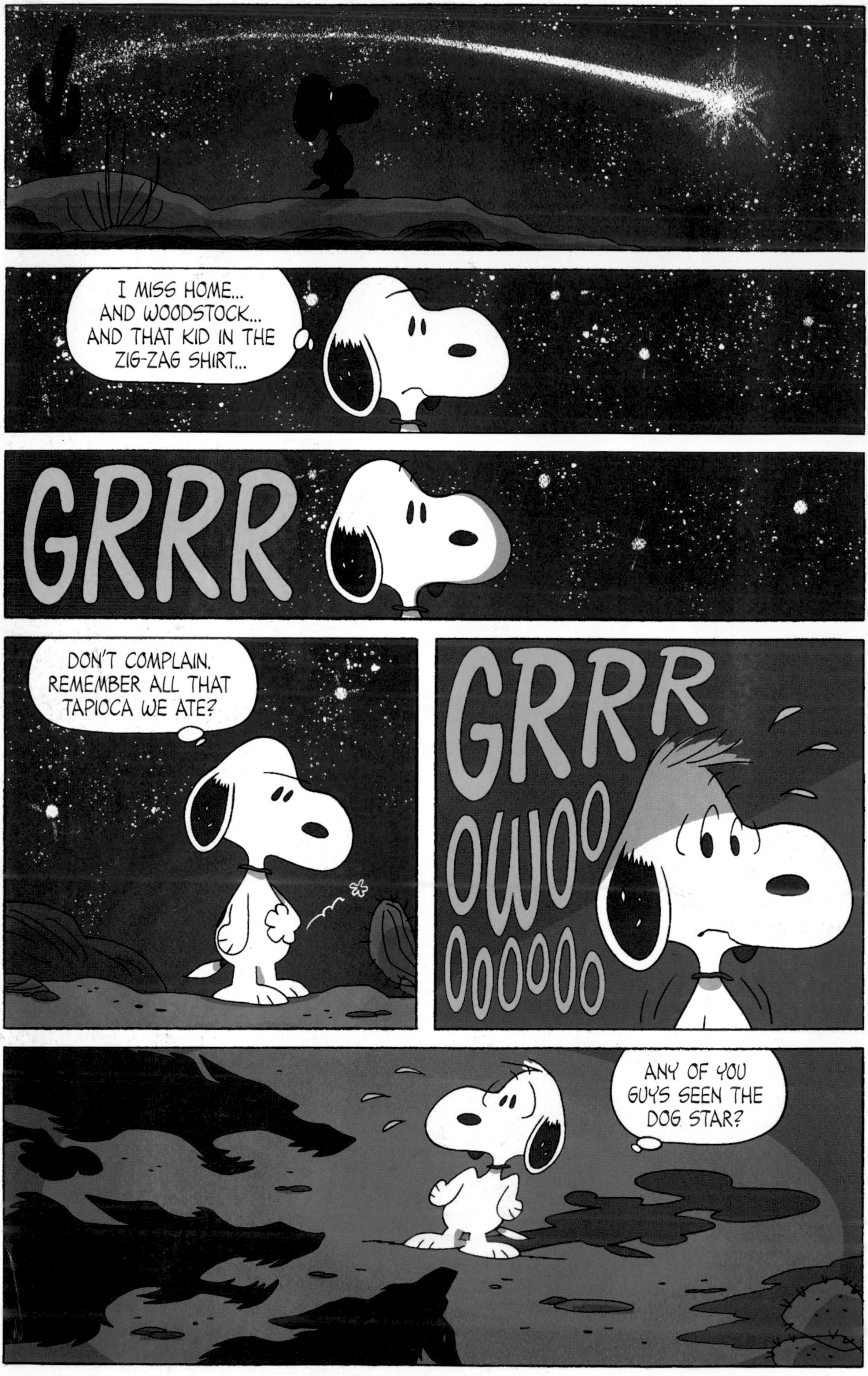
I MISS HOME... AND WOODSTOCK... AND THAT KID IN THE ZIG-ZAG SHIRT...
GRRR
DON'T COMPLAIN. REMEMBER ALL THAT TAPIOCA WE ATE?
GRRR OWOOOOOOOO
ANY OF YOU GUYS SEEN THE DOG STAR?

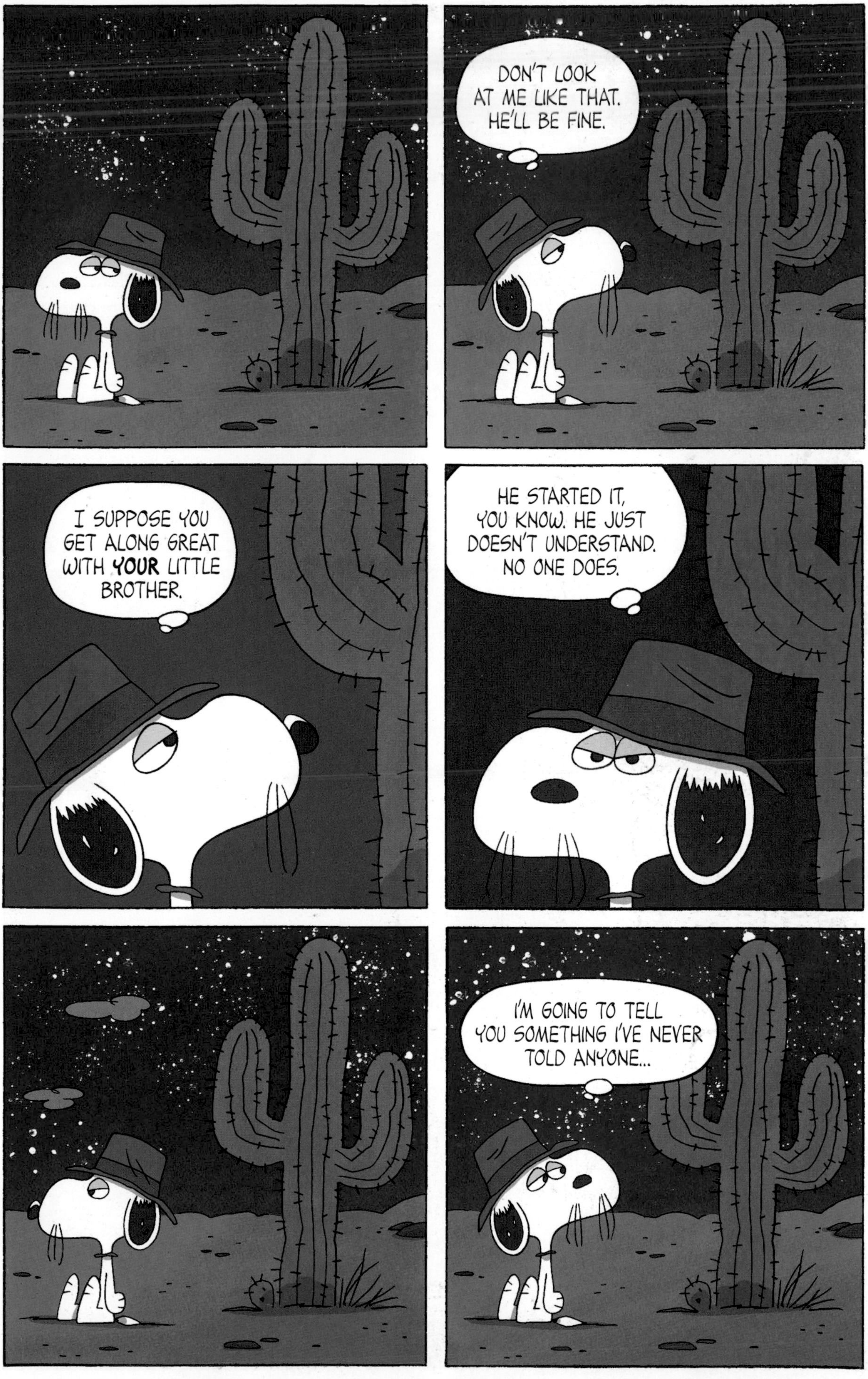
DON'T LOOK AT ME LIKE THAT. HE'LL BE FINE.
I SUPPOSE YOU GET ALONG GREAT WITH **YOUR** LITTLE BROTHER.
HE STARTED IT, YOU KNOW. HE JUST DOESN'T UNDERSTAND. NO ONE DOES.
I'M GOING TO TELL YOU SOMETHING I'VE NEVER TOLD ANYONE...

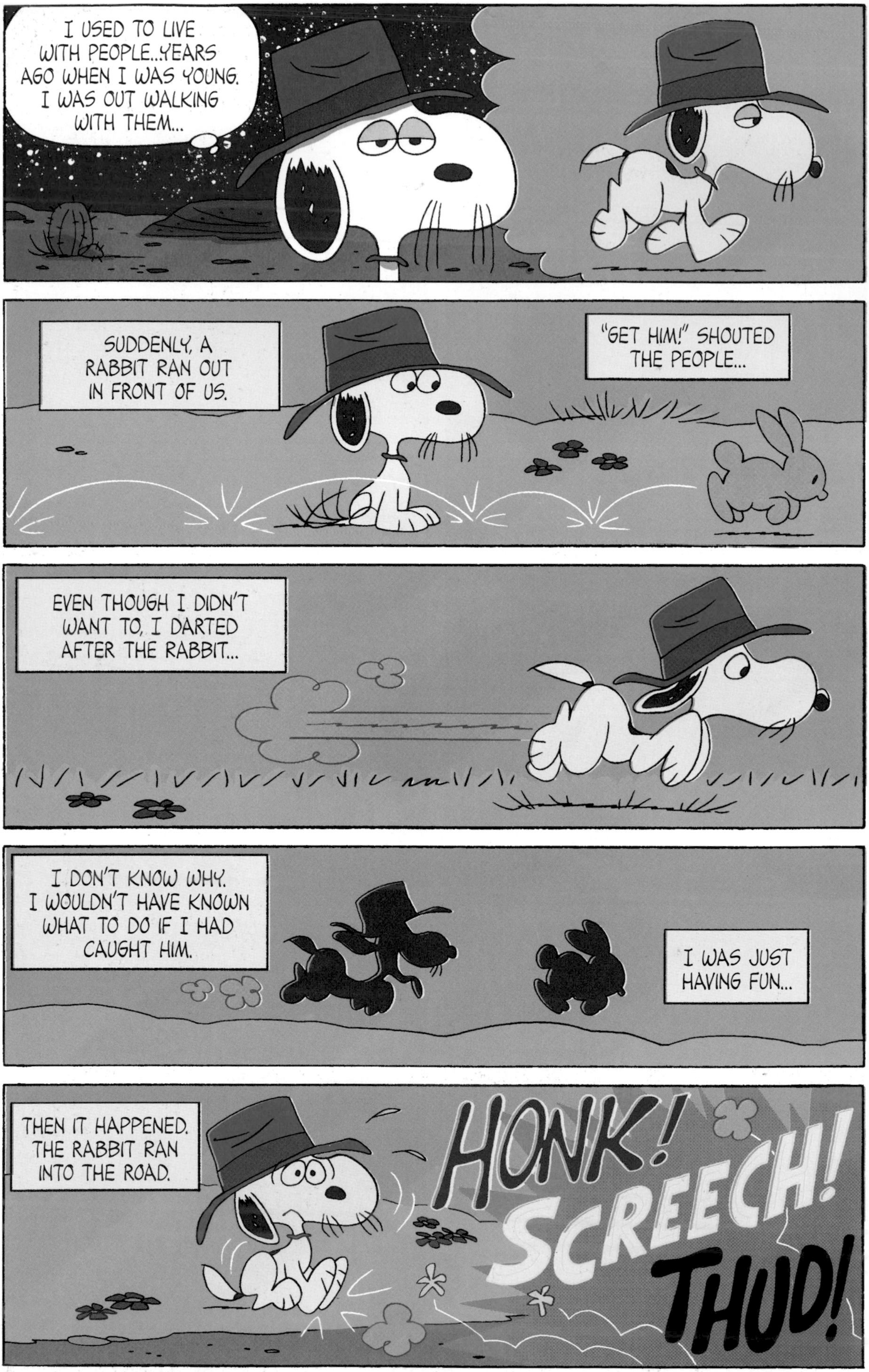
I USED TO LIVE WITH PEOPLE...YEARS AGO WHEN I WAS YOUNG. I WAS OUT WALKING WITH THEM...
SUDDENLY, A RABBIT RAN OUT IN FRONT OF US.
"GET HIM!" SHOUTED THE PEOPLE...
EVEN THOUGH I DIDN'T WANT TO, I DARTED AFTER THE RABBIT...
I DON'T KNOW WHY. I WOULDN'T HAVE KNOWN WHAT TO DO IF I HAD CAUGHT HIM.
I WAS JUST HAVING FUN...
THEN IT HAPPENED. THE RABBIT RAN INTO THE ROAD.
HONK!
SCREECH!
THUD!

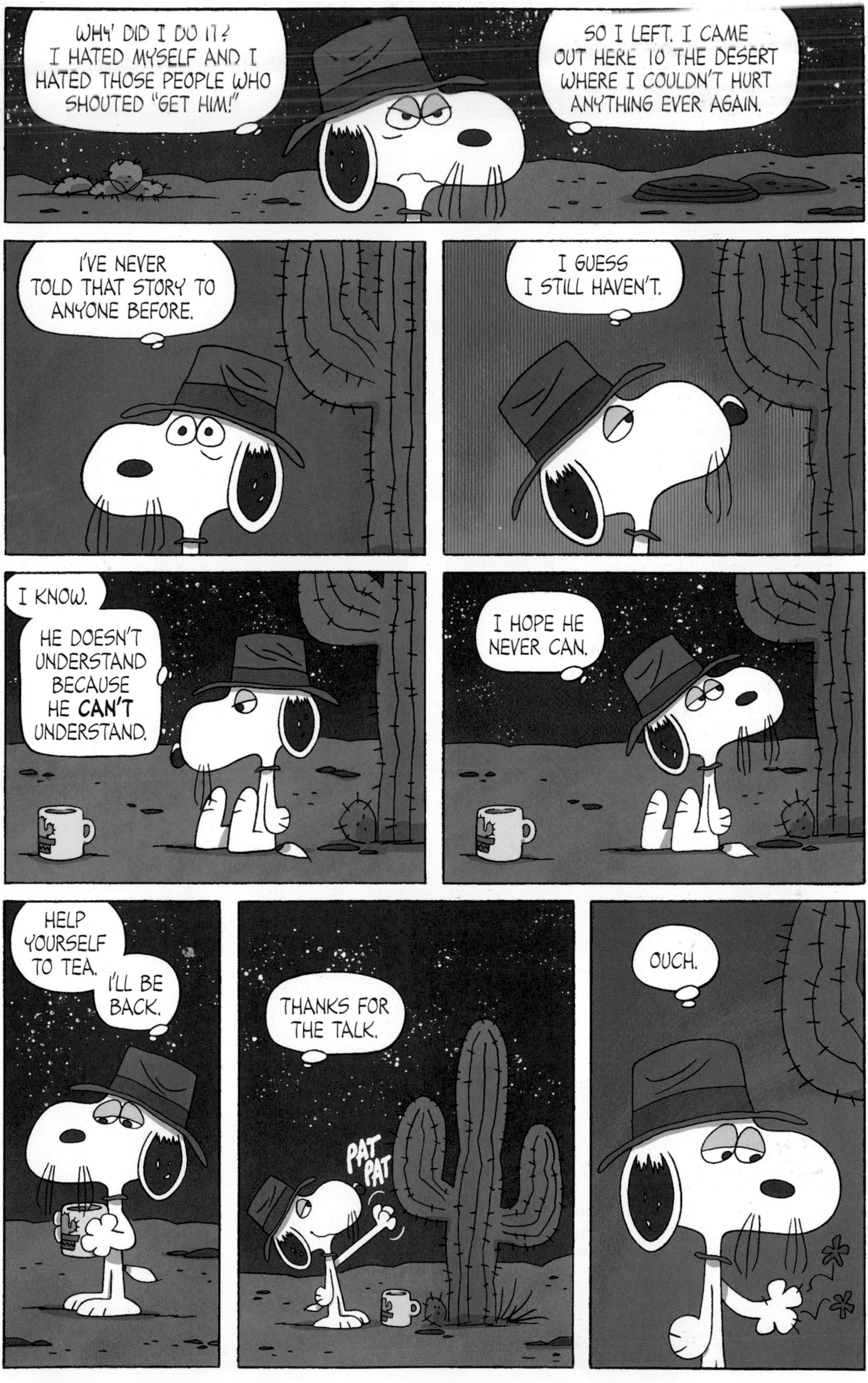
WHY DID I DO IT? I HATED MYSELF AND I HATED THOSE PEOPLE WHO SHOUTED "GET HIM!"
SO I LEFT. I CAME OUT HERE TO THE DESERT WHERE I COULDN'T HURT ANYTHING EVER AGAIN.
I'VE NEVER TOLD THAT STORY TO ANYONE BEFORE.
I GUESS I STILL HAVEN'T.
I KNOW.
HE DOESN'T UNDERSTAND BECAUSE HE **CAN'T** UNDERSTAND.
I HOPE HE NEVER CAN.
HELP YOURSELF TO TEA.
I'LL BE BACK.
THANKS FOR THE TALK.
PAT PAT
OUCH.

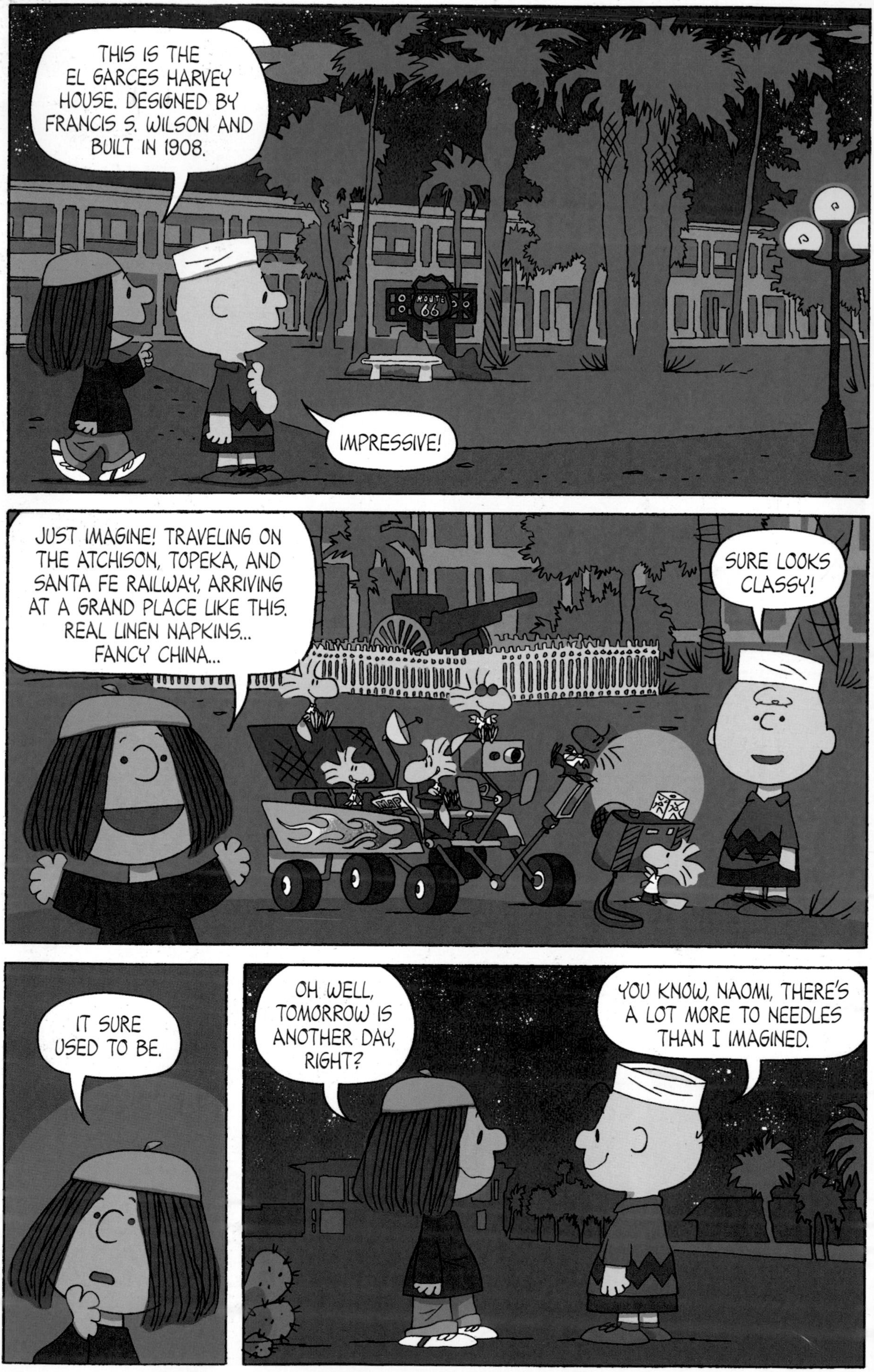
THIS IS THE EL GARCES HARVEY HOUSE. DESIGNED BY FRANCIS S. WILSON AND BUILT IN 1908.
IMPRESSIVE!
JUST IMAGINE! TRAVELING ON THE ATCHISON, TOPEKA, AND SANTA FE RAILWAY, ARRIVING AT A GRAND PLACE LIKE THIS. REAL LINEN NAPKINS... FANCY CHINA...
SURE LOOKS CLASSY!
IT SURE USED TO BE.
OH WELL, TOMORROW IS ANOTHER DAY, RIGHT?
YOU KNOW, NAOMI, THERE'S A LOT MORE TO NEEDLES THAN I IMAGINED.

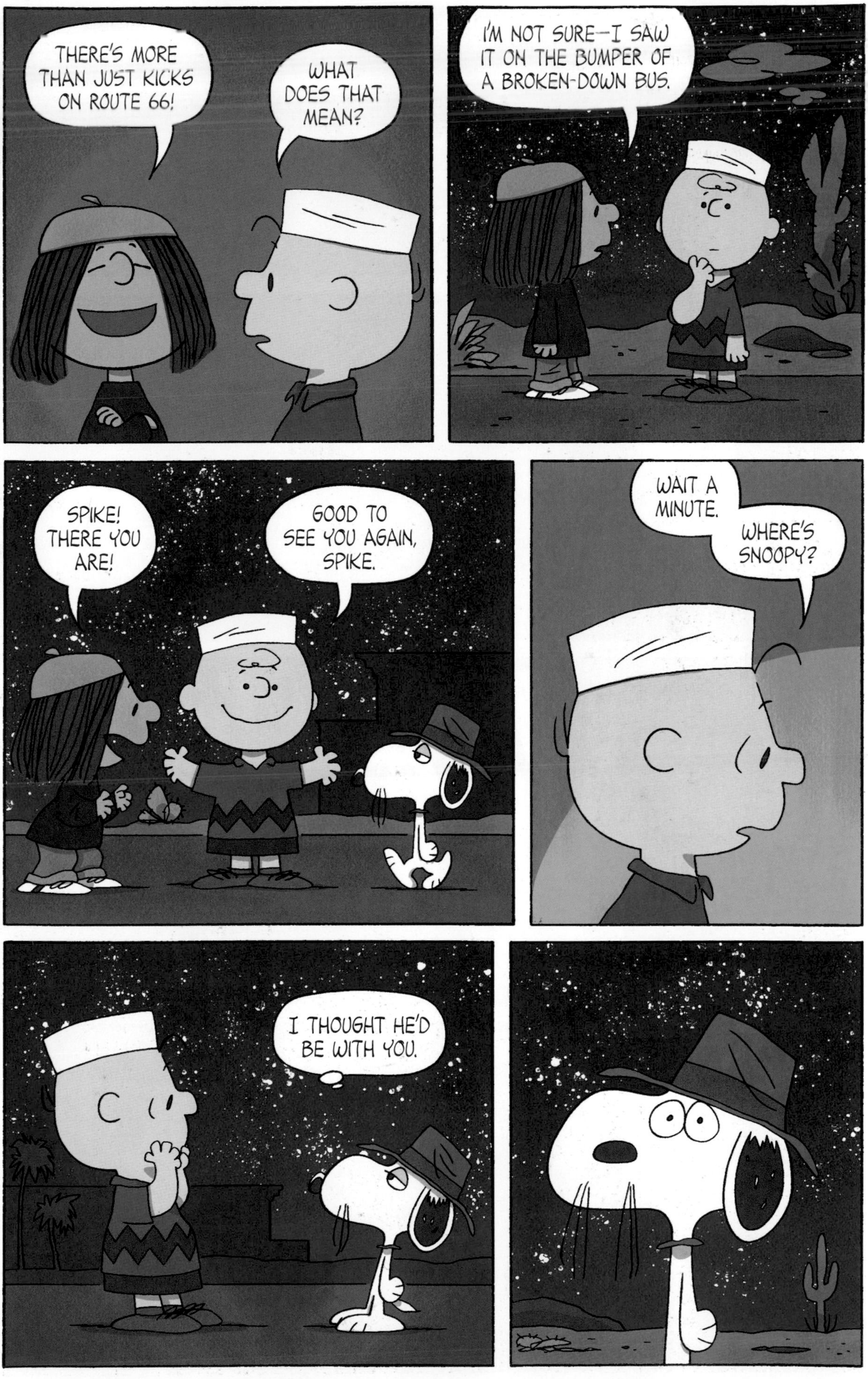
THERE'S MORE THAN JUST KICKS ON ROUTE 66!
WHAT DOES THAT MEAN?
I'M NOT SURE—I SAW IT ON THE BUMPER OF A BROKEN-DOWN BUS.
SPIKE! THERE YOU ARE!
GOOD TO SEE YOU AGAIN, SPIKE.
WAIT A MINUTE.
WHERE'S SNOOPY?
I THOUGHT HE'D BE WITH YOU.

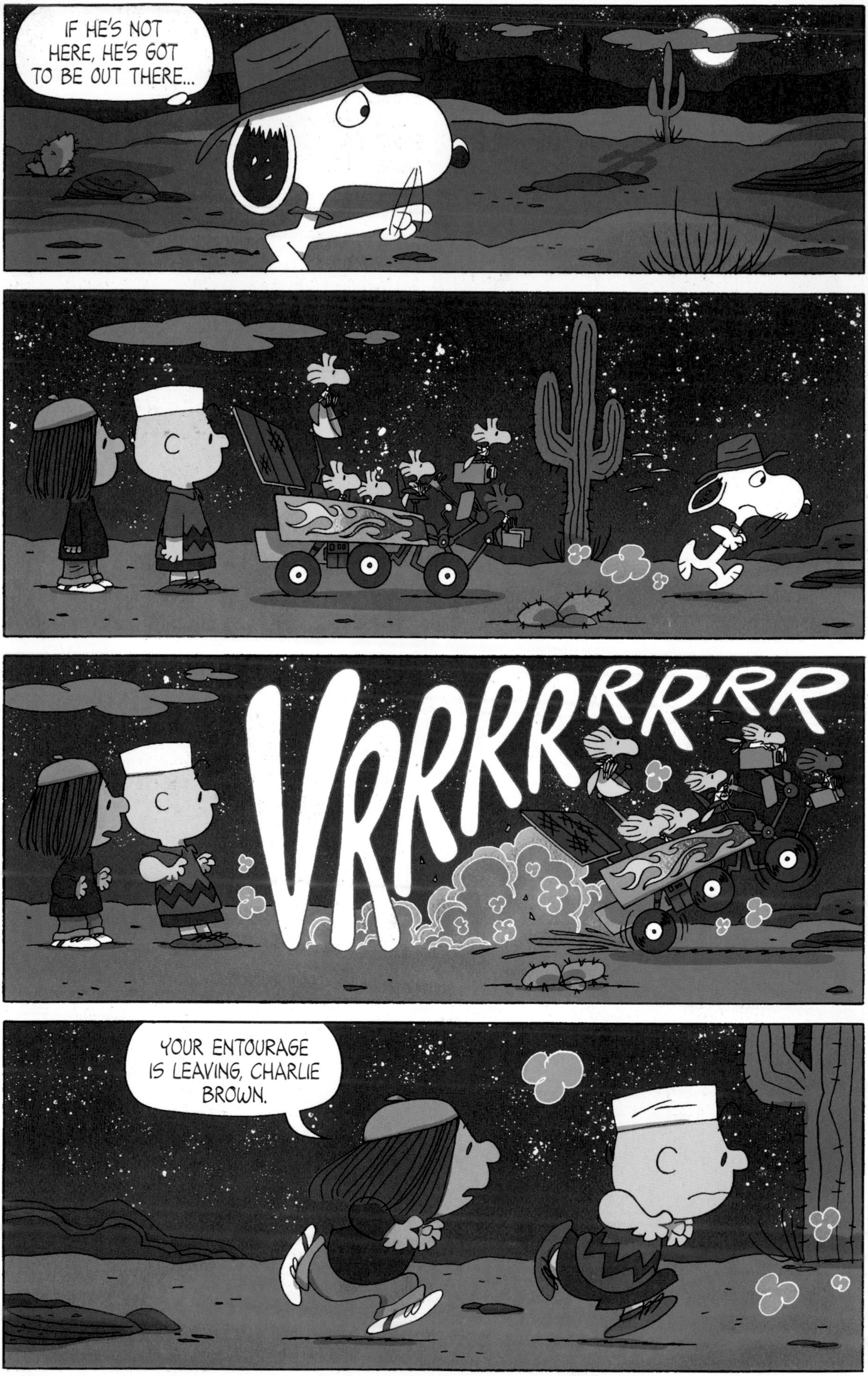

IF HE'S NOT HERE, HE'S GOT TO BE OUT THERE...
VRRRRRRRR
YOUR ENTOURAGE IS LEAVING, CHARLIE BROWN.

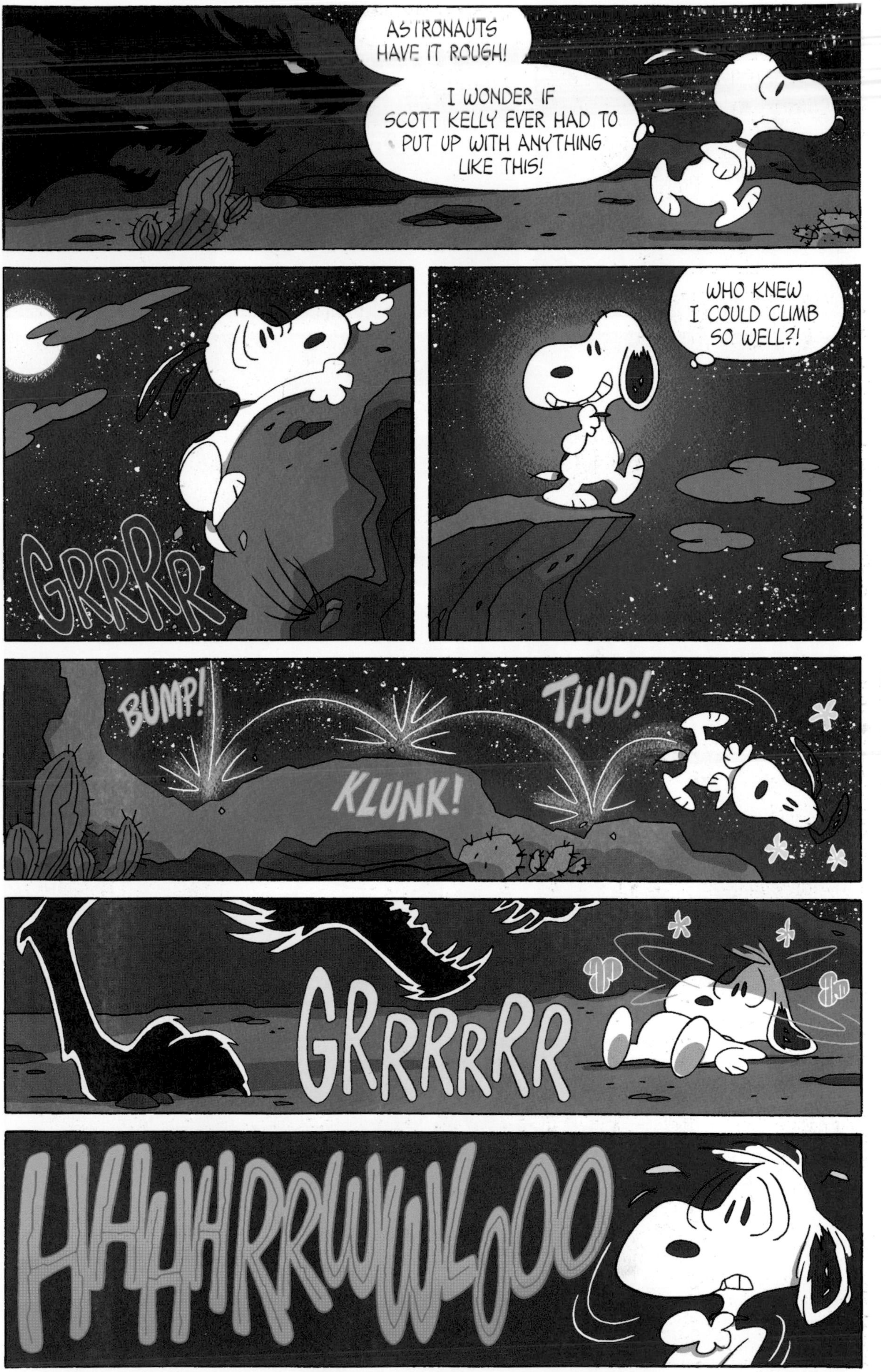
ASTRONAUTS HAVE IT ROUGH!
I WONDER IF SCOTT KELLY EVER HAD TO PUT UP WITH ANYTHING LIKE THIS!
GRRRR
WHO KNEW I COULD CLIMB SO WELL?!
BUMP!
KLUNK!
THUD!
GRRRRRR
HHHHRRWWWLOOO

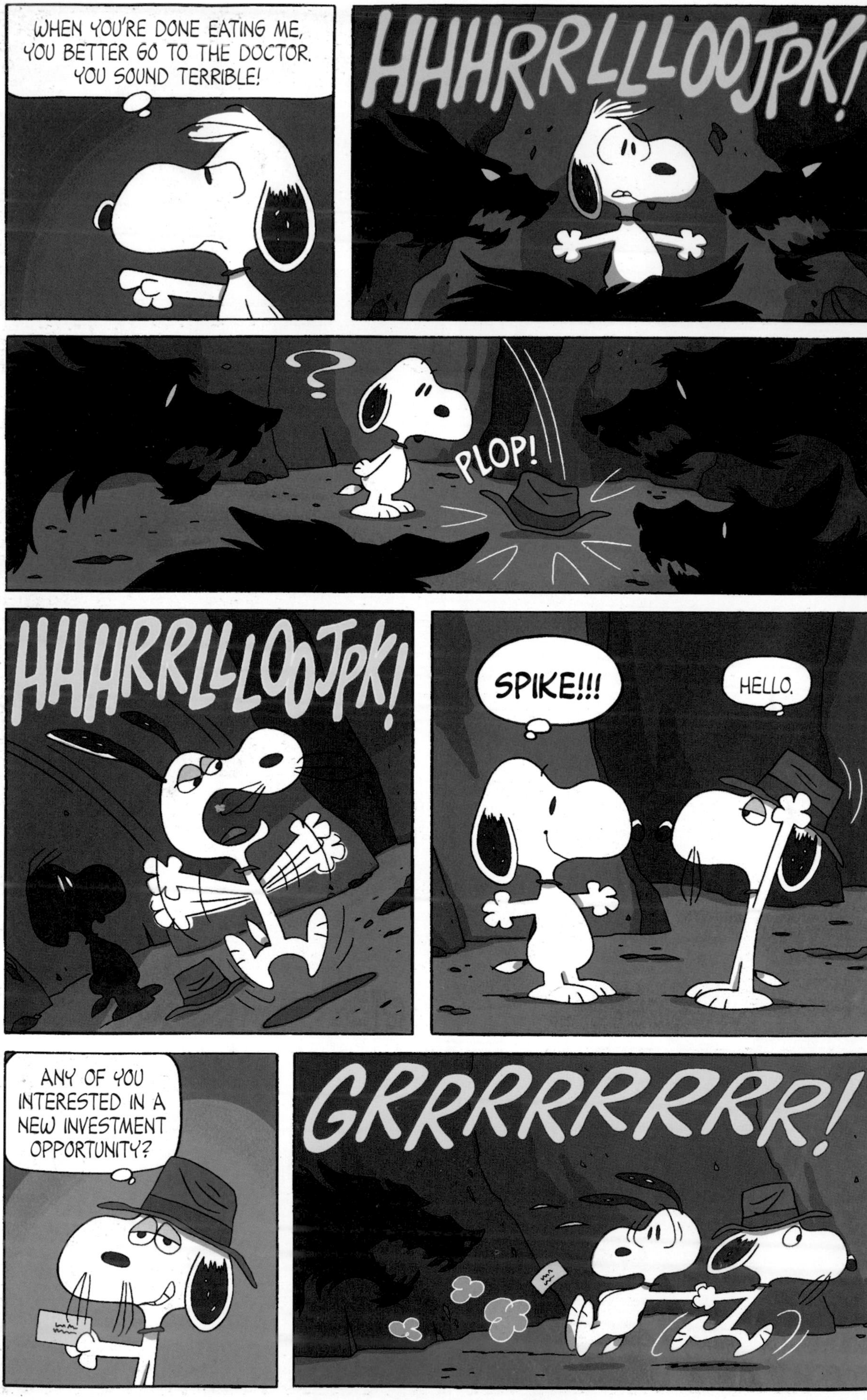
WHEN YOU'RE DONE EATING ME, YOU BETTER GO TO THE DOCTOR. YOU SOUND TERRIBLE!
HHHRRLLLOOJPK!
PLOP!
HHHRRLLLOOJPK!
SPIKE!!!
HELLO.
ANY OF YOU INTERESTED IN A NEW INVESTMENT OPPORTUNITY?
GRRRRRRRR!

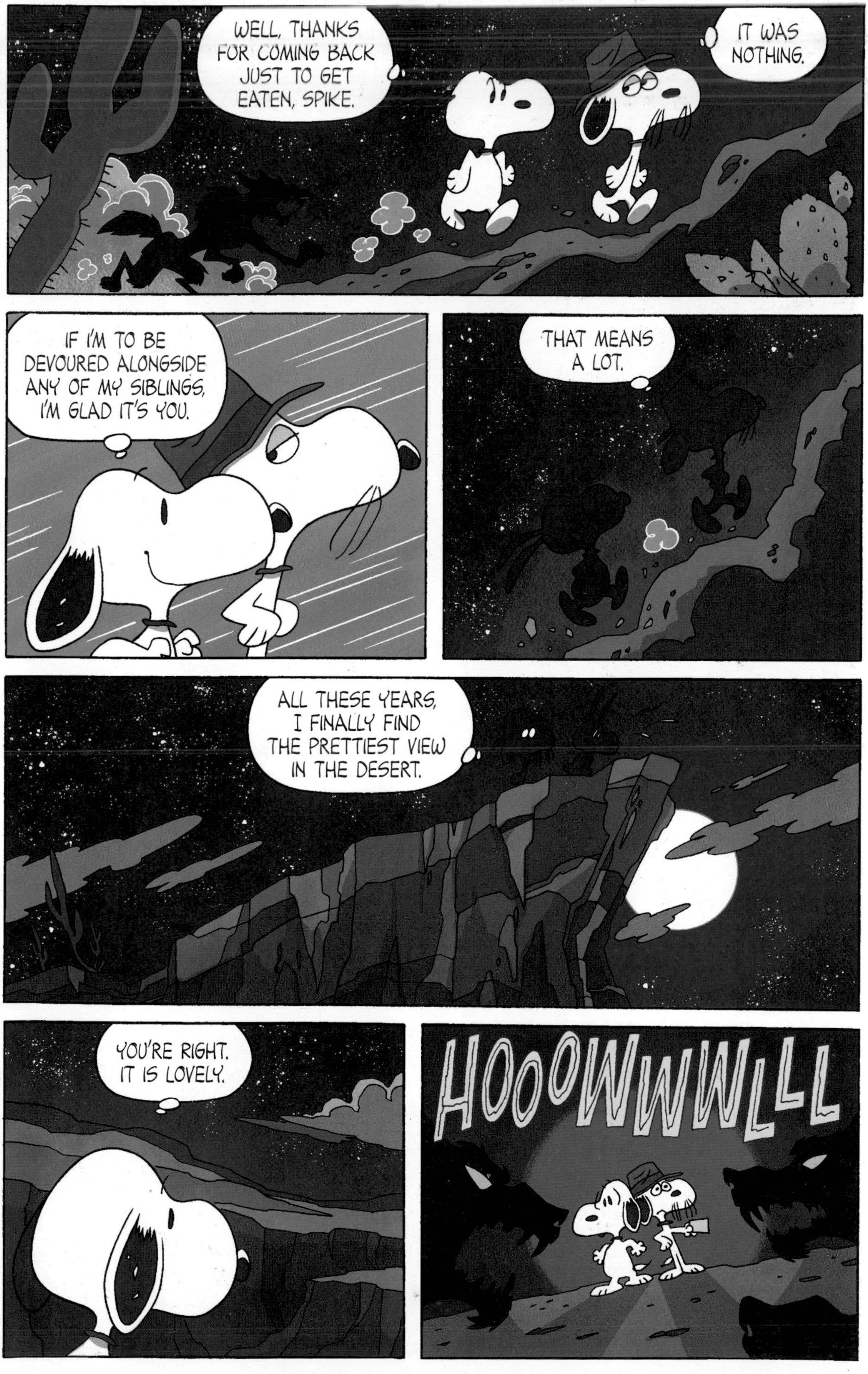

WELL, THANKS FOR COMING BACK JUST TO GET EATEN, SPIKE.
IT WAS NOTHING.
IF I'M TO BE DEVOURED ALONGSIDE ANY OF MY SIBLINGS, I'M GLAD IT'S YOU.
THAT MEANS A LOT.
ALL THESE YEARS, I FINALLY FIND THE PRETTIEST VIEW IN THE DESERT.
YOU'RE RIGHT. IT IS LOVELY.
HOOOWWWLLL

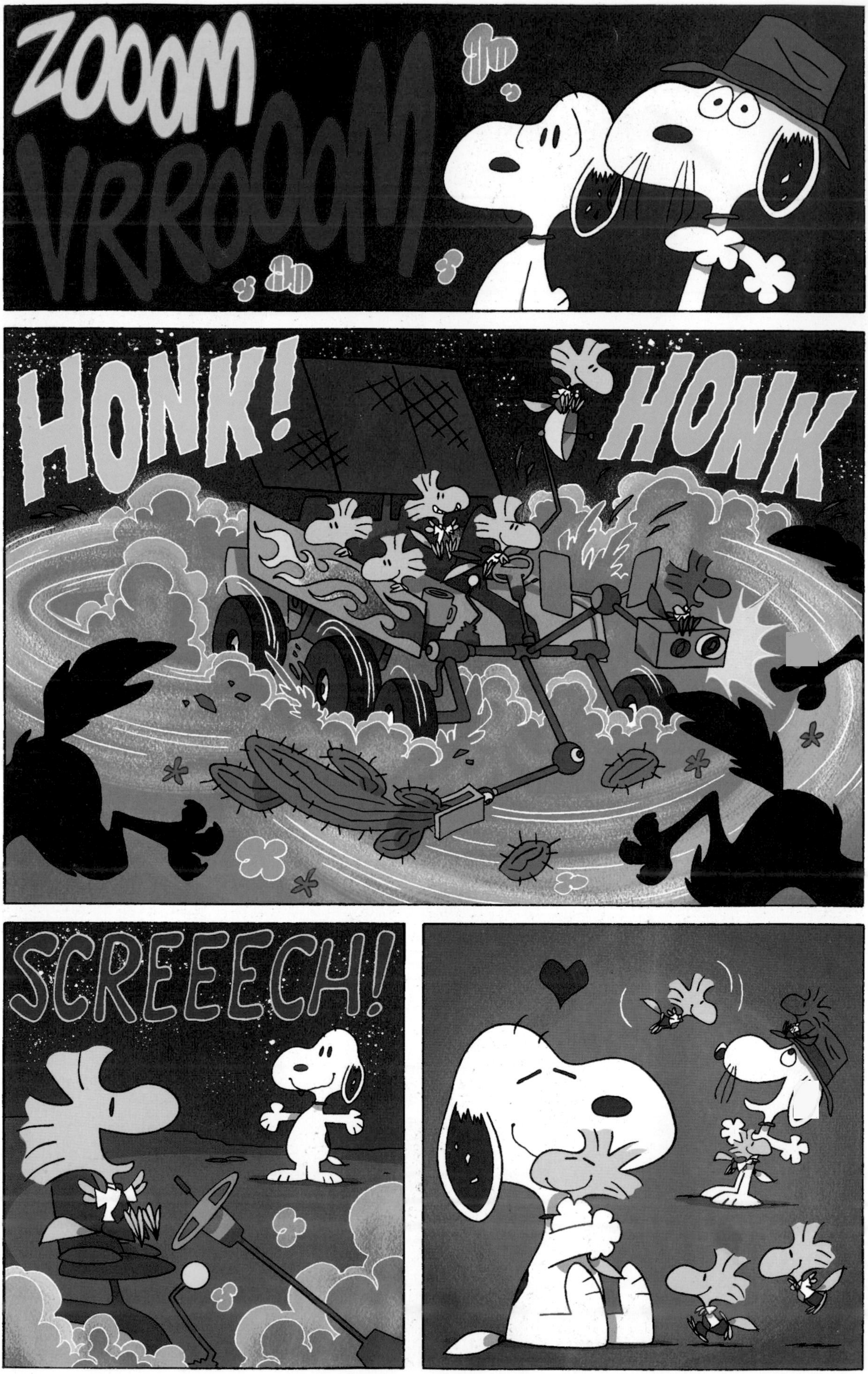
ZOOOM
VRROOOM
HONK!
HONK
SCREEECH!

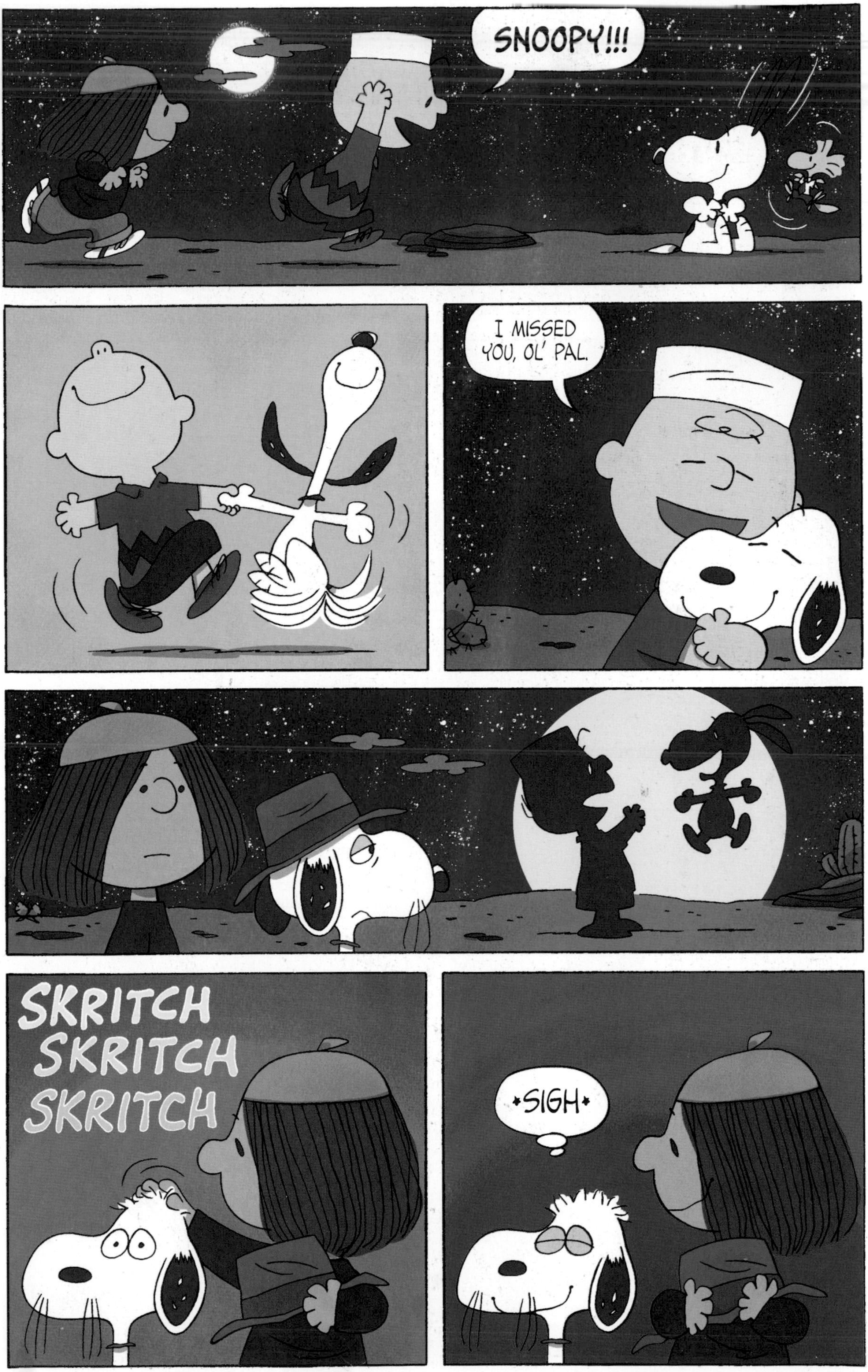
SNOOPY!!!
I MISSED YOU, OL' PAL.
SKRITCH SKRITCH SKRITCH
SIGH

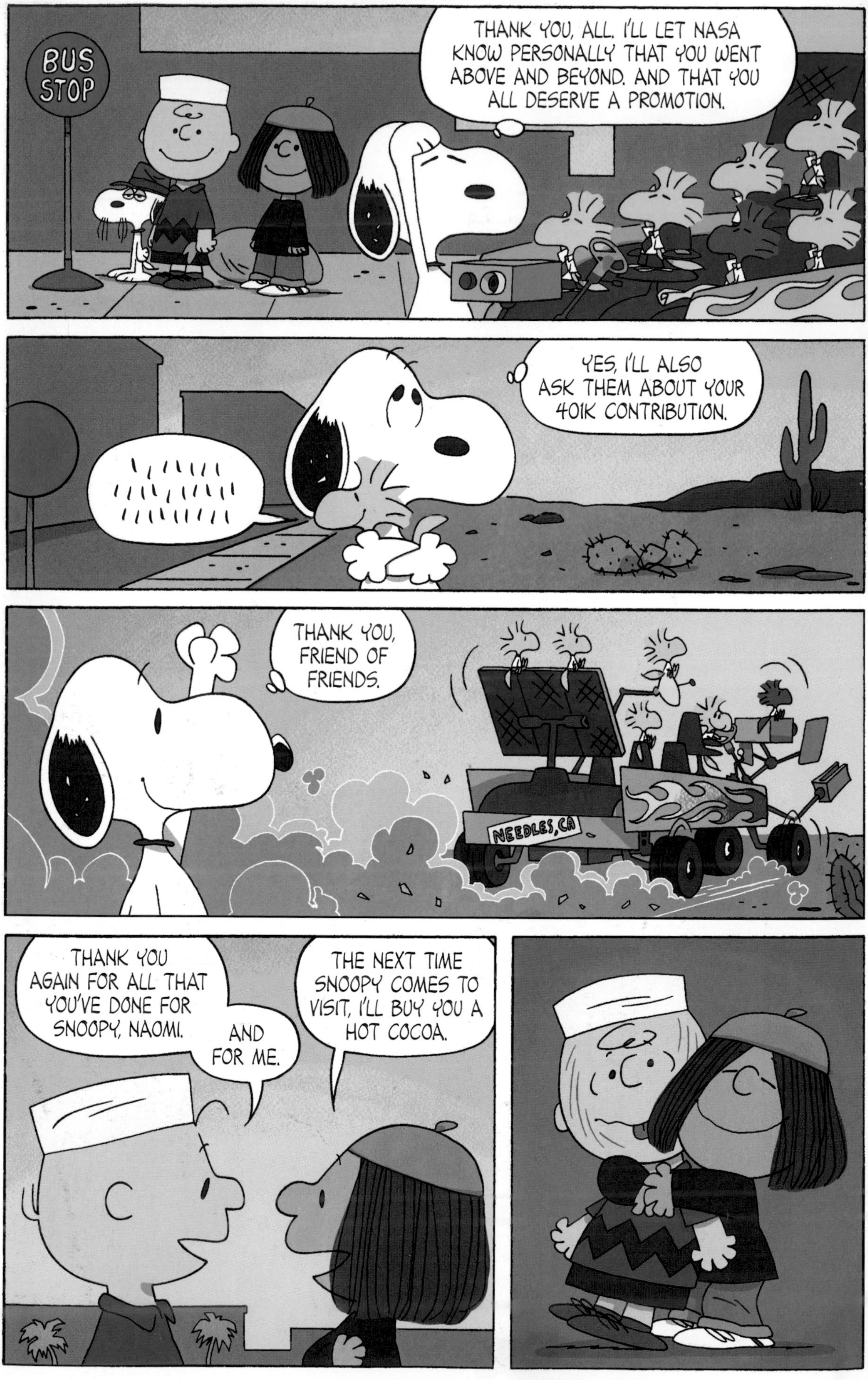
BUS STOP
THANK YOU, ALL. I'LL LET NASA KNOW PERSONALLY THAT YOU WENT ABOVE AND BEYOND. AND THAT YOU ALL DESERVE A PROMOTION.
YES, I'LL ALSO ASK THEM ABOUT YOUR 401K CONTRIBUTION.
THANK YOU, FRIEND OF FRIENDS.
NEEDLES, CA
THANK YOU AGAIN FOR ALL THAT YOU'VE DONE FOR SNOOPY, NAOMI.
AND FOR ME.
THE NEXT TIME SNOOPY COMES TO VISIT, I'LL BUY YOU A HOT COCOA.

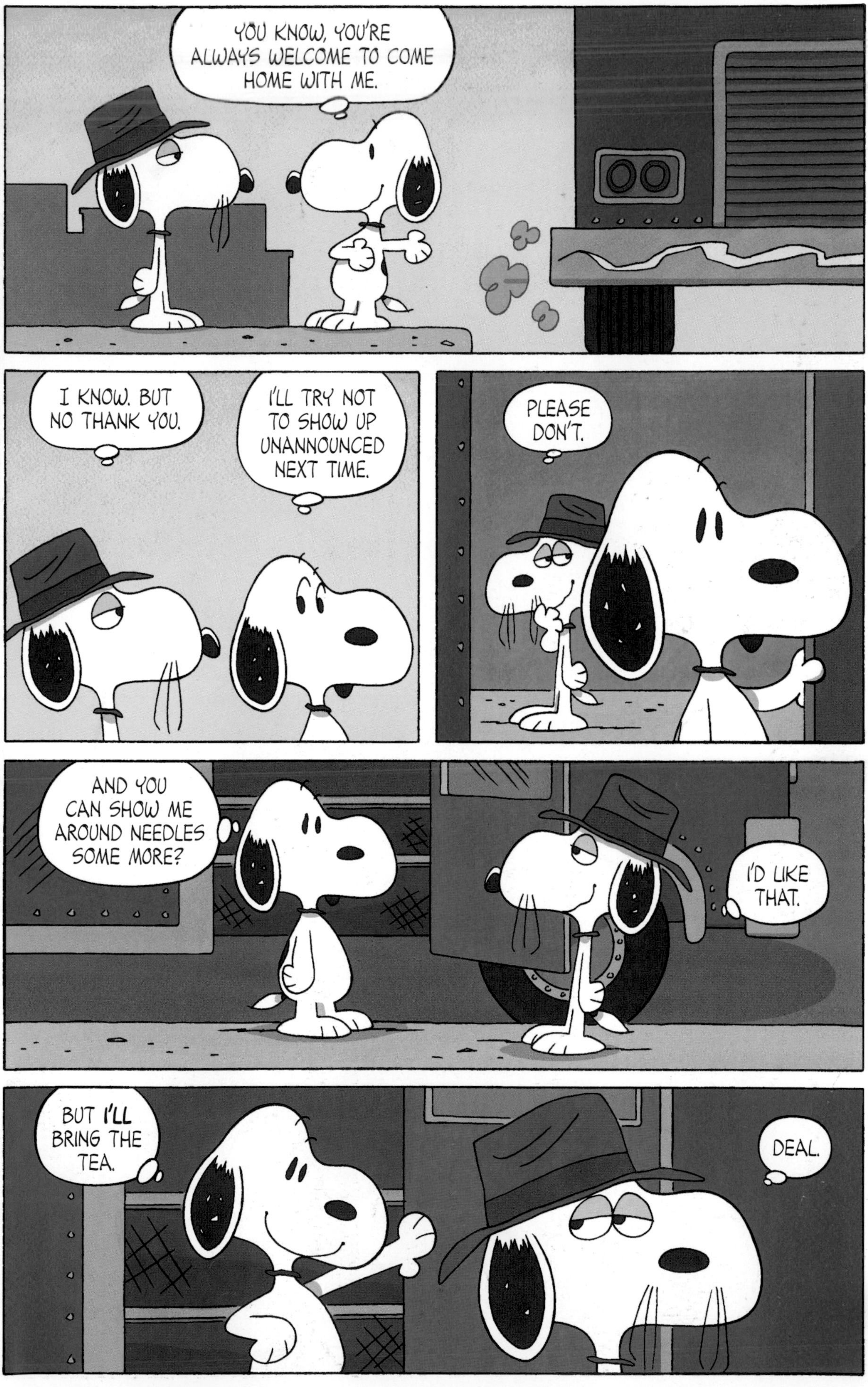
YOU KNOW, YOU'RE ALWAYS WELCOME TO COME HOME WITH ME.
I KNOW. BUT NO THANK YOU.
I'LL TRY NOT TO SHOW UP UNANNOUNCED NEXT TIME.
PLEASE DON'T.
AND YOU CAN SHOW ME AROUND NEEDLES SOME MORE?
I'D LIKE THAT.
BUT **I'LL** BRING THE TEA.
DEAL.

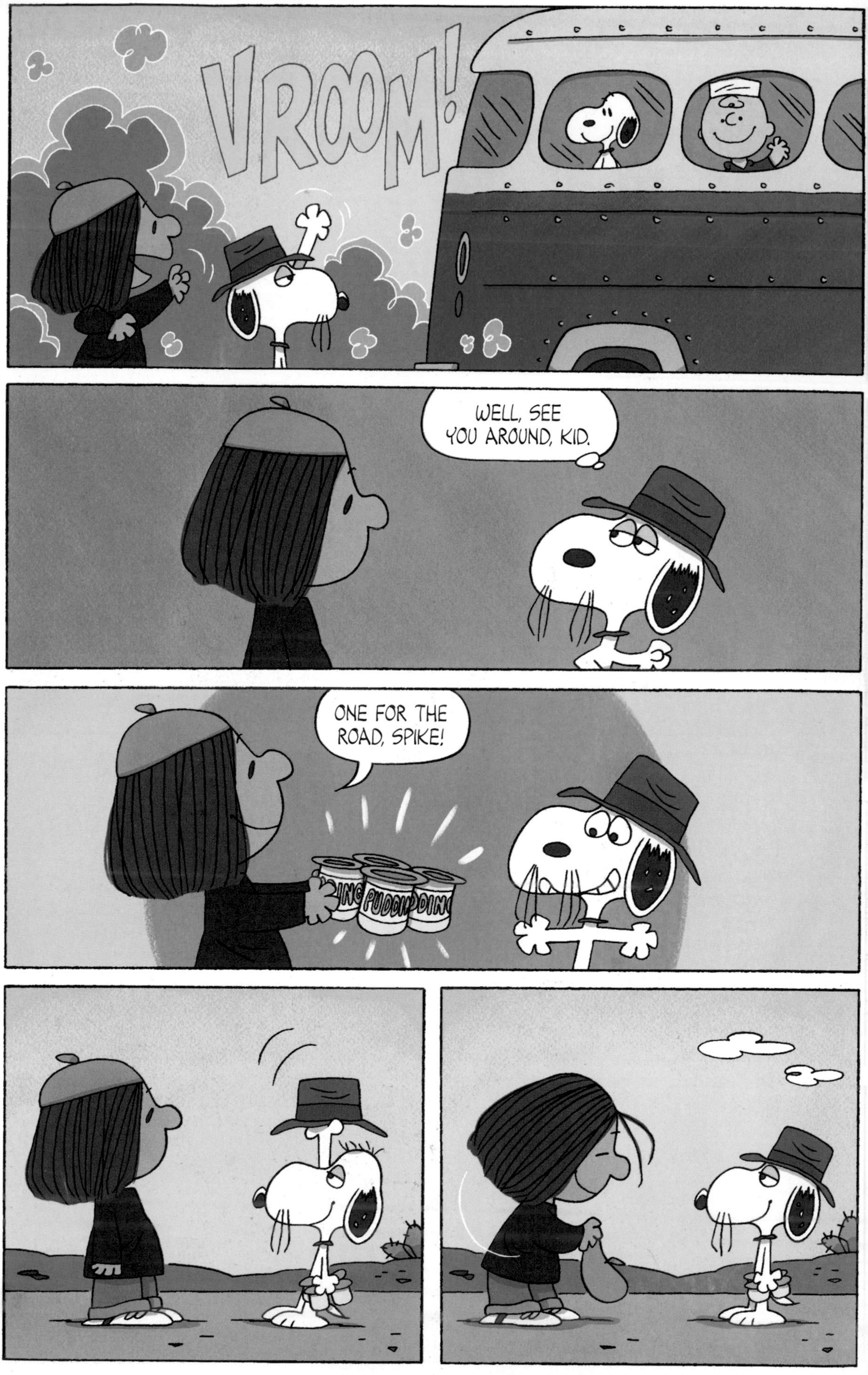
VROOM!
WELL, SEE YOU AROUND, KID.
ONE FOR THE ROAD, SPIKE!
PUDDING

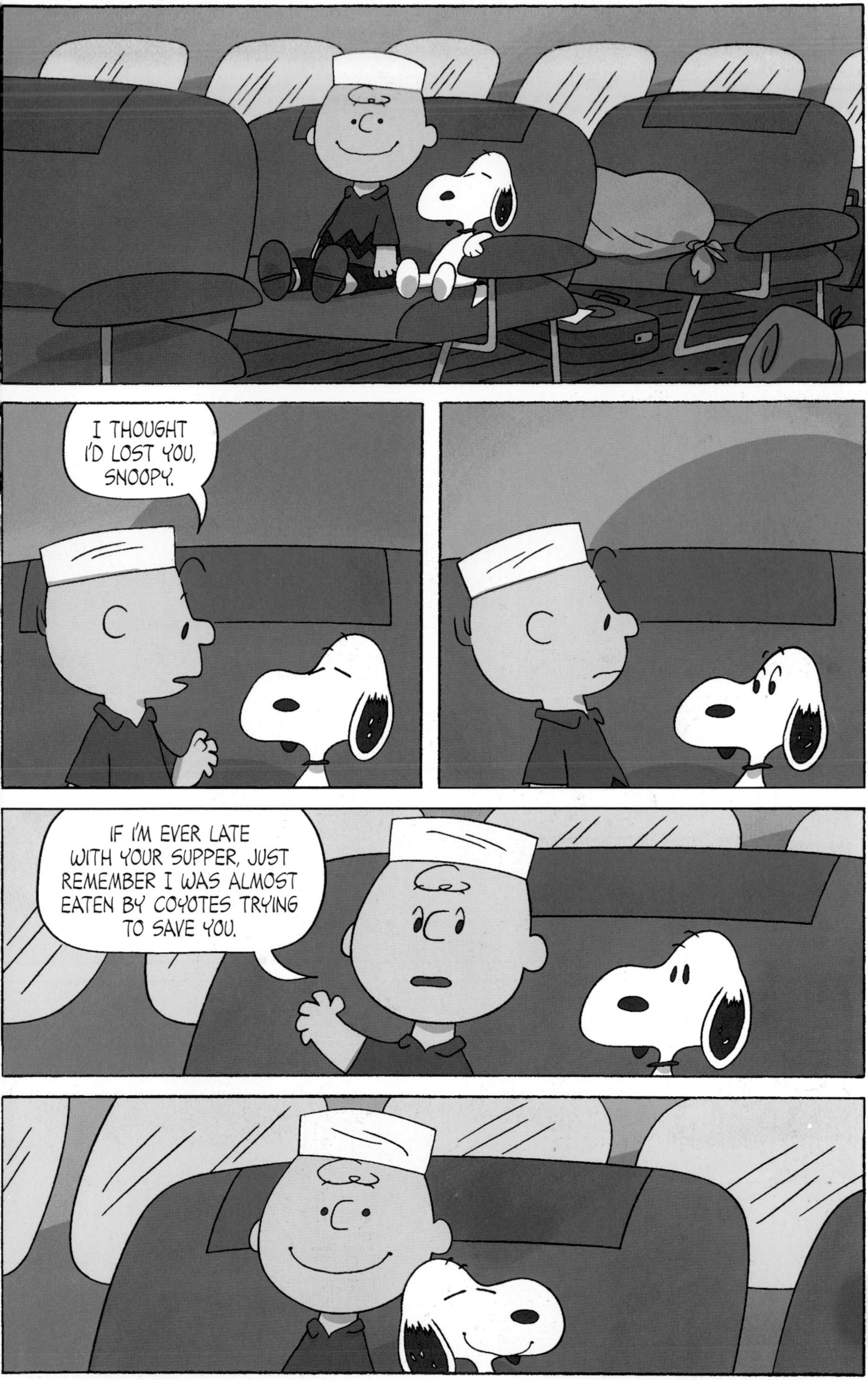

I THOUGHT I'D LOST YOU, SNOOPY.
IF I'M EVER LATE WITH YOUR SUPPER, JUST REMEMBER I WAS ALMOST EATEN BY COYOTES TRYING TO SAVE YOU.

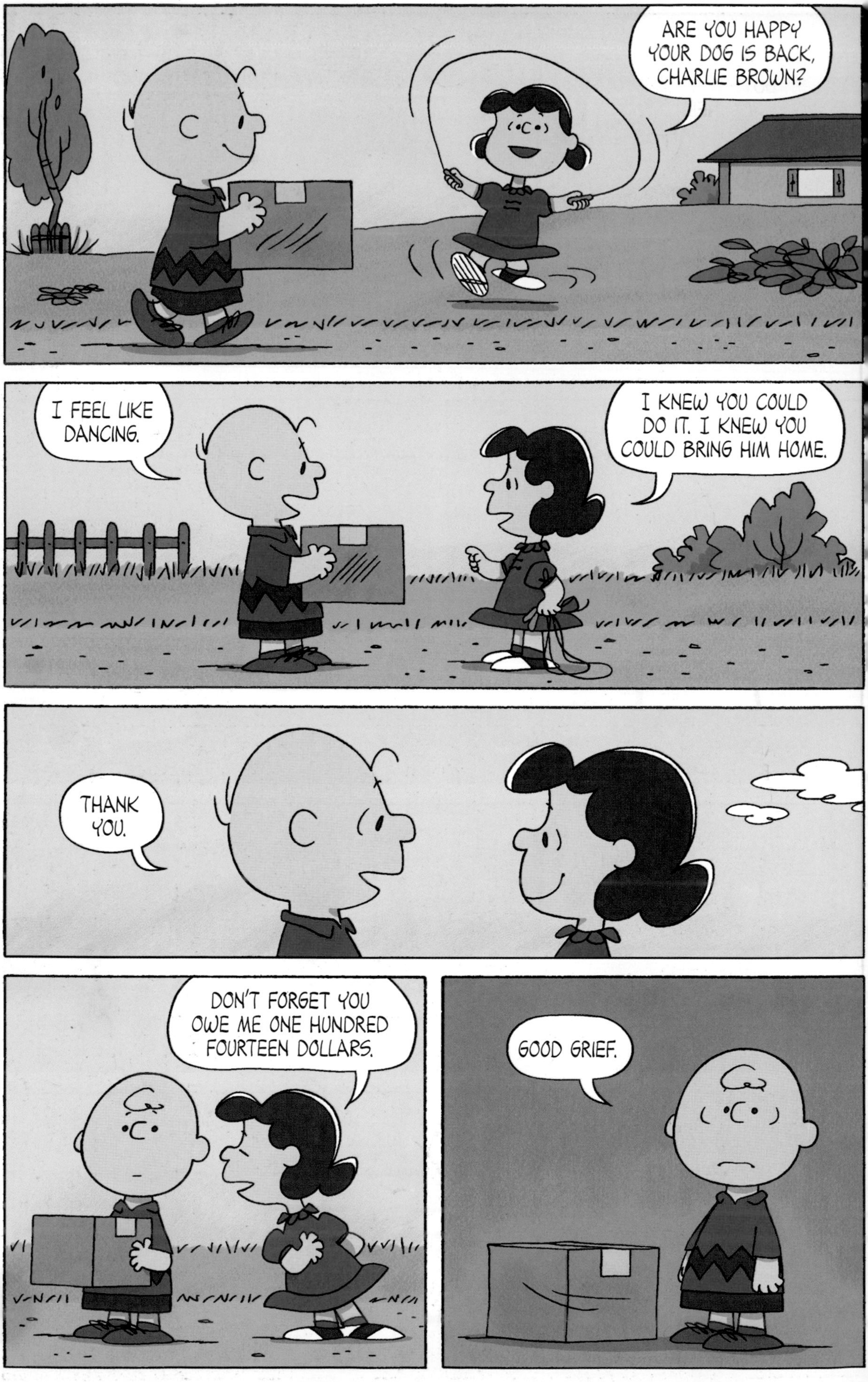
ARE YOU HAPPY YOUR DOG IS BACK, CHARLIE BROWN?
I FEEL LIKE DANCING.
I KNEW YOU COULD DO IT. I KNEW YOU COULD BRING HIM HOME.
THANK YOU.
DON'T FORGET YOU OWE ME ONE HUNDRED FOURTEEN DOLLARS.
GOOD GRIEF.

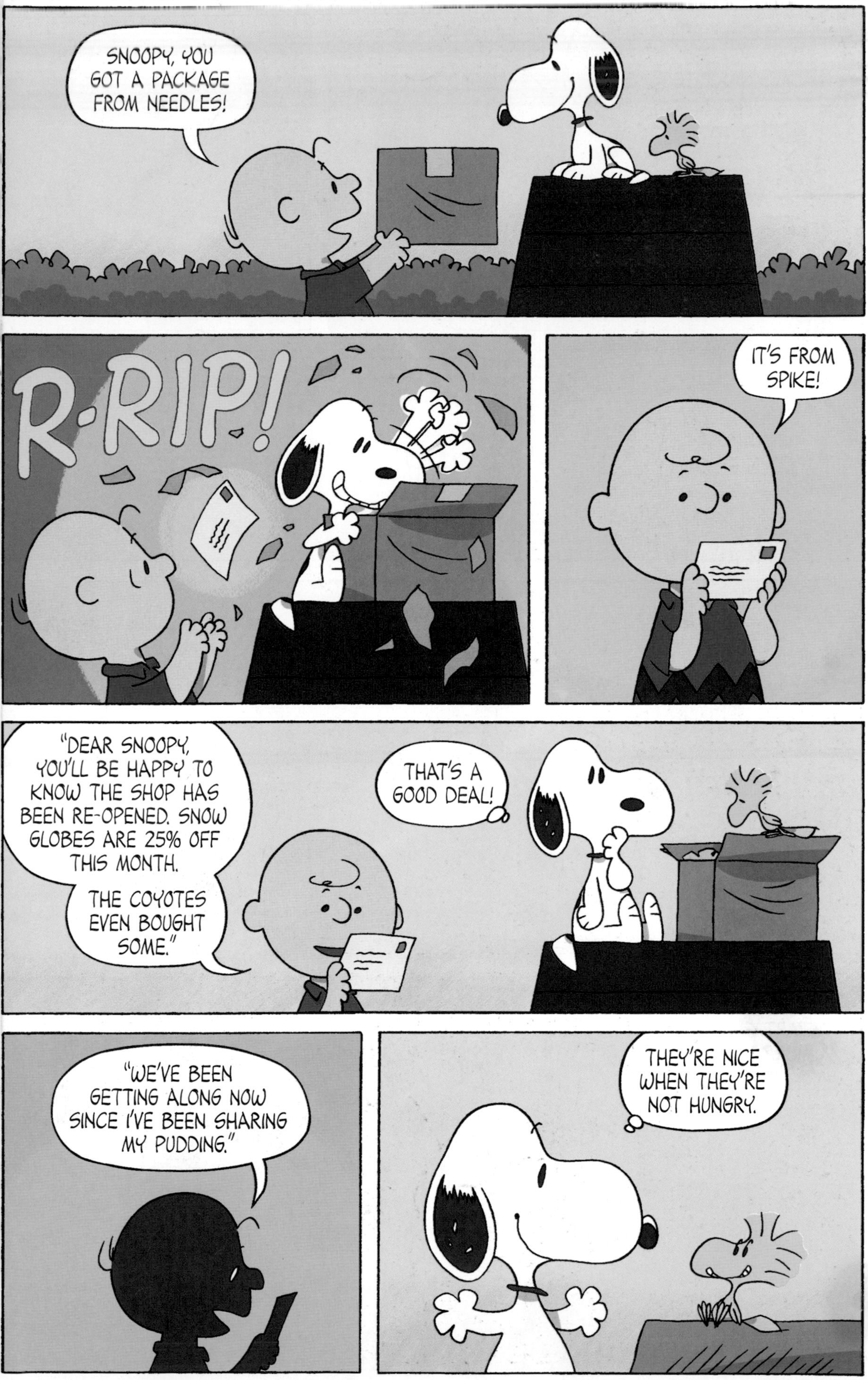
SNOOPY, YOU GOT A PACKAGE FROM NEEDLES!
R-RIP!
IT'S FROM SPIKE!
"DEAR SNOOPY, YOU'LL BE HAPPY TO KNOW THE SHOP HAS BEEN RE-OPENED. SNOW GLOBES ARE 25% OFF THIS MONTH.
THE COYOTES EVEN BOUGHT SOME."
THAT'S A GOOD DEAL!
"WE'VE BEEN GETTING ALONG NOW SINCE I'VE BEEN SHARING MY PUDDING."
THEY'RE NICE WHEN THEY'RE NOT HUNGRY.

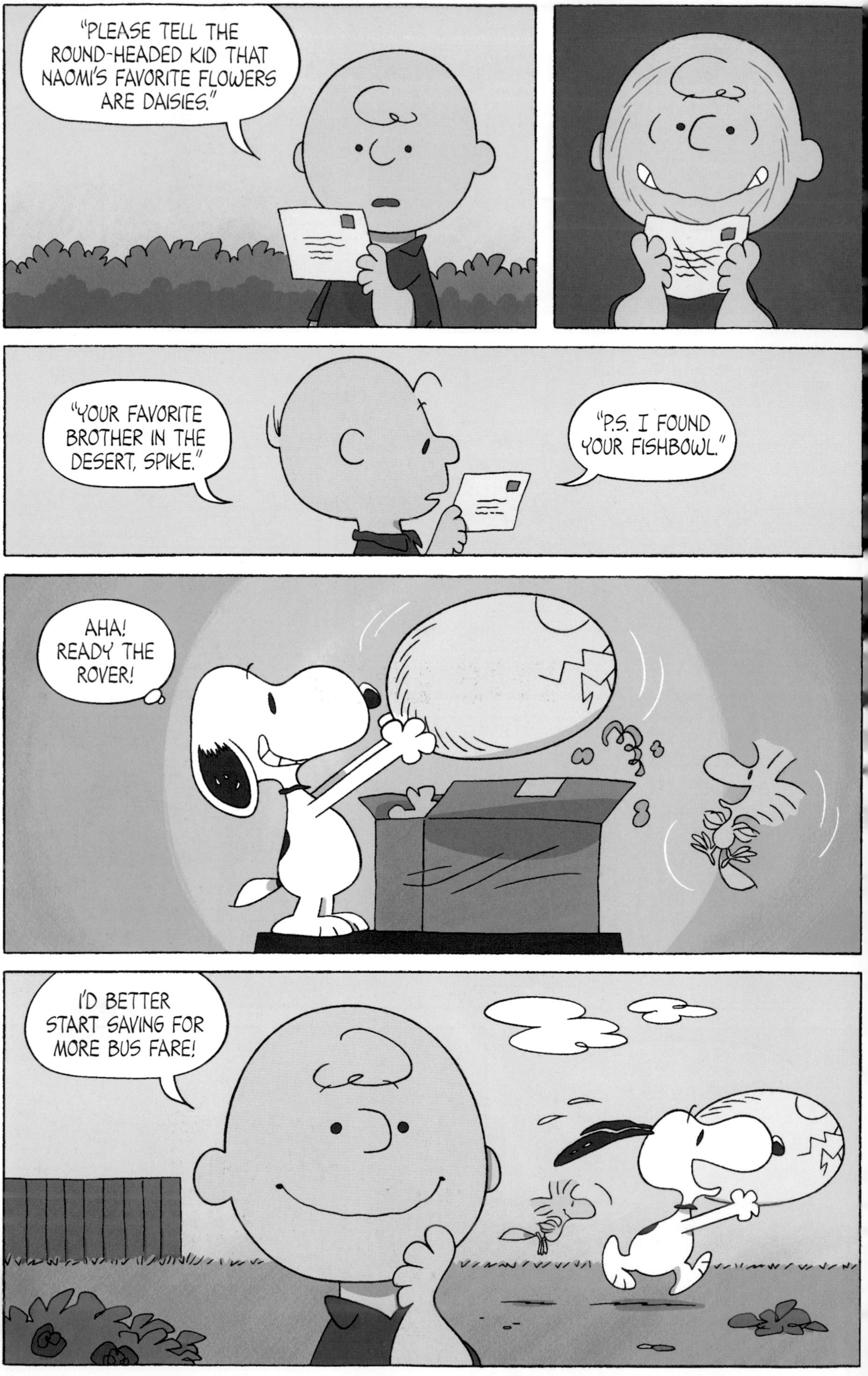
"PLEASE TELL THE ROUND-HEADED KID THAT NAOMI'S FAVORITE FLOWERS ARE DAISIES."
"YOUR FAVORITE BROTHER IN THE DESERT, SPIKE."
"P.S. I FOUND YOUR FISHBOWL."
AHA! READY THE ROVER!
I'D BETTER START SAVING FOR MORE BUS FARE!

THE END

ABOUT THE AUTHORS

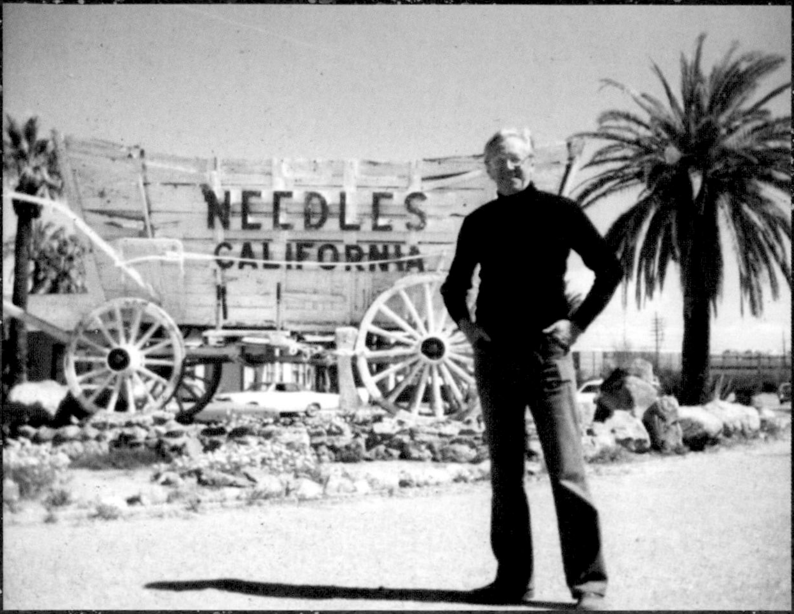
NEEDLES
CALIFORNIA

Photo courtesy the Charles M. Schulz Museum

Charles M. Schulz once described himself as "born to draw comic strips." Born in Minneapolis, at just two days old, an uncle nicknamed him "Sparky" after the horse Spark Plug from the *Barney Google* comic strip, and throughout his youth, he and his father shared a Sunday morning ritual reading the funnies. After serving in the Army during World War II, Schulz's first big break came in 1947 when he sold a cartoon feature called *Li'l Folks* to the St. Paul Pioneer Press. In 1950, Schulz met with United Feature Syndicate, and on October 2 of that year, *Peanuts*, named by the syndicate, debuted in seven newspapers. Charles Schulz died in Santa Rosa, California, in February 2000—just hours before his last original strip was to appear in Sunday papers.

Jason Cooper is head writer at Charles M. Schulz Creative Associates where he has written storybooks, comic books, and graphic novels for *Peanuts*. He relates to Charlie Brown much more than a person should. He wrote this story for his boys, Emmett and Albie.

Cartoonist and animator **Robert W. Pope** has the greatest of fun drawing the *Peanuts* gang for BOOM! Over the years he's also drawn the adventures of the *Looney Tunes* gang, *Scooby-Doo*, the *Powerpuff Girls*, *Johnny Bravo*, and many more for DC, IDW, Disney Publishing and more.

Hannah White is a colorist and artist for Charles M. Schulz Creative Associates; a 2016 graduate of SCAD Savannah, Hannah enjoys her two cats, making comics, and playing video games.

NEEDLES SOUVENIRS

DISCOVER
EXPLOSIVE NEW WORLDS

Adventure Time
Pendleton Ward and Others
Volume 1
ISBN: 978-1-60886-280-1 | $14.99 US
Volume 2
ISBN: 978-1-60886-323-5 | $14.99 US
Adventure Time: Islands
ISBN: 978-1-60886-972-5 | $9.99 US

The Amazing World of Gumball
Ben Bocquelet and Others
Volume 1
ISBN: 978-1-60886-488-1 | $14.99 US
Volume 2
ISBN: 978-1-60886-793-6 | $14.99 US

Brave Chef Brianna
Sam Sykes, Selina Espiritu
ISBN: 978-1-68415-050-2 | $14.99 US

Mega Princess
Kelly Thompson, Brianne Drouhard
ISBN: 978-1-68415-007-6 | $14.99 US

The Not-So Secret Society
Matthew Daley, Arlene Daley,
Wook Jin Clark
ISBN: 978-1-60886-997-8 | $9.99 US

Over the Garden Wall
Patrick McHale, Jim Campbell
and Others
Volume 1
ISBN: 978-1-60886-940-4 | $14.99 US
Volume 2
ISBN: 978-1-68415-006-9 | $14.99 US

Steven Universe
Rebecca Sugar and Others
Volume 1
ISBN: 978-1-60886-706-6 | $14.99 US
Volume 2
ISBN: 978-1-60886-796-7 | $14.99 US

Steven Universe & The Crystal Gems
ISBN: 978-1-60886-921-3 | $14.99 US

Steven Universe: Too Cool for School
ISBN: 978-1-60886-771-4 | $14.99 US

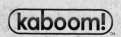

AVAILABLE AT YOUR LOCAL COMICS SHOP AND BOOKSTORE
To find a comics shop in your area, visit www.comicshoplocator.com
WWW.**BOOM-STUDIOS**.COM